ONLY FOREVER

New Haven Series (Book 3)

Samantha J. Ball

This novel is a work of fiction. Names, characters, places, and incidents are either products of the author's imagination or used fictitiously. All characters are fictional, and any similarity to people living or dead is purely coincidental.

Cover photo design by Freepik

ISBN-13: 9798790788123

For my husband.

Chapter One

NEW HAVEN, CONNECTICUT, July 2017

Just another manic Monday.

Julie Rolland shook her head.

No. More like mundane Monday.

How had this new week rolled around so quickly? Couldn't it have waited a couple more days so she could savor her weekend a little longer?

These ridiculous questions entered Julie's mind as she approached Peterson Construction. The tall brick building loomed ahead, not like a beacon of light but rather a tower of torture. Julie stared at it for a few seconds, then huffed in disgust at her dramatic thoughts and shook her head...again.

Her job wasn't terrible. For the most part, she even enjoyed it. She'd arrive at nine, complete regular set tasks, take allotted breaks, then leave at five with everything squared away, ready to be repeated the following day.

What more could she want?

It wasn't what she'd dreamed of doing with her life—working in an office full of opinionated gossips. The women she worked with weren't exactly welcoming; in fact, they barely tolerated her. And the men? They gave her more attention than she wanted.

She could live with that.

Mostly.

Her weekends kept her sane. Evenings spent in the pub with coworkers from other departments—notably Steven, Melanie, Brad, and Jack, and their occasional bowling nights, ice skating outings, and other special occasions, like Steven and Melanie's wedding.

Julie sighed heavily.

That memorable event had been three weeks ago, and now she was avoiding Melanie's brother—Dr. Zac Danvers. She'd met him the previous Thanksgiving, and they'd immediately hit it off. They'd subsequently hung out, sometimes in New Haven but mainly in New York, where he lived and ran his own doctor's practice.

Their casual relationship had been great. Until he'd kissed her passionately at his sister's wedding. Afraid to interpret the kiss the wrong way, she'd taken the coward's way out and not made contact since. Curiously, Zac had done the same.

Was he as confused as her? Surely not?

Because Zac was in love with another woman—at least, he was supposed to be.

The elevator doors swished open.

Julie automatically stepped off, then paused and took in her surroundings. In front of her were the glass-fronted doors to the Administration office. A small smile captured her lips as she swung open the right-hand door —she'd entered the building and ridden the elevator to her floor without realizing it.

"Hey, Julie! What's with the smirk? Don't tell me you've already batted your eyelashes at some poor unsuspecting guy before even reaching your desk?"

"Good morning, Brianna," Julie replied evenly, refusing to take the bait. With her lips pursed, she veered toward her desk without so much as a second glance.

A few hours later, her desk phone rang. Setting aside the supplier's statement she'd been reconciling, she answered, "Julie Rolland, how can I help you?"

"Miss Rolland, this is Kevin Taylor. I saw you on Saturday night." The man had a smooth low-pitched voice, but it wasn't familiar, and his words sounded a little creepy.

"I'm sorry?" she said, her hand darting to the hold button in case she needed to cut him off.

"I'll get right to the point. I'm calling to offer you a recording contract."

What?

Julie froze in her chair. Those were words she never thought she'd hear.

Her hand gripped the telephone handset. Letting go would mean breaking the spell; then, those magical words would simply vanish into thin air.

Though the man continued speaking about his record label and what they looked for in an artist, her concentration wavered.

Could this be a prank call?

She looked beyond the mounting pile of invoices on her desk, searching the entire office for a possible culprit, and saw nothing but a conscientious workforce.

"I assume you're interested."

Though worry gripped her chest, Mr. Taylor's deep voice brought Julie back to the conversation. A complete stranger was offering something she'd only ever dreamed about.

Coherent words escaped her, and she let out a noncommittal squeak which must've been taken as agreement.

"Great," he said. "We'll discuss it further at five o'clock. Meet me at Mary's Coffee Shop. I believe you're familiar with the place?"

"Yes," she managed.

"Good. And, be punctual, Miss Rolland."

Only once Julie registered the silence did the telephone slip from her hand, making her flinch when it struck the desk. Coworkers' heads rose abruptly at the sudden and unexpected disturbance, their hostile gazes boring straight into her as if she'd done it on purpose.

"Sorry," she muttered, squeezing her eyes shut, hating the unwanted attention.

If this was a trick, she'd only have to wait a few hours to discover the joke was on her. No way would she allow herself to get excited about something that seemed improbable.

Humming a tune from Saturday night, she stared at her computer screen. Less than forty-eight hours ago, she'd been singing karaoke in the pub with Jack.

An unfamiliar man had watched her intently as they belted out "Don't Go Breaking My Heart." Although the man's face was hidden by lousy lighting, his expensive-looking suit had appeared entirely out of place. There'd also been an air about him, like a shepherd watching over his flock.

Initially unnerved by his avid perusal, Julie had eventually lost herself in the music and completely forgotten about the man.

Later on, while she downed a well-deserved drink at the bar, someone had settled beside her.

"Has anyone ever told you that you have the voice of an angel?"

Expecting to see her male admirer from earlier, she spun on her seat to find a man in blue jeans with a red shirt, no suit. The newcomer's warm chocolate eyes held undisguised interest.

"You want me to say no, don't you?" she answered, a smile playing on her lips. He was an attractive man.

"It's Julie, right?"

"Yep."

"I'm Sean," he said, smiling seductively. "Let me be the first to congratulate you on your outstanding performance." He motioned to the tumbler in her hand and winked. "I hope there's some rum in that coke. You should be celebrating."

Her eyes narrowed. "Maybe you should worry about your own drink. Oh right, you don't have one."

He chuckled.

"You're right," he said, his tone becoming earnest, "but honestly, the audience's response tonight was phenomenal. Usually, when someone does karaoke on that stage, this room is filled with idle chatter."

His obvious admiration brought warmth to her cheeks. "Is that so?"

"Yep. But you, Julie, you had everyone riveted, including me." He smiled widely. "I probably shouted the loudest for you to sing again."

Laughing, she brushed her fingers over his muscled forearm. "Then, lucky for you, I complied."

After ordering a beer, Sean leaned closer, his aftershave a little overpowering. "You know, the management sells tickets when professionals sing here. So, my question is this...why aren't you already signed?"

"I figure, I was three when I started singing, and I've had twenty-three years to hone my craft. If it hasn't happened by now, it never will."

Thud!

Another pile of invoices landed next to Julie's computer keyboard, startling her out of her memory. Frowning, she peered up into her boss's tight smile.

"I need these documents processed pronto, analyzed by department," she instructed before marching off to her cozy corner office with an unobstructed view of New Haven.

Leafing through the papers, Julie groaned. This would keep her busy all afternoon. No more daydreaming. Besides, long ago, she'd learned words meant nothing without actions. So getting her hopes up was a terrible idea. Especially when she'd been let down more times than she could count.

At exactly 4:45 pm, she shut her computer down, grabbed her purse and slung it over her shoulder. Stuffing her phone into the outside pocket, she tugged down the edges of her skirt and took a deep breath.

No one said goodbye as she tottered in her six-inch heels between rows of desks to the office exit. Not that she expected them to. If she spun around, she knew she'd catch a few women glaring and probably a few men ogling. But...never mind. At least she did a good job, according to the big boss, David Peterson.

A quick visit to the bathroom ensured her thick strawberry-blonde hair shone and her subtle makeup remained flawless. Anxious green eyes stared at her in the mirror, and she forced her cherry-red lips into a smile.

Okay, ready or not.

The walk to Mary's took longer than usual, with every pedestrian light turning red. Fortunately, being delayed gave her time to think.

Mr. Taylor had come knocking on her door. How interested was he really? What sort of offer might this be? Did it mean she was in a position to make demands? Would she be expected to give up her full-time job? Although her daily accounting work didn't stir up any passion, she appreciated the employment security.

She owed everything to David, an old family friend of her foster parents. He'd provided her with her first job—as a front desk clerk—at Peterson Construction, his company. By working hard during the day and studying after hours, she'd earned her accounting qualification. Soon after, she'd been offered an assistant position in accounts.

Outside the entrance to Mary's, Julie inhaled deeply and clutched her purse to her side.

What did she have to lose?

Before she could grab the handle, a man with a familiar woodsy scent pushed open the glass door. "After you, Julie," he said, his low, husky voice washing over her.

Pulse racing, Julie turned her head to confirm her suspicions and gasped. "Jack! What are you doing here?"

"Same as you, I suspect," he said, winking. "Meeting with Mr. Taylor."

***

Jack Carrington held open the door for Julie and smiled as she brushed past him, remnants of her floral perfume stirring his senses. His eyes involuntarily slid shut, then opened to the sight of her heading toward the serving counter. Dressed in a red blouse and short black skirt, she set his heart racing.

He'd met Julie one Friday night, a few years ago. A bunch of Peterson's coworkers had ribbed him about working too hard and never socializing. Caving, he'd joined them for drinks at the local watering hole.

The minute he entered the pub, he'd been drawn to a captivating woman with gorgeous light ginger hair, a perfect hourglass figure, and a smile that lit up the whole room. She'd been standing at the bar counter, a drink in one hand, the other hand resting on a familiar-looking man's shoulder.

Turned out both worked for Peterson's and were part of their group. Jack had been thrilled.

Except, he quickly learned Julie was the resident flirt, and he was better off hiding his attraction. He'd worked hard ever since to keep his feelings under wraps. And anyway, it wasn't like she didn't receive plenty of male attention.

He just made sure it wasn't from him.

Not that it mattered—she avoided him and certainly never showed him any interest. The only time she deigned to be near him was when they sang karaoke at the pub. Jack longed for more of those times, but karaoke stints happened far too seldom to satisfy his desire to be close to her.

Swallowing hard, he joined Julie in the line and checked out the scrumptious pastries.

During Kevin Taylor's call, Jack had been in the middle of working out a complicated job's raw material requirements. The conversation had barely registered, other than: "After hearing you on Saturday night, Jack, I have a proposition I'd like to discuss. Shall we meet at say, five o'clock at Mary's Coffee Shop? I believe you know the establishment?"

The guy had done his homework. How else would he know this place was a regular hangout for employees?

Jack had no idea what the proposal entailed, but it obviously involved Julie, and by deduction, them singing together. Perhaps Mr. Taylor wanted covers sung at his wedding or another such occasion?

That would be cool.

The line finally moved forward, and Mary was free to take their order. Julie ordered a skinny latte, then looked at him. Attempting a pastry with the way his stomach was currently flipping over was a bad idea. "Just a double shot latte," he said instead, pulling out his card.

Julie waved it away. "I'll get my own, thanks."

No point arguing. Living with Charlotte, his sister, or Charlie as Jack affectionately called her, had taught him to rather keep the peace. Safer to pick one's battles when it came to women, and anyway, this wasn't a date.

After paying for his drink, he joined Julie in the collection area and glanced over at the occupied tables. No one appeared to be waiting for them.

The door to Mary's swung open, the latest customer bringing with him a blast of hot July air. Dressed in a custom-made silk suit which screamed 'I'm someone important,' Jack guessed the man to be Mr. Taylor. Judging from Julie's sharp intake of breath, she agreed.

The newcomer joined the queue, then looked around. When his searching gaze landed on them, he lifted a hand in greeting.

Acknowledging the man with a brief nod, Jack turned to collect his order and discovered Julie holding her coffee tightly, a look of indecision on her pretty face. "I guess we should grab a table," he said, noting the slow-moving ordering line. "He'll find us."

"Okay."

Locating a table suitable for four, Jack set his mug down and sat beside Julie. He shifted slightly on the cushioned seat so he could see her face. "I'm not sure about you—" He paused until she looked at him. "—but I found Mr. Taylor's call a little light on detail. I assume this meeting's got something to do with us singing together."

"Um, yes." She regarded him for a second, then peered down at her drink, her lips twisting.

"What is it?"

"Actually, he offered—"

A shadow fell across the table as Mr. Taylor deposited his cappuccino on the table. "Jack Carrington, Julie Rolland, hello," he said, smiling briefly between them. "I'm so grateful you could be here today."

"Great to meet you, Mr. Taylor." Jack stood to grip the man's extended hand.

Julie remained seated while she shook his proffered hand, her smile cautious. "Nice to meet you, Mr. Taylor."

Blue-gray eyes twinkled as they remained on Julie. "Wow, Miss Rolland, you're even more beguiling up close."

Julie ducked her chin, but not before Jack caught sight of her pink-stained cheeks. His chest tightened. So what if she found the good-looking man charming?

Except, the guy was clearly over forty, probably closer to fifty, if his thinning gray hair was anything to go by.

Not cool.

"Maybe we should get down to business?" Jack kept his voice low. "I do have nephews and a niece to get home to."

"Of course." Opening his black attaché case, Mr. Taylor pulled out a stack of paper that looked suspiciously like a legal document and took his seat.

Some time later, Jack pushed his fingers through his hair and linked them behind his neck. Still reeling from shock, he stared at the far back wall, barely taking in the effect of the wallpapered floor-to-ceiling bookshelves.

How was it possible to go from simply singing in the shower and occasionally at a karaoke bar to being offered a record deal? Never in his wildest dreams could he have imagined anything like it.

For a moment, Jack was transported back to the first time he'd been coaxed onto the stage to sing karaoke. Steven MacAlistar, his best friend, had literally shoved him up the steps, forcing him to stand behind a microphone next to Julie. Her eyes had stayed riveted on him as she wrapped her hands around a second microphone, a small smile hovering on her gorgeous lips. Jack still remembered being stunned that she was giving him any sort of attention at all.

Turning to Steven, who was thankfully still on the steps, Jack had frantically hissed, "What am I doing here, man?"

"It's a duet," Steven had replied with a smirk. "You can't leave Julie to do it on her own."

"Why me? What about you?"

A look of horror had crossed Steven's face. "You're kidding, man! I can't sing!" Then, before Jack had a chance to say anything more, Steven had rushed down the steps to his girlfriend, Melanie Danvers' side.

A sideways glance at Julie had revealed her slight frown.

"You *do* know this song, right?"

"'Don't Go Breaking My Heart?' Sure," he said.

"Good."

The grin she'd flashed his way after that one word almost buckled his knees. His already racing pulse had accelerated, and, for a second, he'd wondered if he'd be able to calm his pounding heart.

Then, as they waited for the first notes to begin, Julie's warm gaze had rested on him, helping him relax. Her confident, strong voice had soothed his nerves, and with her focus completely on him, he'd somehow been able to open his mouth to do his part, singing as if it were just the two of them.

While their voices blended seamlessly throughout the performance, Jack had also been aware of incredible chemistry flowing between them.

Back in the coffee shop, he tried to picture what it would be like—being paid to perform with Julie.

If the feeling of peace and harmony he'd experienced, singing with her, could be replicated over and over again, he'd jump at the chance in a heartbeat.

He had his answer.

One thing might still hold him back from agreeing to this, though. Off stage, everything changed. Julie became a different person, seldom looking him in the eye and mostly just ignoring him. She flirted with every unmarried guy around, but never him. Maybe he wasn't her type? For some reason, the idea hurt.

If anyone asked, he denied any attraction, yet the truth was he was drawn to her in a way he couldn't explain. Although they worked for the same company and were in the same friendship group, they hadn't clicked and weren't friends. Yet when they sang, their voices became one, perfectly in sync.

By choosing this fantastic opportunity, would he be risking another broken heart? A high price to pay—to enjoy the moments when everything else faded into the background, leaving him and Julie singing as though only they existed. Feeling like they belonged together, forever.

"I'll leave you two to talk it over." Mr. Taylor's voice broke into Jack's thoughts. "I'm confident you'll both make the right choice to sign the contract. Either way, I need a decision by this time tomorrow. There are other artists I'm considering, and time is money in my business." He smiled, perhaps to soften his words, then pushed out his chair and stood.

"Thank you, Mr. Taylor. We'll let you know as soon as possible," Julie said, then sent Jack a questioning glance.

He nodded.

"Good, and please, call me Kevin."

Picking up his cell and bag, Kevin took a couple of steps before suddenly turning back, his expression stern. "And just to be clear, the deal is strictly for a duo. I'm not interested in taking on another solo artist. If either of you declines, the other forfeits."

Chapter Two

Excitement skittered through Julie as she waited backstage with Jack. They'd been working toward this point for the past two months, and she could still hear Kevin, their manager's words from earlier that day: "You're both ready for this next step. Everything you've been doing has been in preparation for tonight. You know all those informal performances across the city? Great opportunities to test your growing skills. Those countless intensive sessions with our professional vocal coach? They've paid off. Trust me, now's your time to shine."

Talk about a pep talk. One that had certainly bolstered Julie's ego. Jack's too, as far as she could tell.

But what if we forget the words or sing off-key?

The uncharacteristic thought she'd had first thing this morning resurfaced, and Julie stifled a giggle. Their practiced set for this evening was so ingrained in her, she'd be able to do it in her sleep. And she shouldn't be concerned about her bandmate. Jack's confidence in his ability had only grown the more they'd performed. It seemed they fed off one another as they sang, and people had commented on their natural chemistry.

Julie agreed—they had it in bucket loads.

Shortly after signing the recording contract, she'd feared she was making the biggest mistake of her life.

She'd always dreamed of being an artist, but she'd pictured achieving it alone. Doing it with another person, in particular, Jack? Well, that complicated everything. Especially given her infatuation with the man, a fact she had kept—and desperately needed to keep—hidden.

From the moment they'd met, Jack hadn't shown any interest, so Julie had been sure to return the favor. But then, hanging out with Melanie's brother Zac last year had meant more time spent within their close-knit circle. Of course, as one of Melanie's best friends, Jack was included.

The inevitable outcome? Much more time in Jack's presence.

It hadn't mattered initially. Jack had been in a pretty serious-looking relationship, while Julie had spent all her free time with Zac—up until the kissing stunt he'd pulled at his sister's wedding.

Then, after that key meeting with Kevin, Zac had invited Julie to dinner, where she'd told him it was time they stopped looking like a couple. Zac had agreed, making one thing clear—he didn't want to lose her as a friend. She happily obliged, knowing it meant she'd still have an ally when their friendship group socialized.

Although Jack was currently single, it didn't mean Julie was planning on taking advantage of the situation. Nope, she wasn't planning on having her heart broken.

No way.

The problem was that they now spent so much time together, and it was hardly helpful. No, it was as if she were on a journey with a one-way ticket in her pocket. Destination—disappointment and heartbreak.

And *that* was what she was afraid of.

Forget the way his voice complimented hers, the way it felt like they'd been singing together her whole life. Never mind her crazy attraction to the man.

A swell of noise from the gathered crowd drew Julie's attention, and she focused on Jack's appearance. His camel-colored pants, paired with a white button-up shirt, showed off his toned muscles and looked amazing on him.

Suddenly aware she was staring, she snapped her gaze

back to the musicians warming up their instruments and let the buzz of activity distract her. It worked for a while until the awareness she felt every time Jack was around became impossible to ignore.

Thankfully, the opening bars of the music they'd chosen to be their cue came to the rescue. Excitement pulsed through her, and a wide smile lifted her lips.

Not daring to look at Jack, she flipped her long wavy hair over her shoulder and whispered, "It's almost time."

***

Jack slid his sweaty palms down the sides of his pants and stole a sideways glance at Julie. He caught her easy-going smile and frowned. Why couldn't he be half as relaxed? All he could think about was what tonight would be like. Would it be the same as usual or different? How receptive would folks be?

His heart rate quickened at his anxious thoughts, and his stomach somersaulted. He hated having to wait backstage, not knowing how packed the small, theater-like room would be when they walked out onto the stage.

Since being scouted and signed, they'd performed informally at various bars and clubs across the city every week. They'd worked with a hotshot vocal coach and, with no pressure on them, it had been a blast. But now, according to Kevin, they were ready for a more professional appearance.

Jack cast a lingering look at Julie. Her sexy cobalt dress clung to her gorgeous figure giving him ideas. Ideas he shouldn't be having about a woman with a boyfriend.

Did Zac even know how lucky he was?

Taking a deep breath, Jack reluctantly tore his eyes away from her and on to a crowd at least three times larger than what he was used to.

A club setting was intimidating enough...

He moved closer to Julie, dipping his head and catching a generous whiff of her floral-scented perfume. Lavender?

Wasn't that meant to be soothing?

Either way, he liked it.

"Any chance we can change our minds and go back to singing karaoke in the pub instead?" he asked quietly.

She scowled. "Don't tell me you're getting cold feet? I thought you said you were fine with everything?"

"I know. I did," he said, physically retreating at her harsh tone. "It's...I don't want to let you or Kevin down."

Shifting back into his personal space, Julie pointed her index finger into his chest, her expression fierce. "The only way you're going to let either of us down is if you don't join me on stage or if you freeze up when you're out there."

Suddenly a soft smile captured her lips, and the overhead light reflecting in her eyes brought sparkly emeralds to mind. Mesmerized, Jack almost forgot to breathe. Warm fingers moved to rest on his forearm, sending tingles all along his skin.

"Just keep your focus on me, Jack. Pretend we're doing our usual karaoke. Forget about the pressure. We're great together; otherwise, this wouldn't be happening."

"But you were born to do this!"

"So were you!" Julie pursed her lips and peered at him earnestly. "The sooner you realize how amazing your voice is, the better."

He swallowed.

"The first time I heard your deep, powerful voice, it moved me," she said.

"Seriously?"

She nodded. "Almost to tears."

"Wow, okay." Despite the sincerity in her voice, he was still skeptical. "Then I guess we'd better make sure they have a bucket load of tissues in the audience."

Rolling her eyes, she swatted his arm and grinned. "Don't be silly!"

Sassy woman! It wasn't often he witnessed this fun side of her personality. At least, not with him.

Shaking out his hands, he realized she'd removed all his residual tension, leaving him focused on their sheer chemistry instead.

"Welcome, everyone." Kevin's low, distinctive voice redirected their attention back to the stage.

"Thank you for coming tonight. I've recently signed a new act to my label, and I decided their first official performance should be here, in my studio auditorium. I think this intimate, rather cozy venue is perfect, don't you?"

Noisy cheers erupted.

When everyone had settled down, Kevin continued. "So...I'd like to introduce the duo I'm expecting great things from. After you've heard them sing tonight, I'm certain you'll agree—they're simply magical."

Several people hooted.

"Without further ado, please give a warm welcome to Julie Rolland and Jack Carrington. The Jays."

Loud applause broke out, sounding like way more than the seventy-five odd people the venue could supposedly accommodate.

Jack's feet wouldn't move.

Grabbing his hand, Julie dragged him out onto the stage. The spotlights, shining right at him, made it impossible to make out even one face behind the first row. Probably for the best.

She gently turned his head to face her as she handed him his microphone. "Breathe, Jack," she said softly.

Swallowing hard, he took a deep breath and allowed himself a small smile. Her smile, in return, melted all his fears away.

As the musical intro for Lady Antebellum's "Need You Now" began, Julie's steady gaze never left his. She sang the first two lines, and he got lost in the beauty of her sweet voice. Then, like it was the most natural thing in the world, he joined in, singing as if the audience didn't matter. Only Julie, singing to him as if she meant every word, mattered.

Jack's pulse kicked up considerably during the song, and as the last note faded, he found they were still looking intently at each other. He lowered his eyes to break the spell and stopped on Julie's pretty mouth. She grinned at him and spun to face the audience, who were whistling and clapping.

After shielding his eyes from the glare, Jack faced their fans and managed to spot Steven and his wife, Melanie, a few rows from the back. Smiling, he lifted his hand in greeting. Steven gave him a thumbs-up, and Melanie blew him kisses. Jack then shifted his attention to the right, expecting to see Zac, Melanie's brother and Julie's boyfriend. Instead, his heart skipped a beat.

Alexandra Masters.

She'd broken up with him thirteen weeks ago, not that he was counting, so her presence was somewhat surprising. Forcing himself to remain smiling, he nodded in Alex's direction. She immediately waved back, smiling.

A brief scan of the rest of the row, either side of his friends, revealed no more familiar faces. Why wasn't Zac here? Julie deserved her boyfriend's support. Another sideways glance in her direction showed no sign of either disappointment or concern on her face. As far as he knew, the two hadn't broken up. Perhaps she hadn't expected him? Zac was a busy New York doctor after all.

After a few more songs, their set was over. Yet with the deafening response they received before walking off stage, it was easy to forget they weren't the headliners of a concert. For a second, anyway.

Once they reached the corridor where Jack could hear himself think, he said, "Wow, that was awesome!"

"Yes, it was pretty incredible."

Funny, Julie didn't sound nearly as enthusiastic as he'd anticipated.

Without making eye contact, she continued until she reached the bathroom. Then stopping with her hand on the door handle, she gave him a tight smile. "I need to clean this," she said, her hand circling her face. "The studio's idea of makeup and mine...well, let's just say they're not congruent."

To him, she was stunning either way. Trying to gauge why her mood suddenly seemed flat, he studied her eyes for clues. Usually so expressive, right then they were shuttered. Unreadable.

He sighed. "Fine. I'm going to join Kevin and our friends for drinks in the bar. Come when you're ready."

With an imperceptible nod, she pushed open the door and disappeared behind it.

Shoving his hands into his pants pockets, Jack exhaled the breath he'd been holding and pushed down his disillusionment.

Why had he hoped things would change now they were in a band and expected to work closely together? He should've known Julie's behavior toward him, which bordered on mere tolerance most of the time, wasn't going to change any time soon.

She always seemed so happy to play the part, professionally that was. One just had to witness her actions toward him on stage to see it. Yet, when it came to anything personal away from a performance, she shut down completely, as if dealing with him was the last thing she wanted to do in her downtime.

He'd just have to accept things the way they were.

Right?

Chapter Three

"Frankly, I don't have to tell you how Saturday night's performance went," Kevin said, smirking at the Jays. "After all, I do know how to pick stars."

Julie frowned. Had Kevin really dragged her out of her cozy bed just to tell them what she already knew?

It was too early on a Monday morning for this!

She exchanged a brief look with Jack, perched in the other visitor's leather armchair in their manager's office. He seemed equally unimpressed.

Crossing her arms, she barely managed to contain her huff. The last thing she needed was to arrive at work late and have Brianna breathing down her neck. The woman may not be her boss, but she was always looking for ways to make Julie look bad.

"So, on the back of that success," Kevin continued, "you two need to get recording."

A non-negotiable, judging by his tone.

Jack made a choking sound while Julie sat up straighter. "Recording what, exactly?" she asked.

"Well, you can start with the covers you've been singing recently until you're comfortable with the whole process. But ultimately, you need to come up with your own material."

"Huh?" was Jack's less than eloquent response, his expression one of alarm.

Wasn't he aware that singing and songwriting kind of went hand in hand?

Julie hid a smile. Kevin wasn't asking them to become nuclear physicists, only expecting them to write their own songs—a reasonable expectation for members of a vocal duo, she'd have thought.

She smiled over at their boss. "No pressure then?"

"None at all." Either Kevin missed the irony, or he chose to ignore it since his earnestness persisted. "I expect to see you both after work tonight, then before work tomorrow morning, and so on until you have an album full of original songs."

"You've got to be kidding me!" Jack's eyebrows shot to his hairline, and Julie gulped.

"Every day?" she asked, sure she'd misunderstood. What had she gotten herself into by signing that contract? Surely it hadn't mentioned seven days a week?

Kevin shook his head. "Just Monday through Friday. Saturday, I want you here all day." He sent them a fleeting smile. "You can have Sundays off."

When they both began protesting, Kevin coughed loudly, raising his palms like stop signs.

"May I remind you that you signed contracts agreeing to be recording artists and, well, this is the level of commitment required to make it in this industry." His steely gaze flicked between them. "I thought you understood."

Pushing away from his dove-gray desk, Kevin walked over to the large picture window on the far side of his office, no doubt drawn to the sheets of rain falling outside.

Groaning inwardly, Julie shook her head. When had it started raining? Actually, who cared? Getting wet on her way to work would be the least of her concerns if they disagreed on the way forward.

Kevin turned to face them, hands behind his back. "There is another option."

Jack perked up. "Yeah, what's that?"

"You could both resign from your jobs."

Covering her mouth with her hand, Julie dampened the urge to laugh out loud. "That would be taking a rather big risk, don't you think, Kevin? I *do* have rent to pay, never mind living expenses!"

"Yeah, me too," Jack added, like an afterthought.

Julie had no idea of Jack's financial situation, but he *did* live in a great big house with his sister and her family. Maybe he was just freeloading off them.

Whatever. Not her business.

"Then I guess my original schedule remains." From the grim line of Kevin's mouth and the serious expression in his eyes, he wasn't budging.

Julie worried her bottom lip for a bit, then sighed deeply. "I guess if that's what I have to do to pursue my dream, then so be it." She glanced over at Jack. "What about you?"

***

Staring at Julie's lips, a spark of desire shot through Jack. What would they taste like? Would there still be a hint of coffee? The one she'd insisted she needed before this meeting with Kevin.

"Jack?"

His chin jerked up, and he met Julie's questioning eyes. "Are you in?"

What could he say? He held the back of his neck and sighed. No way was he going to let Julie down. In the beginning, this might not have been his dream exactly, but the more he sang with her, the more he wanted this.

"Okay. I'll do it."

The huge, genuine smile she flashed him was worth it. It made his heart stutter.

That evening, they met in the studio's waiting area, just outside the recording room. Jack tried not to notice how Julie's navy dress hugged all her lovely curves.

"How was work?" he asked.

"Not over fast enough." She adjusted the purse on her shoulder. "I've been looking forward to this all day."

"Me too, although I'm hoping it's not going to be too steep of a learning curve." Chuckling nervously, he held open the door for her.

Julie stepped inside, her familiar scent clinging to her. As Jack followed, it took some effort to ignore how his heart picked up pace.

"Hey there." A man appeared from a doorway to the side of a bank of floor-to-ceiling glass. He wore black-rimmed glasses, had a mop of dark brown curls, and sported a goatee. He stuck out his hand. "I'm Carl, your sound engineer. You must be Jack and Julie."

Once the introductions were over, Julie asked the question on the tip of Jack's tongue, "So, Carl, where do we start?"

After being shown the ropes, Jack felt slightly more confident than he had initially. They even managed to record four lines of a song. When Carl played it back, Jack was blown away by how great it sounded.

Julie sent him a knowing smile. "From your look of amazement, I gather you can't believe we're that good."

"N-no. I didn't know... Honestly, I knew you were great, but to hear our voices perfectly blended like that? Now I understand why Kevin's so excited."

Her eyes sparkled up at him. "He's not the only one," she said, touching his arm briefly. Delicious tingles lingered where her fingers had rested. "I'm thrilled to be here too. What I really can't wait to do is get to the part where we record our own songs."

Jack eyed her for a moment, then groaned. "You're serious?"

"Of course!" Julie huffed and shifted away from him to set her microphone back in its stand.

When she faced him again, he heard a soft rumble.

"Sorry." Her hands flew to her flat stomach. "I was too churned up earlier to eat anything."

As Jack glanced at his watch, hunger pangs hit him, too. Was that the time already?

He turned to Carl, still editing on his computer screen. "Carl, would you mind if we ordered in some food?" he asked.

"No, go ahead. I've got some more work to do before we can bring Kevin in for a listen."

"Can I get you anything?"

Shaking his head, Carl lifted a plastic container of what looked like homemade pasta. "Thanks, but my wife always packs me dinner."

"You're a lucky man," Julie said.

Blushing a little, he grinned. "I am. Married two years next week, and I'm still waiting for the honeymoon phase to end."

"Congratulations!" Jack gave a thumbs-up. "I guess if I want dating advice, you're the man to talk to."

Carl laughed heartily.

Julie had a funny look on her face, one Jack couldn't decipher. Was she upset? Why? It's not like she needed any help. She was dating Zac. And, according to his sister, Charlie, Zac was a 'hot doctor.'

Getting takeout became a nightly routine. They ate while killing time between recording and Carl putting on the finishing touches to the final product. Afterward, Kevin would show up to give his stamp of approval.

By Saturday evening, Jack caught Julie pushing chicken pieces around in her takeout bowl, her mouth pursed.

He pointed to her half-eaten meal. "Something wrong with the food?"

"No, it's just..." She shook her head. "I prefer cooking for myself. I don't mind eating takeout once in a while, but this is my sixth day in a row. Honestly, I'm tired of it." She shrugged one shoulder. "Sorry, I didn't mean to sound ungrateful."

"It's fine. I'm not sure what else to suggest, other than we bring packed dinners like Carl."

Julie put a finger to her lips, her face brightening as a smile grew on her face. "Not a bad idea. Would you mind me bringing us homemade food instead?"

"Us?" Frowning, he tilted his head. "You'd be happy to cook for me?"

"Sure, why not?" She dismissed his question with a wave of her hand. "It's easy enough to cook double." Her brow quirked. "As long as you're not a fussy eater?"

"I'm not."

"Maybe..." Julie twisted a lock of hair around her finger. Jack felt a sudden urge to touch those silky strands.

He didn't.

That would shock them both.

"Just to make sure you like my cooking...you could always come over to my place, um, tomorrow night. If you want to?"

He looked at her in surprise. They'd been spending lots of time together this past week. And her barriers when it came to him had lowered a little more with each session. So, did she actually want to be friends?

That was something...except, shouldn't he worry what Zac would think? If Julie was his girlfriend, he wouldn't like the idea of her entertaining another man in her home one bit. Bad enough, they already spent every morning and evening together.

"Forget it," Julie said, sounding a little gruff. Before she turned her face away, he swore he saw a flicker of disappointment. "It was a silly idea," she said. "I'm sure you'll want to spend your free evening with Charlotte and her kids."

"Actually, no, I wouldn't." Although he'd promised his brother-in-law he'd be there for his family, Jack wasn't about to pass up on an opportunity to get to know Julie better. After all, he needed a life of his own too.

Julie regarded him with her brow furrowed, a hopeful look in her eyes. "Really?"

"I'd much rather taste food cooked by you," he said, nodding. "In fact, I'd love to."

***

"That was incredible!" Pushing away his dinner plate, Jack beamed at Julie.

"Glad you enjoyed it."

She scraped the leftovers of beef stroganoff, wild rice, and broccolini to the side of her plate, her knotted stomach easing somewhat.

"I wasn't sure about the rice," she said. "Some people don't like its texture."

"Julie?" The tenderness in Jack's voice made her look directly at him. "I told you I wasn't fussy. I meant it, but I also appreciate great food when I taste it."

He raised his wine glass in a toast. "To you, Julie. If this singing thing doesn't work out, I guarantee you a successful career as a chef. Probably in a five-star establishment."

Heat rose to her cheeks, and she quickly lowered her gaze to the white, rose damask tablecloth she'd bought at a thrift store. "That's quite a statement. You're a hard man to impress, Jack, so thank you."

"What do you mean?"

Ignoring him, she pushed back her chair and rose to her feet. "Fancy some homemade dessert?"

"If it's anywhere near as good as your stroganoff, then yes, please!"

She dished two portions of the hot dessert, scooped vanilla-bean ice cream into both bowls, and carried them to the dining table.

"Here you go."

"Mmm, it smells amazing." Jack's eyes twinkled as they met hers. "Hot chocolate fudge cake, right?"

Smiling, she relaxed back in her seat and nodded. Jack dipped his spoon eagerly into the cake, seemingly delighted when cocoa and orange sauce oozed from the middle. He popped the gooey dessert into his mouth and chewed with his eyes closed.

Seconds later, they shot open. "Wow, best fudge cake ever!"

"Thanks." The compliment warmed her to the core. "It's my favorite."

Afterward, they took coffee into the living room, where Jack occupied one end of the three-seater sofa, and Julie claimed the single armchair. Tucking her legs underneath her, she wrapped her hands around her hot-pink mug and peered over the rim at him.

He slung his arm over the backrest and said, "So tell me, how are we going to come up with the lyrics for one song, let alone a whole album?"

Sneaking a peek to her right, Julie inhaled a deep breath before letting it out slowly. Should she show him? It's not like she had anything to lose. She reached over for the folded sheet of notepaper.

Hours ago, nervous about the idea of Jack's visit, she'd considered the difference between being with him at the studio and entertaining him alone in her home. As a result, a song had bubbled up inside her. One expressing her equal feelings of frustration and relief about never truly being alone with Jack. At the studio, someone was always around—Kevin, Carl, the vocal coach, various visitors...

"I *have* been playing with some ideas," she said quietly, unfolding the piece of paper.

"Seriously? Can I see?"

He stretched out his hand to take the page, but she pulled it back at the last second. "Um, I'm not sure it's ready to be shared."

"Come on, Julie, let me take a look." His stern tone took her by surprise, and she frowned.

"You know I'm always honest," he said, more softly. "If it's rubbish, I'll tell you in the nicest possible way."

"You'd better tell the truth, Jack, otherwise you'll be singing something you hate for the rest of your life," she half-joked, handing it over.

Without a word, he scanned the lyrics keenly, his expression solemn. Nerves gripped Julie, and she closed her eyes.

What if he hated it?

Squinting through one eye, she saw his grin, so she opened the other.

"Wow! You're one incredibly talented woman," he said, stabbing the sheet with his index finger. "This is hit material, in my humble opinion."

"Really? You like it?"

"Don't sound so surprised. I don't just like it; I love it!"

"Thanks, Jack. Coming from you, it means a lot."

At work, everyone talked about him with respect. He was known as a man whose word could be counted on. Dependable and honest, he was revered by all his coworkers. Julie knew she could trust him.

Shifting her legs out from under her, her thumb automatically began circling her wrist tattoo. Anything to distract her from staring at his handsome face with its strong jawline and enticing lips.

This was precisely what she'd been worried about.

During recording sessions, she'd taken to focusing on Jack's toned arms when his attention was elsewhere. The way his fingers loosened, then tightened on the microphone as he belted out his notes had his arm muscles flexing deliciously. That action had her pulse escalating, and she'd struggle to suppress the urge to run her fingers over his tanned skin, to feel the strength beneath.

"I don't suppose you have any more of these gems?" Jack's question broke into her dangerous thoughts.

"I may."

"Don't hold out on me. Let me see. Please?" he begged, his eyes gleaming in anticipation as he leaned forward. He reminded her of a puppy waiting for his ball to be thrown.

Rather than disappoint him, she stood and held up a hand. "Wait here. I'll be back."

Her stomach in huge knots, she returned with the notebook she'd been doodling in for years. She offered him the book. "Remember they're drafts, but hopefully, you'll get the picture."

Opening it hurriedly, Jack seemed to devour every syllable, his smile widening with each subsequent page.

Then he set her labor of love aside, and in one fluid movement, lifted her off the ground, spinning her around in his strong arms. "Julie," he declared, "you're a song-writing genius!"

Giggles burst from her lips as she grinned down at him, completely forgetting to guard her emotions.

Eventually, he stopped turning and stilled, and she automatically slid down against him, her body heating at every point of contact. Molded to his body, her heart rate doubled. She stared up at him. Hazel flecks were visible in his green eyes—they were *that* close.

Their gazes locked, and with his firm hold on her, she couldn't have moved even if she'd tried. His head dipped toward her, just as a flash of desire showed in his eyes.

She panicked.

But she needn't have worried. His hands suddenly

dropped away like she was a bag of hot coals, and he stepped back, a guarded look covering his face. A few seconds of silence passed before she managed to say, "I- I'm glad you like them."

"I do, and I can't wait to sing them with you," he said, his voice deeper than normal. Clearing his throat, he glanced at his wrist. "I'd better go. We have to be at the studio early tomorrow. I don't know about you, but I need at least six hours of sleep if I want to function any better than the walking dead."

An image of him as a soulless corpse popped into her mind, and she almost smiled. Without a doubt, he'd be a hot zombie. She shook her head to clear the image. "I know what you mean. I don't know what possessed us to agree to the early morning session."

"I don't recall Kevin giving us a choice," Jack grumbled, following Julie out of the living room.

At the front door, he gave her a lopsided smile. "So, pick you up at five?"

She nodded, reaching for the door handle. "Sure." The decision to carpool made good financial sense, so she wasn't about to complain. "Goodnight, Jack."

As he stepped past her to cross the threshold, she couldn't help breathing in his spicy aftershave. For a moment, she wished he didn't have to leave.

She shook off the desire.

"Sweet dreams, Julie," he said, glancing back over his shoulder. "Thanks again for a wonderful meal and for trusting me enough to show me your lyrics."

Then he was gone.

Squeezing her eyes shut, she leaned back against the cold, hard surface of the closed door. That had been way harder than she'd ever expected. Twice-daily sessions in a confined space, sharing dinners, and singing together —none of it was helping quell her attraction to the man.

The opposite, in fact.

Never mind the looks he'd been sending her lately. And what about that almost kiss? Why hadn't he seen it through? Had she just misread the situation?

Part of the reason she'd agreed to the duo, at the

record label's insistence, was because Jack had never indicated any interest.

But now... Was he interested, or did he just admire her abilities? Had he just been caught up in the moment?

If only she had someone to talk to about him.

Keep it professional, she decided, clenching her teeth. She'd never flirted with Jack before, and she wasn't about to start now. She needed to make it clear that this was a business partnership, and he was her bandmate.

That was all. If she had to keep telling herself that, she would.

For as long as it took until she believed it.

Chapter Four

The following Saturday morning, Jack drove them to the studio for their session. During the trip, Julie leaned her head against the car's side window and closed her eyes.

She couldn't keep this up—acting like a professional around Jack, avoiding eye contact, and pretending she felt nothing for him. It was emotionally exhausting. Already her nerves were completely frayed, and to top it off, she'd struggled to fall asleep until the early hours. Unable to stop thinking about the wretched man, now she was paying the price!

Kevin's brilliant idea for her and Jack to work together on an original song today was the only reason she hadn't begged off sick. Hopefully, she'd be able to dig deep and find enough energy to survive the process.

Thankfully, the country song playing through the truck's speakers was loud enough to discourage conversation. What would she say anyway? Tell me, Jack, what stopped you from kissing me?

Like she'd go there.

Wrapped in his arms, she'd seen desire spark in his eyes, felt it in his body's response. Had he been embarrassed by his reaction? Wanted her in his bed?

Warmth surged through Julie's body. It had been a while since she'd slept with a man.

The warning office gossip Brianna had given her before introducing Jack suddenly came to mind. "Remember this," she'd said in a condescending tone.

"All the single women at Peterson's want to date Jack Carrington. But rumor has it he lives with his married sister and her kids, and apparently, he's totally devoted to them." Brianna's scowl had deepened before she added, "Everything points to bachelor Jack not dating. So don't you go getting any ideas, Miss Rolland. Got it?"

Unattainable. Untouchable. Out of her league.

She got it.

Yet, from their first meeting, Julie had been thrown by her intense attraction to Jack. Desperate to protect herself, she'd done the only thing she could do, feigned disinterest and refused to flirt with him like she usually did with any unattached, hot male.

When he'd started dating Alex, Julie had continued to ignore him. Even so, his girlfriend had felt threatened. Thankfully, Alex was out of the picture.

Or was she? Jack could still be hung up on her. Perhaps that was the reason he hadn't gone through with the kiss.

Sighing deeply, Julie stole a look at her handsome driver but got caught.

Concern etched his face. "You okay?" he asked.

"Sure. Why wouldn't I be?"

Shrugging, he turned back to focus on the rain-spattered windshield. In the meantime, Julie tried to work out how much longer they'd be stuck in this confined space. A couple more blocks, she estimated, recognizing a landmark.

Filling her nostrils with the scent of his woodsy aftershave did nothing to calm her racing heart. And honestly? Neither did the sight of his chiseled features nor his perfectly muscular body.

The minute they were parked in the underground garage, she jumped out the truck and marched over to the elevator, hitting the call button more than once.

"Why're you in such a rush today?" Amusement colored Jack's voice. "Are you really that eager to get started?"

Refusing to look at him and his gorgeous smile, Julie crossed her arms. "The sooner we get this song done, the sooner I can get home and relax in a warm bubble bath."

"Really?" He sounded surprised. "Personally, I prefer relaxing in front of a game, with an ice-cold beer in my hand."

"Sounds about right," she muttered.

The elevator doors pinged open, and she quickly stepped on. Jack followed more sedately to stand beside her. Shifting her purse strap more securely onto her shoulder, Julie peered at the floor.

"I guess I can see the appeal of a foam bath. In the right circumstances and with the right person," Jack said in a low voice.

Whoa! What was he saying? Her eyes shot to his, and to her astonishment, he winked. Flushing, she spun away from him. If she was going to have any hope of keeping it professional between them, this personal conversation had to stop.

Aware of Jack's gaze boring a hole into the side of her head, Julie ignored him. Instead, she willed her face to cool down and the thundering in her heart to subside.

If he thought she was rude, he didn't say.

***

They'd been talking over song ideas for the past hour. Yet everything Jack suggested, Julie vetoed.

"You really don't need me here, do you?" He tried to keep the frustration out of his voice, but when Julie huffed and folded her arms, he figured he hadn't succeeded.

"I do," she said. "Besides, Kevin insisted, and he's the boss." She had a point, though he wasn't convinced.

The dynamic between them had definitely changed since their dinner. Now all Jack could think about was kissing Julie. So, he'd made a couple of promises to himself: Keep his eyes off her—totally doable, if she wasn't around. And don't fall for her—easier said than done.

Memories from last Sunday night floated in his mind like bubbles, just never popping. The exact moment their gazes tangled, her cute giggles when he lifted her up, the way his pulse raced when their bodies were sandwiched together, and the lavender scent lingering in his nostrils even after he'd left her apartment.

The same one he could smell right now, sitting across from her—so not what he needed!

Stifling a groan, he ran his fingers through his hair and spared her a look. As usual, her head was down, focused on the blank page.

What had Kevin been thinking, wanting them to write a song together? Hadn't he already seen all Julie's songs? They were brilliant. No need for Jack to get involved and have to spend all this time with her. Alone.

After Alex had dumped him, he'd sworn off women. Besides, with Charlie and the kids to take care of, he didn't need another woman always demanding his precious time. His ex's grumbles had never been a secret. He'd ignored them, thinking if Alex loved him enough, she'd understand. Especially since he had a duty to look after his sister's family while her husband, Mark, was away for work. And he wasn't about to break his promise to Mark.

Not for any woman.

Why was Julie being so difficult? Because he hadn't kissed her? Or because she was embarrassed he almost had?

Women! All so confusing!

"Work with me here, Julie. You've written countless songs without anyone else's help. You don't need mine."

She glared at him.

"Okay. I don't suppose my presence while you create your next masterpiece could be enough to say we wrote it together?" He kept his tone light, slightly teasing.

She didn't even smile.

Wow, a nut was easier to crack open.

Releasing a loud sigh, she tapped her pen against her lips. Then her eyelids slid closed, effectively blocking him out.

A clever ploy.

Unfortunately for her, he wasn't going to leave. They had a job to do.

However, it gave him the perfect opportunity to study her beautiful face. Cute creases lined her brow, and her makeup didn't quite cover the dark rings under her eyes. He'd ask what was troubling her, but he doubted she'd tell him.

Her eyes opened, and he immediately averted his to the dove gray wall behind her armchair. Decorated with artists' awards, it was a reminder of why they were here. How many other hopefuls had sat in this very spot trying to write the next big hit?

A thick wool carpet warmed the studio room while dim wall lights cast gentle shadows around the area—no doubt designed to be conducive to creativity, if one was that way inclined.

Bringing his eyes back to Julie's determined ones, Jack suddenly had an idea. "Opposites," he blurted.

"What?"

"I was thinking. I work on a construction site; you work in an office. I'm a man; you're a woman—"

"A bit obvious, don't you think?" She cut him off, smirking.

"Humor me. I like beer, you like wine. I can't write songs, but you can. Opposites."

Julie's eyes brightened, and her head bobbed up and down, making her ponytail swing around.

Every morning she arrived with her hair tied, but by the evening, her light ginger locks were cascading over her shoulders. More than once, he'd suppressed the urge to run his fingers through the shiny, soft-looking strands.

Her brow furrowed in concentration. "I get where you're going." Then, while she tapped out a rhythm on her thigh, her lips moved silently.

A few seconds later, Julie started writing lyrics.

Resting his elbows on his knees, Jack leaned forward. The speed at which she wrote fascinated him. It was like a dam bursting open, flooding the page with words. Riveted to his seat, he dared not breathe too loudly. Five minutes went by while she wrote a couple of verses and even succeeded in getting the chorus down.

Eventually, she peered up at him.

"This could work," she said, a hint of a smile tugging at her red lips—lips he wanted to taste and find out if they were as soft and warm as they appeared.

Shaking away the thought, he grinned and was about to offer congratulations when their cells buzzed in tandem.

"It could be Steven. Mel's due anytime now," he said before checking his phone.

Steven: ***Baby boy just delivered:) Visiting hours 'til 8. Come as soon as suits.***

Chances were Steven had texted Julie, too. "Mel's had her baby," he said anyway.

"Yes." Her flat response and serious expression came as a surprise.

Didn't all women love babies?

Confused, he tried hard to remember if she'd ever expressed a desire to have children. He drew a blank.

"How about we go visit the new MacAlistar?" he said, noting the time on his screen. "We can kill two birds with one stone and grab a bite for lunch while we're out."

"I'll stay and finish this. You go."

Frowning, he angled his head. "You sure? You don't want to see the baby?"

"I'm on a roll here, Jack, so I'll go another time. I'm pretty sure a newborn isn't going to run away." A small smile accompanied her poor attempt at humor.

"Shall I bring you back a sandwich?"

"No... Thanks. I'll raid the bar fridge."

"Okay." He huffed out a long breath. Why was he bothering? She clearly didn't want his help. With anything. Or maybe she didn't even want him around, period. She'd been lumped with him because of Kevin, not by choice.

The thing was...occasionally, he caught her stealing glances at him. And unless he imagined it, when she did, longing filled her eyes.

He collected his jacket from the hook behind the door, then made one more attempt. "You sure you don't want to take a break?"

"Positive." Again, she avoided eye contact, which just confirmed, he'd have to be blind not to get the hint. She wasn't interested in being anything other than a fellow band member. Certainly not his friend.

***

The next five days were spent recording new material, after which Jack decided he was more than ready to go home. It had been another stressful week for the Jays, and as much as he enjoyed singing with Julie, all he wanted to do was unwind. In front of the TV, with a beer and pizza.

In that order.

Jack followed Julie toward the exit and reached out to open the door just as he heard his name. Turning his head, he spotted Kevin marching in their direction, a grim expression on his face.

"Wait up," Jack said, briefly placing a hand on Julie's arm and immediately steeling himself from the tingles that shot up his arm. "I think Kevin wants a word."

She spun around, frowning. "Oh, okay."

Moving back into the lobby entrance, they met Kevin halfway.

"Ah, I'd like a word with Jack, in private," their manager said, looking directly at Julie. "Do you mind?" He seemed a little uncomfortable, which said a lot. Usually, the man exuded a wall of confidence, as though nothing phased him.

Julie smiled, but it was far from genuine. No sparkle glinted in her eyes, and her stiff posture was a dead giveaway. "I'll order an Uber," she said.

"You don't have to do that." Jack looked at Kevin for confirmation. "I'm sure we won't be long, will we?"

"Actually, Julie, that's a good idea. Charge it to the label." Kevin's tone brooked no argument.

"Thanks, I will." She lifted her hand in a small wave and left, her heels clicking on the tiled floor as she went, her hips swaying seductively. Jack couldn't take his eyes off her, watching until she'd disappeared from sight.

"Ready now?"

Jack turned back to find Kevin smirking.

"Let's talk in my office. It'll be more comfortable, and I'll treat you to a cup of my favorite coffee."

Right. Like that or a change of scenery was likely to help lessen his unease. Not when he felt like a schoolboy being sent to the principal's office. But he couldn't really argue with his boss, so he rubbed his palms down his jeans and followed.

A short while later, the rich aroma of freshly brewed coffee beans permeated Kevin's office. Jack set aside his steaming mug—he wouldn't be able to stomach even a mouthful until he knew why Kevin wanted to 'chat.'

"So, how do *you* think things are going?"

"Uh..." Jack gripped the sides of the armchair. Why wasn't Julie here for this? As the most important part of the Jays, surely her opinion mattered... Unless Kevin planned on getting it separately?

"Great, I think. Julie and I are on the same wavelength when it comes to the music. She's an amazing songwriter, and it doesn't seem to take us long to nail down new songs." He chuckled nervously. "At least that's what Carl keeps telling us."

"Not what I was referring to, Jack. I know there's no problem with the songs and the music you're producing. Otherwise, I'd never have signed you in the first place."

"Oh, okay." He frowned. "Then I don't understand."

"I'll be upfront. When I first watched you and Julie perform, I was naturally drawn to your vocal abilities. But do you know the biggest drawcard? You were magical together; the chemistry between you palpable. Chemistry is not something easily manufactured or worked on with practice. It's either there, or it's not."

Blue-gray eyes bored into him, and he tried not to squirm under the intense scrutiny. Instead, Jack met Kevin's gaze head-on, without blinking.

"Something's happened to affect that chemistry over the past two weeks," Kevin said. "I'm afraid it's of major concern to me, and therefore the label. I can easily find other duos who can sing as well as you two. But finding that x-factor? That's what it's all about."

Jack inhaled sharply, panic gripping his chest. "Are you saying you want to drop us? Replace us even?"

Kevin waved his hands across his body. "No. No, I'm not saying that. I'm prepared to give you both a chance to get back your mojo, your rhythm, whatever it is that makes the two of you work so beautifully together. I need that easygoing chemistry back; otherwise, I'll be forced to pull the plug."

"I'll talk to Julie."

"Good." Kevin smiled tightly. "I'm counting on you."

As Jack left Kevin's office, his mind whirled. Ever since that moment in her living room, Julie had treated him differently, distanced herself from him. So, what he needed was to figure out how to restore their laid-back, professional relationship.

He didn't have a clue how to fix what was going on between them on a personal level. Lifting her up in his arms had been a huge mistake. The feel of her warm body pressed against his, his skyrocketing pulse, and the strongest desire to kiss her were memories he couldn't erase. One momentary lapse in judgment, and he'd created tension between them.

As much as he enjoyed his day job, he was loving this music thing more. Some of it had to do with spending time with Julie, but that wasn't all. He'd been bitten by the bug. Performing live on stage? He'd never thought it possible, not when he used to sing in the shower.

Performing with Julie? Incredible. Up on stage, the way women eyed him boosted his ego. Yet there was only one woman he wanted that kind of attention from, and lately, she wouldn't even make eye contact with him.

The dull ache growing daily in his chest made him determined to settle things with her. Apologize, get her back on the same page. He hadn't done anything wrong, but he'd assume the responsibility. If that's what it took.

Chapter Five

Usually, Jack had no objections to spending time at head office. But today, today he had somewhere more important to be than the weekly management meeting.

Stealing a glance at the silver-framed wall clock, he willed the minutes to fast forward another ten.

The hand stubbornly refused.

His gaze flitted across the executive boardroom to his friend Steven's impassive face, then on to the others seated around the cherry wood table. Despite the early hour, CEO David Peterson appeared bright-eyed and completely focused on his son, Brad.

Hands waving about enthusiastically, Brad's voice rose as he described the new client's requirements.

Jack absorbed nothing. All the relevant information would be in his inbox when he arrived at the site office later. Instead, his thoughts wandered to Julie. How easy would it be to pry her away from her desk without causing a scene? She was such a dedicated worker, she might decline his offer to play hooky, especially with him.

When would be the best time, though? Once he left the building, a face-to-face chat would have to wait until tonight. He'd considered calling her yesterday, but chances were she wouldn't have taken too kindly to him disturbing her on a Sunday—her one day off. Especially when she'd been going to such great lengths to avoid him outside of the studio.

"Do you agree, Jack?"

Scrambling to remember anything about the current discussion, Jack's face heated. "Sorry, David...I lost you there for a minute." Or five.

"There's nothing else we needed to cover today, right?" Their boss's penetrating stare was unnerving.

David couldn't read minds, could he? Jack wasn't entirely sure what the policy was about office romances, but— Wait...what was he thinking? Romance? His pulse quickened. He hadn't even kissed Julie. And she had a boyfriend.

He really needed to remember that!

"Yes, no." Jack nodded.

Steven chuckled.

"Pardon?" David's brow was crumpled in confusion.

"You're not like confusing at all, man," Brad said, smirking.

"I meant you're right, David. From my side, there's nothing else to discuss."

Itching to stand, Jack placed his palms on the cool table and slowly started pushing back his chair. He wouldn't be the first to leave, but he'd happily be the second.

After a long questioning look at him, David rose. "Then I think we're done here."

Straightening, Jack extended his hand to each man in turn and said his goodbyes. Halfway down the hall, he heard Brad's voice. "Jack sure was in a rush today. What do you think, Dad? You think he has like a hot coffee date or something?"

David's response was lost in the distance, but Jack couldn't contain his smile as he strode toward the Administration office. If only Brad knew how close he was to the truth.

Standing outside the double-doored entrance, Jack peered through the small glass pane and spotted Julie typing furiously on her keyboard. Every few seconds, she scanned some papers to her left, then continued her data input. Occasionally, her lips twisted, and she scowled, bringing another smile to his lips.

Most women around her were either chatting or on their phones. A few others drank beverages while they worked. No one stopped to chat with Julie, not even the mail lady who dumped the post into her tray. With everyone else, the woman lingered to talk.

What was that about?

A quick scan of the female faces in the large room revealed Julie to be the prettiest, by far. Did jealousy have something to do with the way she was typically treated?

Ages ago, Melanie had explained that Julie's female coworkers were resentful of her stunning looks, and they felt threatened by the way she flirted with unmarried men.

Gazing at Julie now, his heart thumped wildly in his chest. Honestly, she could flirt with him anytime!

Except... How easily he forgot. He might be single, but she wasn't.

He rubbed his hands on his pants, working up the courage to enter the 'den of ladies.' Of course, some men might appreciate being gawked at, but he avoided visiting for precisely that reason.

Fixing his eyes on the only person he actually wanted to see, he swung open the door and marched in.

Unlike the other employees, Julie didn't even respond to the change in atmosphere his entrance created. Surely the sudden quieting down of conversations and the unmistakable hum of whispered comments couldn't go unnoticed by her?

Seemed it did.

"Good morning, Miss Rolland," he said in a low voice, conscious of their audience as he leaned over the top of her wooden privacy panel. Waiting patiently, his heart skipped a few beats before she paid him any attention. When their gazes connected, her gorgeous green, oval-shaped eyes stared back at him. A flicker of surprise crossed her beautiful face, quickly followed by irritation.

"Any chance you can spare a half-hour?" he asked. "I need your help with something."

She didn't immediately respond.

He motioned to the doors. "In private, preferably."

There. He hadn't mentioned a date or coffee. To the rest of the room, he was here on a work-related mission. If the other women wondered what made Julie so special that he'd picked her out for his task, so what.

Her eyes narrowed. "Certainly, Mr. Carrington."

A disconcerting silence descended over the generous office space. Then, after a further few loud clicks of her mouse, Julie stood, grabbed her jacket off the back of her chair, and slipped her phone into a pocket.

"I'm ready." Her mouth remained in a grim line, and she avoided eye contact with everyone, including him.

Pivoting back toward the doors, Jack led the way, his head held high, his face expressionless. The click-clack of Julie's high heels on the tiled floor, along with her lavender scent, followed him out.

As soon as they were through the doors and out of earshot, she shot past him and spun around. Her hands flew to her hips. "What *exactly* do you need help with?"

"We need to talk."

She huffed loudly. "Last time I checked, the phones weren't bugged."

"I meant face to face, and ideally over coffee." He smiled softly, hoping to lighten the mood.

"You still could've called." She sounded angry. "How do you know I can just drop everything to have coffee? I have a job to do."

Her snarky attitude was beginning to irk him.

Tightening his jaw, he worked to keep his irritation at bay. "Are you being particularly difficult because you really do have work to do or because you *don't* want to have coffee with me?"

She glared at him for a long moment, then stalked off down the corridor without saying a word.

Where was she going?

Rooted to the spot, he watched, trying to understand what was going through her complicated mind.

Eventually, she stopped in front of the closed elevator doors and glanced over her shoulder. "Are you coming?" Her steely gaze matched her unfriendly tone.

Just as he took a hesitant step forward, she muttered loud enough for him to hear, "I haven't got all day."

Swallowing down the lump in his throat, Jack rubbed the back of his neck. Maybe this was a bad idea.

***

As the elevator descended to the ground floor of the Peterson building, Julie's mind raced with possibilities for Jack's impromptu coffee date invitation.

No, not a date. A meeting.

She racked her brain. Why did he want to talk? What could be *so* urgent he had to interrupt her workday?

Then it hit her—he wanted to quit the band!

Her hands fisted at her sides, and the butterflies waltzing in her stomach switched to a tango. Stealing a glance at Jack, she noted his clenched jaw and troubled expression. Was he worried he'd be letting her down and, in doing so, crush her dreams?

Sure, things between them had been tense recently, but she definitely didn't want to stop. Singing with Jack, writing songs, and performing with him were what she looked forward to most every day. As the steel doors pinged open, the thought of it all ending abruptly had her almost breaking out in a cold sweat.

Perhaps she needed to rethink her strategy.

Marching in the direction of her favorite coffee shop, she took several deep breaths.

Before she could pull open the glass door to Mary's, Jack's hand shot out. "Let me." He stood so close a hint of his musky scent tantalized her senses, and she had to resist the urge to lean in.

"Thanks," she said, her smile tight, her heart racing.

She strode inside and headed straight for the vacant seats in the corner. Frowning, Jack remained on his feet while she sat. "What can I get you to drink?" he asked.

"Tea. Peppermint, please." As much as she could do with the caffeine, there was no way it would settle in her stomach.

After ordering at the counter, Jack returned with their drinks, the smell of his pumpkin-spiced latte filling her nostrils.

Suddenly she wanted to heave.

Instead, she inhaled a long breath of her herbal drink, praying the mint's calming effect would work fast.

"Kevin's concerned about us."

Jack's statement, as well as the intensity and worry in his eyes, caught her like a trap, and she let out a small breath. "I thought the recordings we've done so far were good. At least that's what he said on Saturday."

"They are."

"What's he got to be concerned about then?"

"The tension between you and me."

"Oh." She should've realized Kevin wouldn't be blind to the strain in their relationship.

Tiny sparks shot up her arm when Jack's hand covered hers. He flinched like he felt them too, but he didn't move his hand away. She tried removing hers, but his grip was firm. If she pulled hard, she'd likely send both drinks flying.

His eyes searched hers. "So, what's wrong?"

"Nothing," she said, looking away. No way could she tell him the truth—*I wish you'd kissed me.*

"That's not true. Julie, look at me." She did but immediately regretted it. His downcast expression tugged at her heartstrings. "Ever since that moment in your living room, things have been strained between us," he said. "You've been different."

Unable to handle his electrifying touch any longer, she slid her hand out from under his loosened grip and leaned back in her seat. She sighed. Now that her hands were tucked safely in her lap, her heartbeat could finally slow from a sprint to a jog.

"I'm sorry if my actions that night gave you the wrong idea or made you feel uncomfortable." He sounded genuinely remorseful. "I wasn't thinking." Lifting his mug to his mouth, he paused before he took a sip. "Don't worry, I won't let it happen again."

The seriousness in his voice broke her heart.

So, he hadn't *actually* wanted to kiss her. He'd been caught up in the moment, instinctively leaning in for a kiss until he'd realized she wasn't Alex. At least, now she knew the truth. The realization tore her apart, but she needed to put him at ease.

"It's okay," she said, keeping her tone neutral. "There's no need to apologize. You did nothing wrong."

He stared at her for a long second, his expression unreadable. Then his attention shifted to the line of customers waiting to be served, and within seconds, he was rubbing his hands over his five o'clock shadow.

What was he thinking?

"Here's the thing," he said, not meeting her eyes. "Kevin told me in no uncertain terms that unless you and I sort out this issue between us, he's going to cancel our contract. According to him, besides our talent, our chemistry was what got us signed as a duo. He's not interested in solo artists." He paused, his tortured gaze locking onto hers. "What can I do to make things right between us?"

She scrunched her brow. "Make things right?"

"You know, get things back to the way they were before...before we had dinner together, and everything changed."

"I'm not sure there's anything you *can* do, Jack."

The beating in her chest became erratic as she eyed her teacup. Should she come clean?

"The thing is," she said, wishing she could've ordered a whiskey and soda instead of tea. "I...I, I'm in—" Chewing on her lower lip, she swallowed the words she was about to utter. Did she foolishly want to reveal her feelings, especially when they were so obviously not reciprocated?

Giving herself a mental shake, she made a show of checking her watch.

"Actually, I'm in a little bit of a rush," she mumbled, slipping off her chair. "I have to get back to my desk."

Jack's face was a picture of confusion.

After shoving her arms into her jacket sleeves, she sent him an apologetic look. "I'll meet you at the studio later. We can talk more then."

"Julie, wait!"

Ignoring him, she teetered away. Then, cursing her

jelly legs—this *so* wasn't the time!—she drew on experience and strode away in her six-inch heels.

Idiot!

What in the world had possessed her to even consider admitting her true feelings? That wasn't the way to fix this problem; ensuring the return of her and Jack's easy rapport—so Kevin didn't end their record deal—that was paramount.

How was she going to do that now she knew Jack hadn't even intended to kiss her?

She'd just have to figure out a way to keep her personal feelings under wraps while maintaining the kind of relationship Kevin expected her to have with Jack.

It's not like she hadn't pretended before. She'd just have to do it again and hope Jack never guessed the truth.

Chapter Six

The minute the clock struck five, Jack jumped up from his desk and grabbed his bomber jacket from the otherwise empty coat rack. With his gut churning, he raced to his truck and was soon on his way to the studio.

Julie had been about to tell him something important before she'd chickened out and rushed out of Mary's Coffee Shop. What though?

Recalling her words for the fiftieth time, he tried to finish her sentence. I'm in...

Too deep?

A sticky situation?

Trouble with the law?

He chuckled slightly manically at his absurd thoughts but then pondered her unfinished sentence further. Could she have been about to say, "I'm in love?"

Yeah, right! There was no way Julie was in love with him. Until they started singing together, she'd flirted with every guy around, never him. She'd barely even looked in his direction. She wasn't interested. Period.

Yet...it didn't explain the look of expectation on her face when he'd almost kissed her, did it?

Or had it been pure panic?

Either way, he still hadn't resolved their issue, and it was only a matter of time before they got their marching orders from Kevin. Or so it seemed.

Unless... An idea took hold, and hope bloomed. Was he seriously bold enough to do something so drastic?

It'd be a big risk and could ultimately backfire on him.

No. He shouldn't. He'd be playing with fire and would likely get hurt.

Julie's car wasn't in the studio's garage when he arrived a few minutes early, so having talked himself into his highly flammable plan, he hightailed it to the lobby. There, he hovered around a corner out of sight but still able to see the entrance.

He didn't have to wait long.

Hidden from view, he soaked up her appearance. Long, shiny hair cascaded over narrow shoulders. Her short tight black skirt and fitted black and white striped blouse were from earlier. *Stunning.* His gaze lowered to her shapely legs, then shot up to her cherry-colored lips. *Gorgeous.*

Heart thumping hard in his chest, he swallowed.

Did he really have the nerve?

Yes, he was going to do this, even if he made a fool of himself. He kept his eyes fixed on Julie's beautiful face and strode toward her.

"Jack!" He didn't care for the frown that marred her forehead as she spotted him. "What's up?"

Determined to be brave, he snagged her hand in his. "Come with me."

"What? Why?"

"Just come," he said gruffly, tugging her forward. She resisted for a second, but he tugged harder, and she relented.

They sped past their usual studio recording area and down the long corridor to the room where they'd written several songs. After pulling Julie inside with him, Jack shut the door firmly.

Grasping her hips, he slowly backed her against the wall. Her eyes went wide, and she planted her palms flat against his chest. "What are you doing?"

Afraid he'd lose his nerve if he waited any longer, he dipped his head. "This."

The instant Jack's lips touched Julie's, he felt a connection like never before. His arms circled her waist, and he drew her closer. Applying gentle pressure, he moved his lips over hers, and she responded with a muffled moan. Her lips parted.

Spurred on, he explored her delectable mouth. Her soft lips tasted sweeter than the syrup on his breakfast pancakes, and when he deepened the kiss, warmth flooded him. He quickly became lost in everything about her, and his heart raced. A kiss had never affected him so much.

Realizing how dangerous it was to continue, he reluctantly ended the kiss and leaned his forehead on hers. He fought to control his breathing for a while but eventually lifted his head. Julie was biting her lower lip.

"Please don't do that again," she murmured, her eyes completely dilated as she stared up at him.

"What?" Jack grinned. "You mean this?"

Like a nail to a magnet, he lowered his mouth to hers, eager to feel the magic again. The ineffective nudges she gave on his chest did nothing to dissuade him. Moving in sync, they quickly settled into another passionate kiss, and rational thoughts fled. All he could focus on was the soft, feminine body pressed up against his and the way she returned his kisses.

It was official—Julie turned his world upside down.

***

This is insane!

Using all her willpower and strength, Julie shoved Jack hard and gave him her fiercest look. "Stop! No more kissing. I. Mean. It."

Looking dazed and probably confused at her sudden change of heart, Jack frowned and took a step back, his hands lifted in surrender. "I thought that's what you wanted."

Crossing her arms, she stared at him. Was he serious? That's why he'd kissed her? Where had he gotten that idea from?

Even if it were true.

"No." She shook her head vehemently, mainly to convince herself. Kisses like those weren't something to be encouraged.

Especially not from Jack.

They needed to work together. Besides, Julie wanted him to kiss her because he felt something for her, not so he could manipulate her into acting the way he needed.

Snatching up her purse from the carpet, she stormed out of the room and made her way to the restroom. She needed a minute to gather her thoughts and rein in her emotions. In private.

A few deep breaths, in and out, didn't calm her racing heart, but they did make her feel a bit better. Shaking her limbs out, she tried to dispel the delicious sensations leftover from Jack's incredible kisses.

No one had ever kissed her like that. His touch, his lips, everything about being in his arms had shaken her to the core. The rest of the world might as well have not existed. His kisses had rocked her world.

Either he was a fantastic actor or...what? She shook her head. No. He was using her to get what he wanted, or rather to keep what he had. Well, she didn't want to lose this record deal either, so she'd have to play along.

It was the only way.

But in order to protect her heart, she'd have to insist he kept his lips to himself in future. Resolution made, she plastered on a smile and slunk into the recording studio. Both Jack and Kevin turned at her approach. Despite Jack's slumped shoulders and grim expression, she held onto her fake smile and continued into the room.

"You okay, Julie?" Kevin's hesitant smile had her wondering what they'd been talking about before she arrived.

"I'm great, Kevin." She turned to face Jack, and brightening her smile, laid a reassuring hand on his bicep. Awareness of his hard muscles beneath his jacket sleeve had her heart thumping erratically. Somehow, she managed to keep her voice steady. "We're ready to get started. Right, Jack?"

He mirrored her smile and nodded, covering her hand with his. "Yes. Let's nail this song."

Just as they were about to start singing, Kevin threw his hands up and shouted, "Wait! I have an idea." He left them hanging for a minute before returning with a burly man wearing a tight-fitting black T-shirt, sporting a serious-looking camera. The man gave them a brief nod.

"I want to film this journey," Kevin said, beaming at the Jays, "so when your first original song becomes a hit —and believe me, it will be a hit—we'll already have music video footage." He turned back to the latest addition to the team. "You need to record their every move, every expression, and every word. I want it all captured."

Nodding, the cameraman positioned himself in front of Julie and Jack.

Even with Kevin's encouraging expression, Julie felt pressure. Pressure to pretend that breathing in the same air as Jack, and knowing the taste of his lips intimately, didn't affect her in the slightest.

Trying to distract herself, she glanced down at her work outfit and groaned. "This is hardly a country look and most definitely not my preferred style of clothing."

Jack scanned her from head to toe. "I think you look gorgeous."

Kevin murmured his agreement, and her cheeks grew toasty.

"Mind if I lose my jacket and reapply my lipstick at least?" she asked before realizing her mistake. Certain her face now resembled a ripe tomato, she quickly added, "It's okay, it doesn't matter."

"I'll give you a minute." Kevin's smirk fueled the heat on her face, which threatened to make her sweat.

Throughout the following two hours, heated glances passed between her and Jack. Evidently, their natural chemistry had resurfaced. A fact that quickly resulted in Kevin grinning like he'd received an early Christmas present.

Three attempts later, the song was recorded.

"Fantastic job, you two!" Kevin planted a peck on her cheek then stuck out his hand to Jack. "Now go home and get some rest."

"Yes, sir!" Jack saluted.

Julie strolled over to collect her jacket and purse. As she turned toward Jack, she had to stifle a huge yawn.

A smile lit his features, and warmth filled his voice. "I feel the same. Although I don't know about you, I'm a happy exhausted."

"Definitely exhausted," she said, trying not to return his engaging smile but barely succeeding. Since Kevin was still within earshot, she added in a low voice, "We achieved our goal. That's the important thing."

Once they were all ready, they exited the studio's recording room together. Walking by her side, Jack placed his warm hand on the small of her back, sending delicious shivers up her spine.

She glanced sideways at him. He was smiling, but the camera wasn't rolling anymore, so why continue creating the illusion of a relationship? Unless he was concerned about Kevin's perception of them?

Fine. She'd run with it while they were in public. Once they were alone, she'd make herself clear.

***

Jack couldn't wipe off his smile. Their careers were back on track! A feeling of euphoria settled over him, and he released a deep sigh.

While accompanying Julie to her car, he pondered what had gone through her mind earlier. Whatever it was, she'd clearly made the right decision to move forward. Kissing her had been the right thing to do, despite her protests.

Alex's words from when she'd broken up with him at Melanie's wedding came flooding back. "You deserve someone who turns your world upside down, who makes the world and everyone in it fade away when you kiss them." That's exactly what had happened when he'd kissed Julie. She was the one he'd been waiting for, uh, only forever. The knowledge struck him deep in his gut.

When Julie shifted next to him, he scrutinized her tense face, then dropped his hand instinctively.

"Everything okay?"

"Perfect." Her tone implied nothing of the sort.

They approached her car just as the doors unlocked

automatically. Jack made sure he reached the driver's side door first and blocked her path.

She stepped closer, hardening her expression. "Do you mind moving?"

Hooking an arm around her waist, he heard her sharp intake of breath when he pulled her to him. "I wanted to say goodnight."

"Jack!" Her voice was breathy rather than cross, yet panic showed clear in her eyes before her gaze dropped to his lips. Obviously, she was having similar thoughts.

He leaned in, his lips nearing hers. Only her finger touching his mouth made him pause, the tiny spark catching him by surprise. He lifted his head an inch.

"Don't," she whispered, her eyes closed.

"Don't what?"

"Don't kiss me." She looked at him then, a plea in her eyes. "There's no camera rolling here. I'll play along. You don't need to convince me. I get it."

What! Had she really been acting the whole time? Dumbstruck, he stepped aside, allowing her access to her vehicle. Once she was inside, she opened her window. "You'll pick me up at five tomorrow morning? Like usual?"

He nodded, staring at her with his head in a spin. The way she'd returned his kisses was not a pretense. Why would she have done that?

Before he knew it, she'd backed out of her parking space, and her car's taillights were fading as she headed out of the parking garage.

Then it hit him—he'd completely forgotten about Zac. Again.

A while later, Jack unlocked his front door, glad to be home. The journey had felt much longer than normal, given his mind had been processing the evening's events. His heart, on the other hand, had soared every time he remembered those incredible kisses.

"Jack, is that you?" Charlie called from down the hall as he eased off his work boots.

"Who were you expecting, Charlie? The Queen?" He kept his voice low as he ventured toward the bedrooms.

The kids shouldn't be awake, but he didn't want to disturb them if they were.

Charlie didn't respond.

He checked her kids' bedrooms first. The boys, six-year-old Peter and four-year-old Daniel were sound asleep, but their eight-year-old sister Amy's bedcovers were ruffled, and her bed was empty.

"Charlie? Where are you?" he called, as quietly as he could.

"The kids' bathroom...with Amy." His sister's voice cracked somewhat on the last word.

Not a good sign.

Charlie was an amazing mother, coping on her own. With her husband, Mark, building homes for the poor in Africa, she couldn't rely on him being around much. So whenever Jack could help, he did, happily. After all, he *had* made a promise to Mark.

Not that Charlie knew anything about it.

Jack's commitment was one of the reasons he'd never had a proper girlfriend until Alex. Women he'd dated previously hadn't understood why a successful, thirty-year-old eligible bachelor still lived with his sister and her family. Nor why he chose to be at their beck and call twenty-four seven.

"Any man who puts family first is a man to hold on to," Alex had told him in the beginning, sealing the deal. Except, in the end, she'd dumped him anyway.

Upon entering the bathroom, he saw Amy leaning against her mom on the floor. The little girl looked peaceful with her eyes closed, but her pale face told another story. A bucket sat beside them.

"Hey," Charlie whispered, her eyes glistening, her smile wobbly.

He knelt on the warm tiles. "How can I help?"

"Uncle Jack," Amy said, her eyes flying open. She smiled weakly. "I've been sick."

"I know, sweetie." He stroked her head, brushing stray locks of silky hair behind her ears. "How about I take you back to your bed?" He gave her a reassuring smile. "You'll be more comfortable there."

"Okay."

With a small grunt, he lifted Amy up. She wound her arms around his neck and leaned her head on his shoulder. Breathing in her berry-scented shampoo, he then peered over at Charlie's slumped shoulders and exhausted expression. "Have you eaten yet?" he asked.

"No."

He suspected as much.

Unraveling her legs, Charlie stood gingerly. "I'll grab something quickly while you get her settled." She sighed deeply. "I don't know what I'd do without you, Jack. You're a lifesaver."

"Any time, Charlie." Precisely the reason he always put her first. She needed him. There was no one else.

They'd been relying on each other for the past ten years, ever since Mom had died shortly after Dad.

Mark might be a wonderful husband, but he was hardly ever around. Acting as a 'stand-in dad' with all the responsibilities didn't bother Jack in the least. He'd always wanted a wife and children, and although this wasn't exactly the plan, he was happy with his lot in life.

Mostly.

Even if he sometimes got a little jealous seeing Melanie with her perfect family, living on their own. Charlie's focus naturally shifted whenever Mark came home. It was only then that Jack felt like an intruder in his own house. Redundant, really.

He lowered a sleepy Amy onto her bed and pulled the princess covers up over her petite body. His fingers brushed her forehead—it felt slightly warm and damp. About to leave to find a wet cloth, Amy's wide eyes and raspy voice stopped him.

"Uncle Jack?" She pushed herself into a sitting position, pain flickering over her face.

"What is it, sweetie?"

"I think I need the bucket," she said weakly, clutching her stomach.

In the nick of time, he had it in position.

While he nursed his niece, his thoughts wandered back to Julie. Would all the time he spent helping his sister bother her?

Was she the understanding type?

Did she even have a family?

He'd never heard her talk about her parents or any siblings. He did, however, have a faint recollection of her having been fostered. So, what of her biological parents? Were they still alive? Did they have any other children?

Realizing he knew next to nothing about her, he let out a deep breath. He needed to remedy that—the sooner, the better.

The rest of the evening went by in a blur, with Amy finally falling fast asleep around three in the morning. By then, Jack was so exhausted he didn't have the energy to decipher the meaning behind Julie's words of 'playing along' and 'I get it.'

All he knew was that kissing her was a catalyst, and every day his attraction grew. He'd had a taste of her soft lips, and he craved more, so this 'no kissing' policy of hers was going to drive him mental.

Then, of course, there was Zac.

Chapter Seven

Julie stepped outside into the cool morning air as the door to her apartment block closed behind her. Her heart skipped a beat. Jack was leaning back against the side of his truck, an overhead light illuminating his chiseled features. The hunter-green bomber jacket he wore accentuated his emerald-colored eyes. Eyes which tracked her progress down the sidewalk until only a few steps separated them.

"Good morning," he said quietly. He offered her a cardboard cup, his dazzling smile making her stomach flip.

"Hi." Sighing contentedly, she wrapped her fingers around the warm container. "I thought coffee was a no-no before singing."

"I won't tell if you don't," he whispered as if this were a clandestine meeting.

Chuckling, she scanned the surrounding area. Not another soul in sight, only an occasional flickering streetlight and the odd chirp from birds who clearly hadn't realized the sun still slept.

Julie eyed Jack over the rim of her cup as she sipped her forbidden latte and noticed dark rings under his eyes. Over the past few weeks, he seemed to have coped rather well with their early mornings, unlike her.

Until now.

What had changed? Was it her 'no kissing' request?

"Did you have a bad night?" she asked.

Samantha J. Ball

"Kind of." He scratched his jaw, frowning. "Amy was really ill, so Charlie and I took turns watching her."

Right. Silly to think Jack was tossing and turning at night because he wasn't allowed to kiss her. She mentally chided herself for being so self-centered.

"Gosh, I'm sorry. Is Amy okay? I don't mind heading over to the studio alone if you're needed at home."

He shook his head. "Thanks, but I left Amy fast asleep. She hadn't thrown up for a few hours, so I think Charlie will cope fine."

"Okay. If you're sure?"

He moved a little closer, brushing a knuckle over her cheek, his gaze fixed on hers. "I like that you're compassionate."

"Thanks," she murmured, his soft touch warming her even more than the hot drink.

Witnessing his pupils dilate, she panicked and looked down... at his mouth.

Mistake.

Her cheeks heated, recalling his kisses, and she quickly propped her cup against her mouth in defense. Then that errant hand of his pushed a stray strand of hair behind her ear, sending tingles down her neck. Each time he shifted closer, his warmth radiated outwards, causing shivers to ricochet through her body. She subconsciously gravitated nearer, too, her heart thundering in her chest.

As she lowered her drink, his eyes closed.

Julie really, really wanted Jack to kiss her. Torn between her resolution and an intense yearning to feel his lips on hers once more, she watched him closely.

Would he honor her request and refrain?

His jaw twitched, and he released a deep sigh before slowly raising his eyelids. Desire burned brightly in his eyes for a second, then it flickered out. "I know. No kissing."

The resignation in his voice surprised her, while equal parts of disappointment and pleasure filled her. He took her words seriously! That meant more to her than reliving those magical kisses.

At least that's what she told herself.

"About yesterday," he said, sounding a little unsure—still in her way as he pulled the passenger-side door open—"I wanted to clear something up. I don't know why you feel the need to act like anyone other than yourself around me, Julie. I wish you wouldn't. Also, I don't kiss beautiful women unless I really want to."

"You think I'm beautiful?"

Instead of answering, he stepped aside, motioning for her to climb up into the cab. As she took a step toward the running board, his hand shot out to stop her.

"And Julie?" Slowly, she met his scorching gaze, her heart hammering hard. "Just so you know, I really wanted to kiss you yesterday, and I really want to kiss you now. But I know I mustn't." Pivoting, he rounded the rear of the vehicle, leaving her to get situated in the cab.

Somehow, with her breath caught in her throat and her mind racing, she managed to fasten her seat belt.

The drive to the studio was quiet.

Julie felt like a fool. She'd only told Jack not to kiss her because she didn't want to be manipulated. Yet clearly, their attraction was mutual, and they worked closely together. Further sensational kisses might lead to a relationship. Was that his intention? Sharing a career and a relationship would be asking for trouble. If one didn't work, what would happen to the other?

No, she'd be wise not to get romantically involved with Jack.

Even so, something else niggled at the back of her mind—Zac's observations from when he visited Melanie at the hospital. Was it possible Jack and Alex were back together? Unlikely. Unless he was a two-timing jerk.

She shook her head. Jack came across as a man of integrity. Whatever their relationship was or became—coworker, friend, or possibly more—honesty between them was imperative. It was the only way they'd survive the world of music together.

Her gut churning with indecision, Julie cleared her throat.

"Something wrong?" Jack took his eyes off the road for a second.

"Is anything still going on with you and Alex?"

"No, why would you think that? You know she broke up with me at Mel's wedding. Months ago."

"I know. It's just that Zac said—"

"I wouldn't believe anything Zac says." Jack's tone was gruff. "Not when it comes to Alex."

Julie swallowed hard. Obviously, she'd hit a nerve. Could Jack still be harboring feelings for Alex? Twisting her hands in her lap, she tried not to feel jealous but wasn't very successful.

Engulfing her hands with his larger one, Jack gave them a gentle squeeze before letting go. "I'm sorry. That came out wrong. It's just that..."

"Just what?" She peered at his profile, wishing she could trace the strong line of his jaw.

He huffed out a breath. "Zac's a little blinded when it comes to Alex."

"What do you mean?"

He gave her a brief sideways glance. "You're his girlfriend. I've probably said too much already."

What? Why would he think that? Of course—he didn't know! It's not like she'd announced her 'break up.' Was that why he'd said he mustn't kiss her?

"Zac's not my boyfriend."

"Seriously?"

She kept up the pretense. "Not since July, actually."

"Wow. I had no idea."

Silence filled the cab. Reaching out to press the button for the radio, Julie noticed Jack's white knuckles gripping the steering wheel.

Was he cross with her?

When a red light stopped them, he faced her, his expression unreadable. "I think Zac's totally in love with Alex, but I'm not sure she has a clue."

Julie stared at him, her pulse quickening. Dare she admit the truth? The light turned green just as she looked away. "You're right. He is."

Jack swung left into the narrow entrance of the

studio's underground garage, backed into a free parking space, and cut the engine.

"Is that why you two broke up?" he asked.

So much for avoiding explanations.

Pushing her palms over her knees, she focused on the concrete pillars holding the building in place. "This is probably going to sound crazy, but..." If he thought any less of her after this, then so be it. It was the truth. "Zac and I were never really a couple."

Jack's eyebrows shot up. "Sorry, what?"

"From the beginning, we made a pact that we'd only ever be friends."

"I don't understand."

"Zac already had his eye on Alex. I liked him, and he needed a friend. So, under no illusions whatsoever, I happily pretended to be his girlfriend. The only reason we 'broke up,' as you called it, was because Zac didn't want Alex thinking he was unavailable. Especially when he discovered she was single again."

Jack rubbed the back of his neck. "But I distinctly remember the two of you sharing a passionate kiss at Mel's wedding. Was that an act?"

She laughed. "Trust me, I was completely thrown by Zac's kiss and mortified. After that PDA, thinking he'd suddenly developed feelings for me, I didn't talk to him for almost a month! But he put my mind at rest the night we called our fake relationship quits."

"Zac saw me kissing Alex and wanted to make her jealous."

"You got it in one."

"So my suspicions about him were right." Jack's smile was fleeting. "What exactly did Zac say about Alex and me? You were about to tell me, but I snapped."

"That you and Alex hugged and shared a kiss after your hospital visit."

"Ah." Understanding lit his green eyes. "We chatted, that's all. Alex was upset about her lack of romantic prospects and worried she'll never have a child." His lips morphed into an easy smile, and he crossed his arms. "I told her that if she was still unmarried at forty, I'd marry her."

Julie gasped, then saw his teasing smirk and smacked his arm. "You didn't!"

Laughing, Jack snatched her hand and laced their fingers. When his smile widened, her insides melted. His thumb began a slow caress of hers, and she struggled to concentrate on anything but his touch.

"I'm glad you know when I'm joking," he said, his voice low. The intensity in his eyes made Julie squirm. If she didn't get away, she couldn't be responsible for her actions.

Breaking eye contact, she glimpsed the neon digits on the dashboard. "Look at the time!" she exclaimed. "We better get inside before Kevin blows a gasket."

Extracting her fingers from Jack's, she immediately felt the loss of his warmth and the security of his touch. Still, she grabbed the door handle and pushed.

***

The next two weeks settled into an effective routine. Every morning, Jack would collect Julie on his way to the studio. There—in what they now referred to as the writing room—they'd hash out new song lyrics over much-needed black coffee. Occasionally, Kevin would conjure up another writer to help the process along, but it was just the two of them for the most part.

Jack noticed a different side to Julie during these sessions—she wore her heart on her sleeve.

He recalled a particular incident from the previous Friday where she'd leaped up from her seat, her pencil flying across the room and her notepad slipping to the floor. "They're not working!" she'd exclaimed.

"What's not working? The lyrics?"

She hadn't heard him—well if she had, she hadn't acknowledged it. Instead, she'd paced up and down the small room rubbing her infinity tattoo, her red lips pressed together in frustration.

Picking up the discarded paper, he'd scrutinized her words:

So come home to me
And I'll make you <u>believe</u>

You're all that I need
My love, guaranteed

"I think they're perfect, Julie."

"Can't you tell the word 'believe' doesn't work?"

"Okay...can I suggest using 'agree' then?"

"Seriously, Jack?" She'd retrieved her pencil and snatched the sheet back. "That's ridiculous!"

Jack had momentarily considered backing out of the room after that. Yet he'd sunk onto his seat and watched her lips twisting, clearly entertaining other words.

Seconds later, her lips had once again lifted into a wide smile, changing her whole demeanor. "See," she'd said, peering straight at him.

"See what?"

"The word I need is *see*, not believe."

But that had been an isolated episode. More often than not, words flowed from her brain directly to the paper, and when they did, her face lit up like she'd won the lottery. Those were the times he could say anything he liked, and she'd agree with a willing smile.

A bone-melting sexy smile.

In her excitement, she'd touch his arm frequently while explaining her thoughts and ideas. Delicious tingles would travel all over his body.

The desire to kiss her remained just below the surface. So, whenever Jack contemplated kissing her senseless or found himself close enough to lean forward and press his lips to hers, he'd remember her request. Putting physical distance between them was the only thing that would work then, and praying the desire would flee.

But it never did.

All too soon, their morning hour together would be over, and they'd be on their way to work. Then Jack would drop Julie outside the entrance to Peterson's and make his way to whichever building site he was working on that week.

Recently, a construction worker had pulled him aside with a knowing look on his face.

"You're looking particularly cheerful today, Mr. Carrington. Who's the lucky lady?"

Jack had narrowed his eyes at the man and replied, "Amy."

"Nice."

"Yeah. She's my eight-year-old niece."

The following day, Hector, Jack's foreman, had laid a calloused hand on Jack's arm and waited for him to meet his eye.

"Looks like someone's brought your light back," Hector had said. "Tell me which lovely woman we have to thank, would you? After Alex dumped you, we thought grumpy Jack was here to stay."

With a tight smile and a non-committal grunt, Jack had continued explaining what needed doing on site.

Every day after work, he would rush home to take a quick shower, then help Charlie put the kids to bed before swinging by Julie's. Once she was safely ensconced in his truck, they'd either ride back to the studio or to whatever occasional gig Kevin had booked.

Most nights, Julie prepared a packed meal for them to eat at the studio during a short break. Jack always looked forward to her surprises, like a little boy on his birthday.

When he'd offered to contribute, she'd dismissed him with a wave. "It's no problem at all. I've always loved cooking and, no offense to your sister, but hasn't she enough on her plate without needing to prepare an additional meal every night?"

Touched by her thoughtfulness and unable to think of any hole in her logic, he'd simply nodded.

In no time, they'd finished writing all the songs needed for a debut album. Then, using their nightly sessions to get familiar with the new material, they began laying down the tracks.

At Kevin's insistence, their stocky cameraman was their constant shadow. But Jack managed to ignore the camera since Kevin no longer had a reason to complain about the Jays. Meanwhile, Julie remained attentive, maintaining eye contact with him and allowing him to periodically hold her hand or place it around her waist.

The one thing Jack longed to do was kiss her again, but he respected her wishes, no matter how frustrated it made him feel.

***

Stacking papers on her desk, Julie hid a smile. The past fourteen days with Jack had been pretty wonderful. He'd been looking at her like she was the only woman in the world, and it made her feel pretty special. Clearing the air with him had been the right call and had broken an invisible barrier between them.

The smell of overly sweet perfume and a jingle of multiple bracelets warned of Brianna's approach. Tensing, Julie looked up.

Tasked with introducing a new employee around the office, Brianna didn't bother to stop when they reached Julie's workstation. Instead, she steered the confused woman right past her desk and on toward Julie's neighbor.

Rude! But Julie was used to it.

At least, she should've been.

"That's the woman I told you about," Brianna muttered loudly, pointing her thumb back over her shoulder at Julie. "The one who flirts with any and every male."

At the woman's wide-eyed expression, Brianna added in an even icier tone—if that were possible—"If you have a boyfriend, then you'd better have eagle eyes. Because, if you bring him here, Miss Rolland will be all over him in two seconds flat. So, you'd better not drop your guard."

A sharp pain gripped Julie's chest, but she ignored it. She'd overheard similar comments before and decided it was ridiculous to be concerned about what others thought. She knew the truth.

Except, the remarks hurt. She meant no harm. Like her mom, she was just friendly. It was in her nature to flirt, or was it because of nurture?

She shook her head. Working out which, wasn't important.

Updating some reports on her computer a short time later, she noticed all the women congregating around Brianna's workstation.

"It's official, ladies," Brianna said, her smug voice carrying perfectly across the office, "I've booked us the Mayflower Spa Resort for next weekend."

A loud cheer went up from the group, and a couple of them glanced in Julie's direction. The sneers on their faces confirmed her suspicions. 'Us' did not include her.

The uncomfortable feeling of pain in her chest returned with a vengeance. Hiding her grimace and wet cheeks with her hands, she groaned. Maybe it was time to look for a new job. Usually, she could take the cattiness and the disdain surrounding her at work.

Today, it was a struggle.

Drawing in a deep, steadying breath to prevent further tears, she then let it out slowly. It wouldn't be hard getting a reference from David. Not when he always complimented her.

"You do an outstanding job," and "You're a real asset to the company, Julie," were two things he'd told her recently. And Jack would happily put in a good word wherever she applied.

But did she really need another change in her life right now?

Only time would tell what would happen with the Jays' record deal. Kevin had spoken of releasing a single first to gauge the public's response, and then after that, if it went as well as he expected, they could potentially do larger concerts and possibly even headline one of their own.

The possibility of touring the country in the future had been hinted at too.

No. Now was not the time to leave the job she'd been doing since she was eighteen. Seven years had flown by, and she'd achieved a lot. Teaching herself accounting at home every night for the first few years had been hard, but she'd been determined to better herself.

Beginning with her very first position on reception, she'd worked her way up to a coveted spot in the accounting department at Peterson's.

She wasn't about to give it up.

With the decision made, Julie bowed her head and got on with her work.

Later, when Jack's attractive face popped into her mind, as it frequently did nowadays, she allowed herself an indulgent half-smile. After all, the others might be planning a leisure weekend without her, but she was the one who got to spend every day with the 'hot guy' they all wanted to date.

Chapter Eight

Sometimes Julie thought she was invisible.

Sometimes she wished she was. Like now when all the women around her were reminiscing loudly about their 'invigorating, relaxing, and amazing' weekend.

The weekend she hadn't been invited on.

Would it be rude to put on earphones? Because the constant chatter and laughter were getting on her nerves.

Counting to ten under her breath, then twenty, Julie chose to picture Jack in his new green and black flannel shirt from this morning. He'd worn it over a fitted gray tee, and the pairing had made his eyes pop. The memory of his heated expression, when he caught her checking him out, flooded her with warmth.

She peered down at her desk. The papers she'd been trying to separate were now thoroughly mixed up.

Great. She'd have to start over.

Before she could begin, her cell buzzed with Jack's text tone. Snatching her phone off her desk, she lowered it to her lap and opened his message: **Hey. Still here. Want 2 meet 4 lunch in the cafeteria?**

Julie glanced at her computer. Almost twelve. An early lunch suited her, especially since she had no desire to re-sift through fifty sheets of paper on an empty stomach. As her thumbs hovered over her phone screen, the hairs on the back of her neck stood to attention, and her head shot up.

Brianna was staring directly at her phone.

Hiding her screen, Julie glared at the intruder. "Can I help you, Brianna?"

"Nope." She smiled sweetly. "Just wondering whose man you've got your hooks into now."

"No one's. Not that it's any of your business." Wheeling her chair backward, Julie leaned forward to grab her purse from the floor. Then, without giving Brianna a second look, she clenched her fist and strode away from her desk.

Thrusting open the double doors, she marched through toward the open-air area. With any luck, she'd find some peace and quiet there.

On the way, her phone buzzed in her hand. Probably Jack looking for an answer to his invite. She checked the screen. Yep, Jack: *Any time from now?*

Huffing, she shook out her shoulders. Imagine the comments if they ate in the staff cafeteria—she'd never live it down. She replied: *Sorry. Not a good idea. See you later.*

Although it reeked of smoke, the outdoor balcony was thankfully empty. Julie admired the view but was unable to focus on any particular building. Down below, vehicles moved along the streets like ants scurrying up and down the lanes, while above, the clouds were steadily darkening. Perhaps the forecast for rain later today was accurate.

Her stomach grumbled. Suddenly, she had a craving for comfort food. Lasagna. Or maybe spinach and ricotta ravioli. Sighing, she glanced at her phone and found no new notifications—her fault she'd be eating alone again, but Jack wouldn't have understood.

Exiting the main entrance of Peterson's, she barely made it fifty yards down the sidewalk when a familiar voice called out her name. Her stomach tightened, and, pretending not to have heard, she quickened her pace.

"Julie!"

Relenting, she slowed down and turned.

"Hey, Jack."

"Where are you off to? Lunch?" He strode toward her,

the lines between his eyebrows marring his handsome face. "Hot date you didn't want to tell me about?"

Was he jealous? Her face heated at the idea.

Inspecting the concrete, she shook her head. "No, of course I don't."

His hand grasped her arm, and her head jerked up. "Why isn't it a good idea for us to eat together then?" he asked, hurt and confusion flickering in his gaze.

"Us eating together is fine." She gave him her most beguiling smile. "My problem is eating with you," she said, pointing back up at the office building and adding, "In there."

It took a moment before comprehension dawned, and he released his hold, his expression softening. "I see." A teasing tone entered his voice. "You're not ready for the office gossips to declare us a couple."

She laughed. "You're funny!"

"I love hearing you laugh." Amusement flittered across his face. Then his expression turned earnest, reminding her why this wasn't a good idea, and her smile slipped.

"Seriously though, the ladies at work already give me a hard enough time, Jack. If I have lunch with you, I'll never hear the end of it."

"Well, I know an excellent, out-of-the-way Italian restaurant near here." His fingers brushed her cheek. "Does that appeal?"

"Yes," she whispered.

Jack offered her his arm, his eyes twinkling. She hesitated, looking back at the revolving doors. "Don't worry, the coast is clear," he said, chuckling.

She punched his bicep playfully, then flinched and had to rub her tender knuckles. She marveled at how quickly she'd forgotten about the work he did on construction sites.

Linking her arm with his, she eyed him. "You think I'm being ridiculous, don't you, Mr. Carrington?"

"Cut it out, Julie."

She batted her eyelashes. "What?"

"You know what, *Miss Rolland.*"

She giggled. Bumping into Jack on her way out of the office had certainly improved this day by leaps and bounds.

***

Gino—an old family friend of Jack's parents—practically lifted Jack off the ground the minute he and Julie stepped into the restaurant. Then, after several long seconds and a few firm pats on Jack's back, Gino released him.

"What 'as it been, Jack? A year? I thought you'd dropped dead, and your sister forgot to tell me!"

Gino's hearty laughter echoed around them while Jack's laughter was more reserved, a little guilty. There was a time his family would visit at least once a month to enjoy Gino's mouth-watering meals. But since Italian hadn't exactly been Alex's favorite food—

"I'm sorry, Gino. It's been too long."

"And who is this bella donna?" Gino asked.

Feeling a strange need to protect Julie, who stood slightly behind him, Jack took her by the hand and drew her next to him. Gino might be twice their age, but he was a good-looking man who took great care of himself. From Jack's experience, ladies usually swooned in the older man's presence.

He snuck a peek at Julie. Yep, her flushed face showed she was no exception. Or could it be that, like him, she felt the rightness of their joined hands?

"This is my friend, Julie." Jack smiled warmly at her as he made the introduction. "Julie, Gino."

A wide smile appeared on Gino's tanned face as he captured Julie's other hand, bringing it to his lips. "Enchanted. Jack is a 'andsome young man and a great catch. You two make a perfect couple."

Looking suddenly uncomfortable, Julie shook her head. "Oh, we're not a couple."

Gino frowned and raised his eyebrows at Jack.

"Actually, we are." He hoped Julie understood his explanation and wouldn't argue further. "We're in a band together, just the two of us, so we are a couple."

Julie's brow furrowed. "As musicians, yes," she said,

giving Gino a tight smile.

Jack's heart sank. Okay. Clearly, they needed to talk about their relationship, define it, and agree on what to tell people.

"No matter, come, come." Gino motioned for them to follow him, his chirpy voice lifting the slightly strained mood. "I'm sure you're both 'ungry." He directed them to an area toward the back of his establishment. The table he indicated had the most privacy but was close enough to the kitchen to get the best service and would've been Jack's preferred choice anyway.

Once they were settled with cloth napkins on their laps and water glasses filled, Gino handed them menus. "Pedro will be over to take your order in a few minutes. I'll make sure 'e knows to give you everything you want."

"Thanks, Gino." Jack beamed at the older man.

Before leaving, Gino laid a hand on his shoulder and leaned down to whisper, "This one's a keeper. I feel it in my bones."

Jack peeked at Julie, but she appeared engrossed in her menu. "Anything catching your eye?" he asked.

Peering over the top of the card, she nodded. "Everything." She giggled, a carefree sound he didn't hear often enough. "I do love Italian food. Do you have any recommendations?"

"Everything."

"Not helpful," she grumbled, half-smiling.

"I'll tell you what. Why don't I ask the chef to prepare a few taster portions of his favorites? That way, you can enjoy a few dishes rather than just one."

Her eyes lit up like sparklers. "You can do that?"

"In case you didn't notice, I have an 'in' with the owner."

"Right, I forgot." She blinked. "I'll leave you in charge of satisfying my appetite then."

He stifled a groan—pity she was only referring to food.

Soft music played over the speakers, and waiters bustled about attending to other customers scattered around the restaurant.

"Julie?"

Guarded, her eyes met his.

"We need to talk about our relationships," he said, keeping his tone light. "Professional and personal."

"What do you mean?"

"Well, it's only a matter of time before word gets out about us being in a band. Then the ladies at work, the ones that bother you so much, they'll potentially become an even bigger issue for you."

Looking down at her clasped hands, she sighed. "You're right. I can't bury my head in the sand and pretend they're never going to know."

"Do you have a problem with them knowing about you and me?"

"You and me?"

"That we spend a lot of time together," he explained.

"I suppose not. I guess I am concerned they'll use me as a reason to sully your reputation or something."

"How do you figure that?" he asked, confused.

"You're the golden boy, Jack. The man every available woman wants to date. Associating with the 'office flirt' isn't going to look good for you. Not to mention whoever you do end up dating will most likely feel constantly threatened." He opened his mouth to disagree, but she hurried on, "I know that's why they're not friendly toward me. They worry I'm going to lure their boyfriends away, but I honestly don't know why they think I have so much power."

Jack found it refreshing how Julie seemed to have no clue just how beautiful and sexy she was. Initially, her habitual flirting had put him off, despite his physical attraction, until he'd gotten to know her better.

Reaching over, he covered her hands with his. "You don't need to worry. If you agree, I'll talk to David about us this afternoon, set the record straight. I know he'll be supportive."

"Okay." She twisted her lips, looking like she wanted to say something more but didn't.

"What's bothering you?" he asked, squeezing her fingers. "You can tell me. I want us to be honest with one another."

"It's just...I get our professional relationship—to a large extent, it's dictated by the record label. What Kevin says, happens."

He nodded.

"But as far as our personal relationship goes...you... you agree we're just friends, right?"

He searched her face for any sign that she was withholding her true feelings, yet her eyes and expression betrayed nothing. They were like a locked drawer.

If only he had the key.

His heart sank. Again. Maybe that's why she'd said 'no more kissing' because it confused her like it confused him.

"Yes. Just friends," he agreed while his heart ached.

***

Like Jack, Julie dished a selection of Gino's food onto a beautiful blue Italian plate. Fresh mozzarella and tomatoes; fried calamari; spaghetti with black olives and anchovies; chicken and mushroom risotto; penne with eggplant; stuffed filet mignon and breaded veal cutlets.

Delicious flavors filled her mouth as she sampled the fare. In between mouthfuls, she caught Jack's eye and said, "Tell me more about your family."

"What do you want to know?" His gruff tone made her feel bad for asking. She probably should've stuck to a less personal subject. But she was curious.

"I know you have a sister, obviously, but I've never heard you talk about your mom or dad."

A flicker of emotion, pain maybe, crossed his face before his expression grew pensive. "My dad died shortly after Charlie turned fourteen. I was seventeen at the time." He cleared his throat. "Dad's death devastated my mom. Sometimes I think she died from a broken heart. In reality, it was cancer that took her three years later."

Aching for him, she gave his hand a brief squeeze. "I'm sorry, that must've been very tough, being so young, and losing both your parents so close to one another."

She could tell he'd been reliving the past when his glazed eyes found hers. "I guess one good thing came from my dad dying when I was a teenager," he said, his voice scratchy sounding. "It made me want to step up, be the protector for my mom and my sister."

"How did you do that?" she asked quietly.

"Well, instead of pursuing my dream of a college football scholarship, I left straight after graduation and managed to get a job on a construction site." He gave her a lopsided smile. "One day, David visited the site and took an instant liking to me. The rest, as they say, is history."

She smiled too. "I'm sure it's more than him just looking at your face and deciding, 'That Mr. Carrington, he'll do nicely for my next Head of Construction.'"

"You're right." Jack frowned. "A lot of hard work, sweat, and tears were involved. But it was worth it in the end. I owe all I've achieved to David."

"And now you're about to become a famous singer."

"Somehow, I think it's your gorgeous face that'll come to mind when people hear our music, not mine." He smiled, appreciation twinkling in his eyes.

When her cheeks burned suddenly, she glanced toward the large picture window, looking for the sun. Instead, a silver metallic car parked on the street was the only thing shining. Thick clouds blocked out any rays that might otherwise have been present.

She removed her suit jacket and placed it over the back of her chair. "Don't be so sure it's me they'll be focusing on. I predict a ton of female interest when your picture starts circulating. I may even get jealous."

"What? You jealous?" He snickered, shaking his head. "I don't believe it."

She pursed her lips, and his expression became serious, his gaze intense. "Nothing seems to phase you, Julie. I think you must've had a very tough upbringing to be as strong and confident as you are."

"If only you knew..." she began, warmth filling her veins at his unexpected compliment. It was nice to know he thought so kindly of her. Not many people did.

Breaking eye contact, she peered at the photo of an abandoned house on the wall above Jack's head. Probably taken somewhere in rural Italy, it reminded her of the rundown place she'd lived in as a young child.

Julie conjured up the vision of her mom, passed out on their dilapidated orange sofa, an empty bottle of alcohol dangling from her hand. Her breath reeking of some long-ago consumed liquid while smoke seeped out of her pores. She recalled wanting to gag. But instead of trying to help her mom, she'd rushed out of the living room and dived under her bed covers. At the time, she remembered thinking, if she pretended everything was fine, maybe it would be.

Except, that was the day social services had knocked on their front door hours later. She'd never forgiven herself for not trying to wake her mom up from her alcoholic stupor, for not calling 911 and getting help. Instead, she'd buried her head in the sand and hoped for a miracle.

"Hey. Earth to Julie." Jack's deep, smooth voice interrupted her memories. "You okay?"

She shook her head to clear the cobwebs, focusing on the present and the amazing man sitting in front of her, his voice filled with concern.

"Yes. Yes, I'm fine. Let's just say I grew up in less than stellar circumstances, and past experiences have definitely influenced my behavior and outlook on life."

His interested and caring expression made her want to tell him her history. He didn't push, and that made her feel safe.

"My mother was a prostitute," she admitted in a low voice. "She died of alcohol poisoning not long after I was removed from our home by child protective services. I was ten years old."

Jack grasped her hand briefly, his eyes reflecting her hurt. "I'm so sorry. Did you go into foster care?"

Feeling weirdly emotional, despite the passing of time, she stifled her tears before they had a chance to surface. "Yes. I was moved from one foster family to the next until I was sixteen."

"I bet that was hard, never having a permanent family."

"It was, but the Andersons were wonderful." She gave him a wobbly smile. "They treated me like one of their own children for the two years I stayed with them, even though they had four already."

"Wow. I take it you've been living on your own since you were eighteen then?"

"Yes. The Andersons are old family friends of David. They arranged a job at Peterson's for me. After a few months, I was able to rent an apartment on my own."

"Talk about having to grow up in a hurry. I know all about that." His eyes held sympathy and understanding.

She nodded, her thoughts returning to the past.

When she'd first moved into her place, she'd taken freedom to a new level, indulging heavily in wine and casual relationships. One night she'd been so drunk, she'd woken up alone in a stranger's bedroom. Although that wasn't unusual, the black eye and bruises on her wrists were. Right then she'd decided to stop drinking and, more importantly, avoid sleeping with random men.

Time to redirect the conversation.

"How come you live with your sister?" she asked.

Irritation flashed in Jack's eyes. "Actually, it's my house." His harsh tone took her by surprise. She hadn't meant to pry and annoy him in the process.

"A few years after our mom died, I was able to buy out Charlie's half of her inheritance."

"Oh." Feeling stupid for her assumption, Julie stared down at her plate. The flavors of pancetta and mushroom still lingered in her mouth.

When had she finished the last of her delicious food?

She took a few large sips of her diet soda, watching Jack from beneath lowered lashes as he finished off some seafood pasta.

Leaning back in his chair, he smiled tightly. "Don't worry, I've heard it all before."

What did he mean? Did he think she thought badly of

him because he was over thirty and not living on his own? Honestly, she admired him. His dedication to his sister and her kids was commendable. If only she had someone like Jack to take care of her, love her the way he clearly loved his sister.

Jack's priority was his family, not her. They had a record deal together, but it wasn't like he needed the extra money. And he didn't strike her as a man who sought out fame either. In all regards, she was wrong for him. The two of them together, as a couple, made no sense other than professionally.

So what was she doing here? Digging herself in deeper, becoming more attracted to her bandmate by building a personal relationship with him. And liking the man more with each passing minute.

So not a good idea.

"I'm sorry, Jack, I didn't mean to come across as judgmental. Your business is none of my business."

Proud of herself for keeping her voice neutral, she grabbed her purse from the seat beside her and pulled some bills from her wallet. She laid them on the table.

"I'll see you later," she said, taking one last look at his wounded expression before hurrying from the table. From behind her, Jack's words rang in her ears.

"Julie, wait... That's not true."

Chapter Nine

A boulder sat in Jack's stomach. All he could think of was Julie hightailing it from Gino's, without giving him a chance to elaborate. As far as he was concerned, his business *was* her business. In all respects.

At least, he wanted it to be.

He should've known she wasn't trying to judge him.

Unfortunately, other women had, and it made him defensive. Only a very special lady would willingly accept his unique situation. Especially knowing his level of commitment to his sister and how it impacted the free time he'd have left to spend afterward in a relationship.

Could Julie be that person?

He sure hoped so. His professional life, and possibly his personal life, depended on it.

But maybe he was wrong? Maybe she was just like the rest? It could explain why she ducked.

Driving to collect her from work, his phone pinged.

Julie: ***Not feeling well. Need to skip tonight.***

Frowning, he activated his phone's voice text and replied: ***Oh no! Food poisoning?***

No. Gino's was fantastic. See you tomorrow.

At least something had been good. If he guessed correctly, though, she was avoiding him. He prayed he hadn't blown it, taking offense at her innocent question over lunch. Otherwise, they'd be back to square one, struggling with tension between them.

Studio time dragged.

They got down some of Jack's parts, but the time wasn't that productive without Julie's harmonies. A positive was Kevin's early dismissal which meant Jack was home to assist Charlie with her kids' bedtime routine—for which she was very grateful.

Long before dawn, his nephew Peter started throwing up. In order to look after the sick child, Jack swiftly requested a day's leave from Peterson's and canceled his studio time.

When he told Charlie, she burst into tears.

The alarm on his face must've been evident because she quickly smiled and said, "I promise, I'm only crying because I appreciate you so much!"

The following morning, Jack awoke to a message from Julie: ***Don't worry, taking my car in. See you at the studio?***

Separate journeys? Yep, classic avoidance.

He buried his disappointment. ***Sure. See u there.***

At the studio, Julie was already doing her vocal warm-up exercises in the glassed cubicle, and when he joined her, she barely acknowledged his presence.

Great, they were definitely back at the beginning! Good thing Kevin wasn't around yet.

Knots turned in Jack's stomach. Every time he fixed the situation, he somehow managed to mess it up again. Two steps forward, six steps back.

An uncomfortable half-hour passed before he cut the mic in the middle of singing his line and closed his eyes. He counted to five, then signaled to Carl. "I need a minute or ten," he said in a measured tone to the sound engineer.

"I'd rather we keep going," Julie said, sounding annoyed. "We're nearly done with this song."

Too bad. Until this mess was sorted, Jack wouldn't be able to concentrate, and it was going to reflect in the music. Luckily, with their cameraman absent, this disaster wouldn't be documented.

Pulling off his headphones, he grasped Julie's hand and spoke in a low voice, "We need to talk. Alone."

"Fine." Scowling, she snatched back her hand.

He led them to the adjacent song-writing room, letting her enter first. Then he shut the door, spun the lock, and ran his fingers through his hair. Puffing out a long breath, he turned.

"What's up?" Julie asked, her eyebrows scrunched together. "Your heart isn't in it today."

"If you knew that, why'd you insist we continue?"

"I guess I didn't want Carl reporting back to Kevin. Everyone has bad days. I was cutting you some slack."

"Well, don't!" he snapped, immediately regretting his harsh tone when hurt entered her eyes, and she folded her arms.

Great, he wasn't getting this right either!

"I'm sorry, Julie," he said softly. "There's a lot on my mind."

She peered at him for a few seconds, concern on her beautiful face. "So how about we call it a day and continue tonight?" The warm hand she placed on his arm sent electric pulses all along his skin.

He sucked in a breath.

Covering her hand with his, he looked her straight in the eye. "I wanted to clarify something first. My business *is* your business. We're in this together; we're a team, partners."

Confusion flitted across her face. "I'm not sure I follow. I was referring to your personal business on Monday. Whatever way you choose to live is up to you. Just as I don't expect you to tell me who I can or can't date or sleep with, I don't expect to be able to tell you who you can or can't live with."

Sleep with?

He jerked his hand away. What was she talking about? Was she sleeping with someone? Had she slept with Zac? She'd said they weren't attracted to each other, but maybe that didn't matter to her. She flirted a lot, but Jack had no idea if she took it further.

He scowled. Maybe there was a valid reason for the way the women in the office behaved toward her.

He had to be sure, though.

"Are you...involved with someone else?" His breath caught in his throat as he waited.

"No!" she responded, her eyes widening. A few beats passed until she shook her head vehemently and added, "There's no one."

He believed her—she had no reason to lie to him.

"Okay." It seemed she'd meant the 'just friends' bit too. He ignored the sharp pain in his chest and let out a long sigh.

A glance at his watch had his heart picking up speed. Their time was up—Carl would be anxious to finish, never mind that they were also expected at their other jobs soon.

"Here's the thing, Kevin expects us to be a couple. So professionally, that's the image we need to portray to the public, regardless of what's happening in our personal lives. If he thinks there's trouble in paradise, he'll get nervous, and I don't need to tell you what that might mean."

"I understand." Her voice had an edge to it. "You're concerned about my behavior. Again. Don't worry, Jack, I'll behave."

***

"That's a wrap!" Kevin beamed as he made his way over to them. "Another song down. Only eight more to go."

Julie made a face and withdrew from Kevin's side embrace. "Seriously? Did you have to remind us?"

Jack shot her a worried look before shaking Kevin's hand and smiling reassuringly. "She's kidding."

"Glad you know it." Putting a smile on her lips, Julie slipped her arm around Jack's waist and squeezed tight. "Actually, I can't wait to record the next song." She hated being told how to act, and deceiving Jack into believing she was pretending wasn't something she wanted to be doing.

In reality, she wasn't pretending at all, and that deceit in itself was burning a hole in her heart.

She shifted her focus to their boss. "Have you decided which one that'll be?"

"No, they're all so good. I'll let you know as soon as possible, though." He rubbed his jaw. "Why don't you two take a couple day's break? I'll have made a decision by Saturday."

"Sure. Sleeping late would be a treat. I could do with a break from the early mornings."

"Yeah, me too." Jack sounded less than thrilled. Did he relish getting up at the crack of dawn?

In the parking garage, she stood outside her car, holding her keys. "I guess I'll see you on Saturday."

"I guess... Unless..." Jack's hand went to the back of his neck.

"Unless?"

"We could still meet tomorrow morning...have some coffee and talk." His eyes lit up. "There's a wonderful place by the lake where I like to watch the sunrise. If I picked you up as normal, I could show you..." he trailed off, his expression turning uneasy.

Hoping to ease his discomfort, she smiled gently. "I'd like that."

"Okay, great."

She nodded. "It's a date."

***

Ridiculous!

Jack frowned—this was the third time he'd changed his shirt. He was acting like a teenager on his first date.

He took a critical look at his reflection through blurry eyes. His black and blue plaid shirt peeked out from under his navy denim jacket. Wearing his smarter, deep blue jeans meant he'd have to change when he arrived on site, but Julie was worth the effort.

His hand skittered over his scratchy chin, and he groaned. Maybe hitting the snooze button hadn't been the best idea. But Julie's sexy voice, beautiful face, and kissable lips had plagued his dreams. The result was interrupted sleep.

He couldn't imagine why any hot-blooded male wouldn't be attracted to the ginger-haired beauty. Beneath that flirtatious personality was a tender-hearted, wonderful woman he was just beginning to know. Sharing the wonder of 'his spot' and its natural beauty on their first date would be a pleasure.

He chuckled. Julie brought out the romantic in him. Alex had often complained, good-naturedly, that he was 'great with entertaining his nephews and niece, but not so great at romance.'

Well, he wanted to find ways to make Julie smile because the way her eyes lit up, as a result, made his knees go weak.

A short while later, he approached her place and eased his foot off the accelerator. Julie had said this was a date, but had she meant it?

Jack knew the deal—they had to pretend to be a couple. Yet, for all he knew, this could just be another practice session for her. So she could perfect her role.

Sobering thoughts.

When he pulled up alongside the curb, his heart raced at the sight of Julie in a short navy pinstripe skirt he hadn't seen before. She looked hot!

Smiling, she yanked open the passenger-side door and slipped onto the bench seat. "Hey, Jack."

Her soft voice washed over him like sunshine on a cold day, and his mouth went dry. He struggled to think straight as she tugged at the edges of her skirt—a skirt that flirted dangerously high on her gorgeous legs. Swallowing hard, he dragged his eyes up to her pretty face and flashed her a smile. "You look incredible." His voice came out huskier than intended.

"Thanks." Her cheeks reddened slightly. "You'll drop me off at work afterward, right?"

"I will."

After shifting the truck into drive, he indicated to the cup holders containing their to-go coffees. "Help yourself."

"Thanks." She released a contented-sounding sigh. "I slept in, so this is just what the doctor ordered."

He gave her a sidelong glance. "Wasn't that an apple a day?"

"That too." She chuckled, and he smiled with her.

During the silent ride to the lake, they sipped their

java while the darkness slowly lifted. Jack fought to keep his nerves in check. Every time he thought he'd managed, he caught a whiff of Julie's floral scent or glanced in her direction and caught her studying him. Her scrutiny made him shift uneasily on his seat. Eventually, he risked taking his eyes off the road long enough to look right at her.

"What's up?" he asked.

"Just enjoying the view."

His heart rate quickened, and he did his best to give the road his full attention. "There's not much to see until the sun wakes up."

"Mmm. I beg to differ." A gentle tease underlined her words.

Okay, she was definitely flirting. A rush of heat whooshed over him, and his clammy hands tightened on the steering wheel. That was a good sign, right?

He tried not to think about it too much because he didn't want to get his hopes up.

At their destination, he killed the engine and turned to her. "Wait there, will you?"

She nodded, and he hopped out, grateful to be in the cool, fresh air. Then, inhaling deeply, he rounded the vehicle to the passenger-side door and pulled it open.

Offering her his hand, his heart thumped in his chest as she stepped to the ground. Her enchanting smile captured his attention while her soft, warm hand remained enfolded in his. Awareness shot through him, and it took him a few seconds to gather his thoughts.

"Uh, what size shoe do you wear?" He hoped he'd kept his tone unemotional and practical.

Her smile faded. "Five. Why?"

"I think Charlie's boots are still in the trunk. They're a six, but they should fit."

He led her round to the tailgate to grab more appropriate footwear. Julie stared at the dirty rubber boots, then gave him an incredulous look. "You want me to wear those? With my skirt?"

"Unless you'd rather risk twisting an ankle or ruining your fancy shoes," he smirked.

She huffed out a breath. "Fine."

Using an app on his phone to illuminate the way, he navigated the narrow, makeshift path in the low light. Occasionally, he glanced over his shoulder to check on Julie's progress.

Holding the small flashlight he'd given her, she trudged across the uneven surface with her lips pursed.

He hid a smile. "You managing?"

"Yep, I just wish you'd warned me. I could've worn my own off-road trail shoes. These boots are rather cumbersome."

"I'm sorry, but we're nearly there. Trust me, it'll be worth the inconvenience."

"It had better be," he heard her mumble.

They turned a corner, and suddenly the lake emerged, and he stopped to let her catch up. The dawn broke as the first rays of light appeared, glinting off the surface of the water and making it glimmer.

"We're just in time," he murmured.

"Yes, we are." Julie's eyes danced, no doubt awed by the sight in front of them.

After motioning to a nearby log, he followed her to the weathered chunk of wood. He tried to push off leaves and other debris before they sat down, but there wasn't much clean space in the end. Ultimately, the rather cramped seating meant their legs and forearms were pressed together.

Not that he was complaining.

Remembering to breathe, he took in the magnificent view. The bright yellow globe of the sun peeked out from the middle of the lake, its halo of deep orange fading to peach in a semi-circle around it. Spears of light cast reflections onto the shimmering water, revealing faint ripples as the breeze blew.

Julie shivered beside him.

Without hesitating, he put an arm across her shoulders and drew her to him. Her soft sigh as she leaned into him set his pulse racing. He wanted to savor every moment alone with her. Birds chirping in the tall trees surrounding the lake were their only company.

Once the sun had fully emerged above the horizon and the surrounding area had taken on its true colors, he turned to find her gaze on him.

"That was breathtaking," she whispered.

Aware of the ravishing woman beside him, his heart skipped a few beats. His attention drifted to her lips, then back to her eyes, and the air around them crackled with anticipation.

When Julie bit her bottom lip, a sudden desire to taste those sexy lips hit Jack. Without thinking, he dipped his head and heard her suck in a breath. She reached up, and her hand covered his cheek. He stilled.

"Have you forgotten?" she asked quietly.

His eyes darted to hers. Although narrowed, they reflected his desire.

"You promised," she murmured.

"No kissing?"

She nodded. "Also, we should head back."

He jerked back, disappointment washing over him. "I guess a promise is a promise. And you're right. It is time to go."

Chapter Ten

"I'll be back," Julie called over her shoulder as she exited the recording studio with her hips swaying provocatively.

Jack grinned. Did the woman have any clue how sexy she was?

He turned back to the man in the control room. Carl's head was down, no doubt checking the sound levels of the lines they'd just recorded.

Someone cleared their throat directly behind him, and Jack spun around. "Kevin, you startled me!" he muttered.

"Apologies, that wasn't my intention; I'm just pleased to see you and Julie looking so cozy. You make a striking couple." His boss's expression was smug. "The fans will love that you're together, and it'll get them rooting for the Jays even more."

"Uh, we're not actually dating." Jack glanced toward the door, aware Julie could return at any second.

"You're not?" Surprise flickered across Kevin's face. "Could've fooled me. Why not?"

"Julie wants to keep things professional."

"I see the way she looks at you, Jack—no way it's like a professional. I've worked in this industry long enough to know when a woman has feelings for a fellow band member. Julie's in love with you; I'd stake my life on it."

Yeah, well, Kevin might be happy to take a gamble, but he wasn't about to risk his career on a hunch.

What if he was wrong?

"I won't deny the mutual attraction," Jack said, "but as far as anything more? I'm not sure I'd agree."

Kevin scratched his temple. "How do *you* feel about her?"

Checking out his favorite sneakers, Jack shrugged. "I think...I think I'm in love with her."

"Uh-huh."

His head shot up. Was that all?

"What would you suggest I do?"

"Take my advice, young man. Tell her how you feel because I believe you two are made for each other."

Of course, Julie chose *that* exact moment to stroll into the room. "Who's made for each other?" she asked, looking between them.

Chuckling nervously, Jack remained tight-lipped and prayed Kevin wouldn't reveal anything.

"You two, of course!" Kevin's eyes were full of mischief.

Great! Jack shoved his hands into his pockets and reflected on how he'd been anything but lucky in love. Initially, he'd really liked Melanie but ever since high school, she'd held a torch for Steven. So eventually, Jack had bowed out, deciding they were better off as friends. Then he'd thought Alex was the one, but it turned out not to be true.

Now, there was Julie.

Whatever Kevin's opinion, Jack wasn't about to jeopardize his professional relationship or friendship with her.

The stakes were too high.

Although...wasn't there a saying? Third time's a charm? Nope, he wouldn't go there. After a mental shake, he concentrated on Kevin's voice.

"I was telling Jack how perfect you are, as a couple."

"Oh, okay, thanks, Kevin. Your seal of approval is important." Julie sounded sarcastic.

And why the odd facial expression?

"Also, your first release is next week," Kevin said, his tone earnest, "and I'm counting on it being the label's biggest hit yet. We all have a lot riding on your debut, but I have a good feeling about it. So, I don't want either of you worrying. Alright?"

They both nodded.

Peering briefly at his wrist, Kevin took a step toward the door. "Sorry, I have a meeting scheduled."

"Of course." Jack waved him off. "Go."

Julie's focus stayed fixed on Kevin until he left the room. Then she turned to Jack. "Everything okay?"

"Yep. Why wouldn't it be?"

"I don't know. You just seem skittish."

He stifled a sigh. "I'm fine. Other than our boss hovering like a papa bear, reiterating how important it is for the Jays to portray the *right image.*"

Julie stepped closer, her jasmine scent assailing his nostrils. As her fingers caressed his cheek, his pulse accelerated. He slipped his hand around her waist, nudging her nearer until there was only a little space between them. Blood rushed through his body as their gazes tangled.

"The right image means us as a perfect couple, I assume?" she whispered.

He nodded, his brain reminding him that he wasn't allowed to kiss her, but his heart urging him to do just that. The second he closed his eyes to gain some control, her soft lips pressed against his cheek, and he froze.

"Luckily, it comes easily to us, right?" she said in a gentle voice. "We wouldn't want to disappoint our fans now, would we?"

Opening his eyes tentatively, he observed her mischievous expression. Then he wrapped his other arm around her waist and leaned in to whisper in her ear, "You're such a tease."

Julie giggled, and he couldn't help hugging her to him, reveling in the feel of her soft body pressed to his and inhaling the fruity smell of her shampoo.

Abruptly, he dropped his arms and stepped away. Otherwise, he'd have broken her rule and kissed her. Shifting his attention to Carl, Jack gave the signal to continue the track.

Time to get back to work. The sooner, the better.

His blood pressure couldn't take any more tonight.

***

Julie missed the safe, loved feeling of being in Jack's arms. Not that she knew what 'loved' meant exactly since her mom had generally never been sober long enough to give her a proper hug. But she'd imagined the experience would be exactly like that.

Hearing her mom say, "I love you, my girl," never felt right unless accompanied by either a kiss or a hug, or both. Unfortunately, those actions never materialized when it came to her mom.

According to Julie's reading, lack of physical affection —first from her mom, then her various foster parents— meant that she craved it. Consequently, she'd gone looking for it in all the wrong places, turning to drink and one-night stands. But, ultimately, the deep need for true affection hadn't been fulfilled.

Older and wiser now, she knew she'd never find what she was looking for in those situations.

What Jack didn't understand was that she wasn't teasing. Being with him was easy, considering his wonderful, kind, and caring personality. The fact he was so attractive was just a bonus.

Frankly, she'd been stupid to insist on keeping their relationship professional. Things had become personal —for her at least. The more time they spent together, the closer they became.

Telling Jack not to kiss her hadn't been fair.

When her eyes instinctively traveled to Jack's lips, she had an overwhelming desire to taste them once more, to feel the way she had the last time.

"Julie? You okay?" Jack's voice cut into her reverie.

She stared at him, confused.

"You missed your intro."

"Oh."

You'd better concentrate, Julie! Don't think about kissing your hunky bandmate, she told herself as she grabbed her mic.

To apologize, she sent Jack her most dazzling smile.

As if guessing her thoughts, he grinned in response. Her legs turned to jelly, and she held fast to the mic stand, focusing on Carl behind the sound desk instead.

Five retakes later, Jack sounded tired.

"Uh, Jack?" Julie waited for him to look at her. "It's late. Let's finish this in the morning."

"You sure?"

Nodding, she let Carl know they were stopping. The engineer smiled widely and wasted no time in switching off his equipment.

By the time they'd gathered their belongings, the only lights left on were the ones in the studio's vocal booth.

"Guess we're being kicked out," she said, laughing.

"Looks like it."

In the parking garage, Jack paused to stifle a yawn before reaching for the truck's passenger door handle.

"Maybe you shouldn't have sacrificed an opportunity to sleep late just to show me the sunrise," Julie teased.

"Never." He smiled sheepishly. "It was worth not getting another hour of shut-eye to share something special with you."

"Well, I'm honored you gave up your precious sleep for me, thank you."

He gave her a puzzled look. "Any time."

Belted in her seat, she felt Jack's burning stare. "What's wrong?"

"Nothing," he said.

Her brows lifted.

"Actually, I just wanted to clarify that every minute I spend with you, I consider an investment in our future."

"Oh," was all Julie could think to say.

***

At work, the next day, "Oh" once again tumbled from her lips as she read the internal press release sent by Mr. Peterson's personal assistant.

Date: Tuesday, October 31

It is with great pride that I wish to draw your attention to two of our outstanding employees, Jack Carrington and Julie Rolland. The singing duo, known as the Jays, are releasing their first original song today: "The Face Behind the Mask."

Those who've visited venues across the city and heard their incredible voices singing timeless covers will be excited to tune in to hear their song live on WWYZ at midday. Those who haven't heard them will be in for a treat.

So, I'm authorizing an office-wide downing of tools from 11:55 to 12:15 to encourage everyone to listen on their office computers.

David Peterson - CEO of Peterson Construction

Now all the twittering and whispers Julie had heard around the office made sense. She lifted her gaze slightly and caught numerous pairs of eyes riveted on her—male ones expressed their curiosity, while female ones appeared judgmental and disbelieving.

When the email addressed to 'All Employees' first appeared in her inbox over an hour ago, it hadn't seemed like a priority—not with her focus on a bank reconciliation that had been taking far longer than necessary.

Honestly, she'd been rather preoccupied, what with their song officially reaching the radio waves today, and Kevin predicting a number one.

"Kevin's a seasoned label exec, Julie," Jack had said when he dropped her off last night. "He knows what he's doing. We have to trust him." Jack's long embrace and subsequent kiss to the side of her head had been an enormous comfort.

Right now, though, all these eyes on her hardly seemed fair. If only Jack was with her, holding her hand and whispering words of encouragement. Would his coworkers be blasting their radios over the sound of drills and hammers? She highly doubted it.

A commotion at their department entrance had Julie whipping her head around. Brianna was scowling at a delivery man who she'd obviously intercepted on entry. A huge bouquet sat in his arms.

"It's *my* responsibility to distribute all incoming gifts

in this office," Brianna stated loudly, a restraining hand on his arm.

"I'm sorry." The burly man shook his arm free from her hot-pink talons and seemed to focus his attention directly on Julie. "My boss gave me express instructions. I'm to personally hand these to the named recipient. And only her."

Julie swallowed. That stunning floral arrangement couldn't be for her, could it?

The closer the delivery man came, the hotter she got. She tried to block out his ample form by staring intently at her desk, but the sweet scent of the flowers reached her nostrils anyway.

"Miss Julie Rolland?"

She looked up.

"These are for you."

Her heart sank. As if there wasn't enough attention on her already. Now this.

"Thank you," she mumbled, quickly relieving the man of his delivery. The lavish display of lilies, pale pink roses, and light green hydrangeas took up half her workspace.

How in the world would she carry it out later, let alone get any work done around it?

"So—" Like an annoying stone in her shoe, Brianna appeared at her side. "—who are the extremely generous flowers from?"

"I've no idea." No way she was going to read the message in Brianna's presence.

Julie's cell buzzed on her desk. But before she could answer Jack's call, Brianna's hand stretched toward the floral arrangement, blocking her view. Way too late, she realized Brianna's intention.

Panic gripped her chest, and her breathing became labored. Assuming it was Jack who sent the flowers, what had he written?

"Let's see." Brianna pulled the card out of the envelope. "You're a woman of many talents, Julie. You deserve every success, today and always." Brianna's distaste was perfectly evident in her tone.

Pushing to her feet, Julie gave Brianna her fiercest look and stuck out her hand. "Would. You. Please. Give. That. Back?"

With a smirk, Brianna dumped it in her hand. "Gladly. I bet you thought it was from Jack. Well, you should be so lucky. You probably sent it to yourself." Turning on her heel, she marched away.

Julie let out a deep breath. The timing of Jack's call was too much of a coincidence. The flowers had to be from him.

A text lit up her screen. Jack: *Have u got them yet? I wanted u 2 know I'm thinking of u.*

For a moment, her heart went warm and fuzzy. Then she recalled what had just happened, and she rushed a reply: *They're gorgeous! But if you ever send flowers to my office again, I Will Kill You.*

***

Jack groaned. Not exactly the response he'd been going for. Why hadn't he thought about what kind of reaction flowers would evoke in Julie's workplace?

On several occasions, she'd said she tried to keep a low profile.

Now he'd gone and blown it.

On the other hand... after today, with any luck, she'd be viewed differently. The women she worked with wouldn't necessarily stop being jealous, but they'd surely have to be envious of her incredible talent. Her voice was angelic—he'd defy anyone to say otherwise. She was not going to be able to hide under a bushel any longer. She had to step out into the light and take the admiration and interest coming her way.

"Jack!" One of his men wore the biggest grin he'd ever seen. "Jack, you have to come—you're on the radio!"

What? How did they know? He'd kept quiet about his other job and the song's release. Curious, he trailed the man to where the rest of the crew were gathered.

Julie's sweet voice filled the surrounding air, and pride consumed him. She sounded fantastic, but he already knew that. There was something about hearing it outside of the studio, though.

Literally, music to his ears.

All too soon, only Jack's voice was audible. He glanced around, humbled at the expressions of surprise, awe, and admiration. A couple men were so caught up in the music he couldn't tell what they were thinking. Then when his solo verse ended, Julie's voice blended with his, and no one uttered a sound. It was almost comical watching grown men bewitched by a song.

The last note finally faded out, and the presenter came on again. "Well, folks, that was 'The Face Behind the Mask' by the Jays. I don't know about you, but I feel a number one coming on."

Shouts and whistles pierced the air, coming not from the radio but from the surrounding small crowd.

After being slapped on the back for the tenth time by yet another guy in a fluorescent jacket and bright yellow hard hat, Jack eventually edged away. "Thanks, guys," he said, "but it's time to get back to work. Mr. Peterson promised to stop by this afternoon sometime, so it wouldn't look good if you bunch were hanging around staring at me now, would it?" He kept his voice light, teasing.

Murmurs and snickers filled the air, but the men slowly picked up their tools and sauntered back to whatever they'd been doing before, some still wearing broad smiles.

Turning to head back to his office, Jack came face to face with Steven.

"I knew you two could sing, man, but seriously?" A grin split Steven's face as he raised his hand for a high five. "You totally blew me away!" After their palms connected, Steven dragged him into a quick embrace.

Jack took a step back, his neck heating, a half-smile on his face. "Uh, glad you like it, man."

Would he always feel a little embarrassed about this kind of effusive praise?

"Like? I loved it! Melanie and I can't wait for you to become famous because then we'll be known as the best friends of the Jays. How cool will that be?"

"I think you're getting a little ahead of yourself, man."

He peered behind Steven. "I thought the boss was coming. Did he send you instead?"

Steven's smile dimmed somewhat. "David's in the car. I bailed when he got a call from his irate wife."

"Probably wise." Jack chuckled just as Steven's eyes shifted over his shoulder, his expression becoming somber.

Jack swung to face their boss, who wore his typical neutral expression, which was as difficult to read as always. Did David regret his ringing endorsement of the Jays' music?

"Here's the man of the hour. Congratulations, Jack!" David held out his hand and grinned—something Jack hadn't often seen him do. "I'm so impressed with both you and Julie. And I must admit, when I put that radio station on, I had to keep reminding myself that I actually know the Jays."

Jack shook David's hand while returning his smile. "Thank you. The last thing we'd ever want is to let you down." He rubbed the back of his neck and shared a brief look with Steven before adding, "Although I'm not sure Julie appreciated being the center of attention so much. But I am certainly grateful for your support."

David's brow scrunched. "What do you mean? Was she given a hard time because of the email I circulated?"

Email? That explained how everyone knew.

Jack shook his head. "Not that I'm aware of. I sent flowers to mark the occasion, then received a text giving me the impression she wasn't very happy with the attention." He frowned. "Uh, come to think of it, I'm guessing your shout-out went down about as well as torrential rain at a picnic too."

A mortified look crossed David's face. "I'll have to apologize. Embarrassing her was not my intention. I honestly thought her coworkers would be excited to know about the singing star in their midst."

Steven jumped in. "Let's just say Julie's not the most popular woman in her department, at least as far as the other women are concerned."

Jack nodded his agreement.

Samantha J. Ball

"I see. In that case, I feel a promotion coming on for Miss Julie Rolland."

David's concern was touching. Yet Jack's stomach dropped as he pictured Julie's response to being made a manager or being put in charge of accounts. All it would do would be to give her fellow coworkers even more reason to hate her.

That would not make Julie happy at all.

Who would be the one dealing with the fallout then?

Him and his big mouth.

Chapter Eleven

After one last sniff of the sweetly-scented flowers gracing her small dining table, Julie shrugged into her coat. Jack was due any minute.

All afternoon, she'd fretted over the harsh words in her text. Especially once their song played on the radio and her coworkers had bombarded her with lovely comments. Of course, one person said nothing—Brianna. Not that Julie had expected any praise from her.

The doorbell rang, and as she went to answer it, butterflies bounced in her stomach. She felt a tiny bit lightheaded. Hopefully, there'd be some decent canapés at the masked party tonight.

Before pulling the door open, she caught a glimpse of herself in the hallway mirror. The off-the-shoulder gray and white silk dress with wide-lace olive trims wasn't too formal, but it suited her style. The skirt fell loosely to her knees while the rest of the dress hugged her body, and her classic pointed-toe stilettos were the exact green of seafoam.

The doorbell rang again.

Breathing deeply, she donned a welcoming smile and opened the door to Jack in a gray suit and loose olive tie. He wore it effortlessly with the jacket sleeves pushed up to his elbows.

Her heart skipped a beat.

The man was hot!

"Hey, don't you look handsome?" Her voice came out breathy.

Jack just stared at her, and her smile faltered. What was he thinking? He didn't *seem* angry. Was he, though?

Pushing a stray strand of hair behind her ear, she pointed to his tie, then her dress and mustered up another smile. "Someone must've told you what color to wear."

"Uh, yes," he responded slowly, glancing down at the white shirt covering his muscular chest. Then his gaze locked onto hers, and he cleared his throat. "But they didn't mention how beautiful you were going to look."

"Thanks, Jack." With heated cheeks, she stepped across the threshold, forcing him to shift back a few steps. His gorgeous green eyes continued to peer at her.

Was that worry or uncertainty shining in them?

Crazily, she thought she'd be the anxious one.

Reaching out to snag the end of his tie, she moved close enough to inhale his woodsy scent. It set her heart racing. His hands shot to her upper arms and held them lightly in place, his eyes never leaving her face.

She swallowed. "Jack, I need to apologize for my text. The flowers were thoughtful and very much appreciated. It's just...all the attention was overwhelming. I panicked and took it out on you."

The tender look he gave her nearly melted her bones. "No, *I'm* sorry. I should've thought about your lack of privacy at work, never mind the unwanted interest the delivery would bring. I'll remember for next time."

"There'll be a next time?"

"Of course, but I'll make sure they get sent to your apartment instead."

She shook her head. "No. Don't do anything different. I'm not going to hide anymore. This career I've chosen will shine the spotlight on me, whether I like it or not. I need to take the good with the bad. So, if you want to send me flowers at work, go ahead."

He pulled her into a quick, tight embrace then released her. "That's my girl. I'm proud of you," he said, his voice husky.

"Your girl?" Pleasure flooded Julie at his insinuation, intentional or not.

Smiling, he threaded his fingers through hers. "We'd better go." He caught her eye and winked. "The guests of honor can't afford to be late now, can they?"

***

"Wow, this place is amazing!" The excitement in Julie's voice made Jack smile.

"Yeah, it is," he said, grabbing their masks off the back seat of his truck and turning back around.

Julie, her eyes sparkling right at him, quietly snuck her hand into his.

He wasn't about to complain.

"They call it 'The Castle' for a reason," he told her, leading them toward Kevin's chosen party venue. "Partly because of the fieldstone walls which were uniquely mixed with glass features, and—" He halted, waiting until she looked at him, then he pointed up. "Do you see the array of A-frame and gable roof shapes?"

"Yep."

"Well, you'll also notice the sprawling structure isn't symmetrical at all."

Julie chuckled. "You sound just like a property expert, Jack. I guess you can take the man away from the construction site, but—"

Not wanting to sound like a know-it-all, he zipped his mouth and started walking again. A few steps later, she squeezed his fingers.

"Is that an *actual* turret?" she asked, her voice filled with awe.

"Correct." His lips twitched. Maybe she hadn't been mocking him, after all.

"Incredible! I can't wait to see the inside."

Jack's smile grew.

Online pictures of the place hadn't done it justice. The well-placed lighting really brought the unique building to life, making it all quite magical. And judging from Julie's expression, she thought so too. He imagined her thinking that being here was like being in a fairy tale.

Was he her knight in shining armor? Because she was definitely his princess.

"Wait, I almost forgot," he said, dropping her hand.

"What?"

Facing Julie, he carefully slipped her mask over her head. "Perfect," he breathed, resisting the urge to run his fingers through her loose, silky strands. Instead, he secured his own mask. "Ready?" he asked.

A cute giggle escaped her lips. "I am, now that we're incognito."

He couldn't help laughing. "I hate to break it to you, but Kevin supplied the masks. Our cover will be blown the minute he arrives."

"Oh." Her adorable smile fled. "I hadn't realized."

Outside the entrance, at the top of the wooden staircase, Jack paused, his stomach clenching. For the next few hours, they'd need to be on the same page. The issue was how to broach the subject without upsetting Julie.

"What did you forget this time?" she teased.

He forced a smile. "Haha. Nothing." Except, tonight was all about appearances and first impressions. This song release party was specifically to introduce the Jays officially. So, the thought of needing to dictate the way Julie should act instead of allowing her to just be herself, well, that didn't make him feel great.

"You realize representatives from the music industry will be here, right?" Jack brushed his free hand over his head to the back of his neck and held it. "Bottom line is...we have to play our parts. Kevin's promoting us as a couple, not just two random band members." Even if, in reality, they were just close friends who'd shared a couple of sensational kisses.

"I know that, Jack." She scowled. "You don't have to keep reminding me to behave."

"As long as we're on the same page."

She huffed. "I promise I won't cause any problems."

The woman was so cute; he wanted to gather her in his arms and kiss her senseless. Yet that wasn't possible.

He stifled a groan. She had to understand exactly

what he meant, though. "So, no flirting with other men?"

Her pretty eyes narrowed. "Seriously?"

"I know it's in your nature to be friendly, but men do tend to get the wrong idea."

"You want me to change?"

Holding her gaze, he ran his hands down her arms and linked their fingers. "Never. You're perfect just the way you are."

The sultry smile she shot at him made her eyes shine like emeralds. "Now now, Mr. Carrington, flattery won't work on me. Just be grateful I like you."

She might like him, but pretending to be into her and having to protect her from male advances would be his absolute pleasure. The easiest task he'd ever been set in his life.

Only one issue—his heart and how to keep it from getting broken into a thousand pieces.

***

"Now, this is a place I can see myself getting married in," Julie said the second she stepped inside the building. The magnificent venue had a cathedral-type vaulted ceiling with exposed cherry wood beams and a luxurious feel. Kevin certainly had good taste.

"You're thinking of getting married?" Jack's voice sounded a little strangled.

"Of course!" She grinned, twirling to take it all in. Rather than the traditional white fairy lights, the green and orange ones twinkling on the wooden wrap-a-round balcony produced a spooky atmosphere. So cool. "Someday," she added, more solemnly.

For a minute, she allowed her imagination to run wild. Herself, a bride in a white silk dress, embroidered with millions of sequins and translucent pearls. Her groom by her side, enjoying the all-encompassing view from above. She pictured the groom in her mind's eye—he looked an awful lot like Jack.

Mentally shaking the image from her head, she honed in on the fire blazing in a fieldstone fireplace across the room. No wonder it felt so cozy in here, despite the stone floor. Good thing they'd left their coats at the entrance.

Realizing Jack still hadn't commented, she turned to examine his eyes since the skull mask he wore did a good job hiding his expression otherwise.

"Don't you?" she asked. Then when he seemed confused, she clarified, "Don't you want to get married?"

"No. Not in my situation. I mean, it's rather unique, don't you think? I'm sharing a home with my sister and her children, helping her raise them while their dad works abroad. Getting married would change those dynamics, and I'm not sure that would work. So no, marriage isn't on my radar for the foreseeable future."

She stared at him. The way he described his life didn't exactly leave any possibility of a serious relationship.

Suddenly, she didn't feel happy anymore.

"There you are!"

Kevin's smooth head was immediately recognizable, and Julie tensed. Predictably, he wore a gold 'Phantom of the Opera' style mask—the man was a huge fan. Hopefully he had good news, especially after Jack's depressing revelation.

Cupping his mouth with his hand, Kevin spoke without raising his voice. "Congratulations, you two. You hit the number one spot!"

"Fantastic!" Jack said, mirroring Julie's thoughts.

The men shook hands, then Kevin squeezed her shoulder gently, his smile bright. "If I'm right, it'll stay up there until Christmas."

"We couldn't have done it without you, Kevin."

Julie nodded. "Jack's right."

"Ah, you're welcome. You're enormously talented and deserve it." Seemingly distracted, Kevin scanned the large room, then returned his attention to them. "Now remember, this night is for you. Socialize, but don't give up your identities. Most importantly, have fun."

Torn between elation because of their success and crushed by Jack's thoughts on his marriageability, Julie was glad her face was currently masked. When the music cranked up and couples gravitated to the dance floor, her foot automatically tapped along with the upbeat music.

Jack peered at her feet. "You want to dance?"

"I thought you'd never ask."

He laughed out loud. "The music started all of two seconds ago!"

"Exactly."

Moving to the rhythm was almost therapeutic. And though she longed to dance with Jack alone, it would give them away. So, one song after the other, she swapped partners until finally, the music slowed down. Thankfully, there was no need to keep track of Jack—the women he chose to dance with wore such frightful masks.

Moments after making herself comfortable in the terrifying arms of a Count Dracula, Jack appeared. "Mind if I cut in?" The smoldering look in his eyes, along with his hand snaking possessively on her waist, implied he wasn't going to take no for an answer.

Dracula sent her an inquiring look.

"Only if you don't mind, Count?" She spoke sweetly and gave him her most persuasive smile. When his fangs made an appearance, she held her breath.

"Sure," he muttered before releasing her and stalking away.

Wasting no time, Jack drew her into his arms. "About time. I think I've shared you enough."

She glared at him. "You know I'm not a plaything to be passed around, right?"

"No, but you're precious to me, and I'd much rather you were safe in my arms."

A deep sigh escaped her lips at Jack's endearing words. She'd rather be secure in his arms too.

A moment later, it was as if she'd tempted fate. Light-headedness suddenly hit her, and she slumped against him. All that kept her upright were his strong arms.

"Hey, are you okay?"

"Yes," she managed, his concern touching her heart. "Sorry about that. Probably the effect of being in your arms."

He must've smiled because his eyes lit up like a starry night.

"I'm teasing." She smiled weakly. "I couldn't face food earlier; my stomach was so tied up in knots. I just need something to eat."

A flicker of disappointment entered his gaze, and it dulled somewhat. "Okay, dancing can wait. Let's find you some proper sustenance."

Once her energy was restored, Julie's face covering started to feel more than a little uncomfortable. Beside her, Jack fidgeted with his mask too.

Surely it was time?

After checking her watch, she smiled. Ten on the dot. The music faded away magically, and everyone stood around looking expectant. Up on the grand stage, Kevin commandeered the microphone. "Right, folks. It's time to reveal the faces behind the masks."

A cheer went up, along with loud applause.

Julie sent Jack a knowing look. "I guess we won't be anonymous for much longer."

"Sad, but true. Not that your mask is weird or anything, but I'd rather see your beautiful face."

Visualizing the cat mask was easy. Julie had stared at it sitting on her dining table for the past week—glitter on its black ears, white on its cheeks, and an ornate gold-trimmed design. Oh, and an extract of sheet music on its forehead. Which song it belonged to was still a mystery.

So, not scary at all.

She shoved Jack playfully on the arm. "I'll have you know I've had multiple compliments tonight. *Gorgeous* was mentioned quite a lot."

"I'm not so sure they were referring to your mask." He sounded a little jealous.

Slipping her arm through his, she reached up to whisper in his ear. "Don't worry, you're the only one I've had my cat eyes on."

Jack's response was drowned out by Kevin's booming voice, saying, "Each of you were given a number upon arrival. I'll call out some of those numbers. If I mention yours, form a line next to me. You'll then be handed a new number from one to twenty to identify you."

Unsurprisingly, she and Jack both got called forward. She received a plastic number three, Jack a number nine.

"Somewhere behind these masks are the two faces you really came to see tonight." Kevin waited until the murmurs, rippling around the room, ceased. "Okay. We're going to start with Julie Rolland."

An almighty roar of 'three' came from the hundred-odd, masked people occupying the room. Mindful of the fact her mask didn't cover her mouth, Julie squashed her grin.

How had they known?

She glanced over at the other women in the lineup—none were strawberry blonde! Perhaps she should've plaited her hair to make it less distinctive. Or worn a wig.

"I'd like to say you're all wrong." Kevin's lips tipped up, thwarting his attempt at keeping a straight face. "But I guess Julie's colorful locks set her apart, much like her incredible voice." His focus moved to her. "Number three, would you lift your mask?"

Praying her makeup hadn't smudged, Julie dutifully removed her disguise and smiled.

Wolf whistling muffled the enthusiastic clapping while numerous reassuring smiles eradicated any concerns she'd had about her appearance. The crowd looked kind of freaky anyway. Breathing a sigh of relief, she risked a glance at Jack.

He was watching her intently.

Desperate not to spoil Kevin's game as heat rose up her neck, she dragged her eyes away, back to the assembled group.

Discovering Jack's identity took a lot longer. Kevin had cleverly chosen men of a similar height and build. The groans grew louder with each incorrect guess, and Julie had to stifle her laughter.

Eventually, only one man remained.

Drums rolled and trumpets sounded.

Taking off his mask for the final reveal, Jack gifted everyone with his charming smile before striding across the stage to Julie. He slung his arm over her shoulder and leaned in to press a light kiss on her cheek. The feel of his warm lips on her skin, however brief, made her heart rate shoot through the roof.

"At last," he said in a low voice, his face so close to hers. "I honestly thought they'd be bright enough to get the hint."

"The hint?"

"You know." He lifted his olive tie.

"Oh!" She grinned. "Dead giveaway, really."

"You'd think," he smirked, his eyes fixed on her.

Julie turned her body to face his, her hand itching to trace his stubbled jawline. If she leaned in a little, she could press her lips to his. Resisting the pull to do just that, she set her focus higher. Their gazes tangled, and her breath hitched.

"Yep. If it were up to me," she murmured, "I could've picked you out from your eyes alone."

Chapter Twelve

"Miss Rolland?"

Both Jack and Julie turned around.

Recognizing the reporter immediately, Jack's heart sped up. The woman had quite the reputation for creating juicy gossip, and a clever investigative reporter like her could easily sniff out their fake relationship. Not even the most private of people came away unscathed when she started digging.

What was she doing at their party?

Did Kevin know about this?

"Yes?" Julie said, evidently unaware of any potential disaster.

"Mind if I ask you some questions?" The woman's sweet, soft voice did nothing to alleviate Jack's concern.

"I'm not sure this is the time or place for an interview," he said, scowling. He pulled Julie to his side and kept an arm around her waist. "We're in the middle of a party here."

"Actually, it's perfect timing." Kevin appeared from out of nowhere, a smile plastered on his face, his tone cajoling. "You'll talk to her, won't you, Julie?"

When Jack shot Julie a questioning look, she just shrugged her shoulders. Not wanting to come across as controlling, he dropped his hand because no matter what he thought about the idea, ultimately, the choice was hers.

"Okay, sure." Julie nodded at the woman holding the

microphone.

"Great. Come, Miss Rolland, it's a little noisy in here," the reporter said, gravitating toward the exit doors. She clearly expected Julie to follow like a puppy.

Instead, Julie glanced over at Jack, uncertainty flickering in her eyes. Fisting his hands, he took a step forward. If he accompanied her, he could keep her from being eaten alive by this piranha.

Kevin gripped his arm with a restraining hand. "She'll be fine."

"Yes, I will be." Julie's voice held a slight quiver, despite the confident look on her pretty face.

Jack's protective instinct deepened, but he had to respect her decision. Not to mention the warning look Kevin sent his way.

"Okay, okay." Raising his hands in surrender, Jack watched Julie until he lost sight of her.

Things went a little crazy after that when Kevin dragged him over to a group of music industry officials who apparently only wanted to 'chat.'

"Are the Jays working on any other original music?"

"When will we hear it?"

"Who's writing the new lyrics? Miss Rolland again?"

Peppering him with more questions than he was comfortable answering, Jack felt harassed by the men. And these weren't even reporters. Was Julie coping with a similar onslaught? Or would the vulture reporter slip toward more personal topics? A feeling of unease rose in him. They hadn't been prepped for any of this!

Eventually, the men turned to Kevin to satisfy their questions, leaving Jack to make his escape. He searched for a dimly lit, secluded spot, his breath settling when he found one.

His relief was short-lived. It only took a second before a group of women flocked to him, pushing and shoving each other like star-crazed fans.

"Me first!" grunted a petite blonde who managed to muscle her way to the front. "Please sign this for me, Jack." She handed him a napkin with a red kiss printed on it. Feeling his face heat, he looked away into the face of an attractive brunette.

"Could I have an autograph too?" She stuck a slip of paper and a marker pen under his nose.

"Mind if I keep this for now?" He waved the pen at the grinning brunette.

Her head bobbed. "Of course! Have it," she said, then giggled to her neighbors. "Jack Carrington's got *my* pen."

Each fan had something to sign, even if it was just their hand. One crazy woman tore off a strip of her white satin sleeve and handed it to him. "Would you write me a message, please? My name's Lucy."

When he returned the piece of material, she smiled widely. "Thanks! I love you, Jack."

He frowned. Not the person he wanted to hear that from!

The whole experience was utterly surreal. Kevin had obviously invited those who he figured were 'suitable' attendees from the Jays' growing fan base.

After signing yet another mask, Jack caught a glimpse of Julie in the corner, surrounded by a pack of masculine admirers. Her smile seemed a little forced, and the men stood way too close.

Time for this informal meet and greet to end.

Jack turned his most charming smile on the women still vying for his attention. "Ladies," he said smoothly, "I'm afraid I have to go. My girlfriend needs rescuing."

He didn't get very far.

"Mr. Carrington," the annoying reporter purred, blocking his path. She resembled an eagle about to pounce on its prey. "My talk with Miss Rolland was very illuminating, but it's always best to get both sides of the story." Her Botox smile didn't fool him one bit. "That said, I'd like to interview you now."

Jack reined in a heavy sigh. No doubt Kevin would've sanctioned this too. Hopefully he wouldn't blow it since he and Julie had never talked about 'matching their stories.'

Standing in the private room with only the reporter and her camera crew present, Jack felt like he was on trial. The woman shoved a microphone in his face.

"How long have you and Miss Rolland been singing together?"

"The first time was almost exactly two years ago, but after that only very occasionally until we got signed."

"Did it really start out as just a dare in a karaoke bar?"

"Yes."

"Who wrote 'The Face Behind the Mask?'"

"That was all Julie—she's an amazingly talented songwriter."

The woman nodded, a small smile on her otherwise intense face. "If your first song is anything to go by, then I don't doubt it."

Slowly relaxing his shoulders, he smiled too. This wasn't so bad, after all.

"Something everyone's particularly interested in, especially your fans, is how your love story began."

Tension returned like a boomerang. Was this a trap? Definitely a test. "I think you'll find Julie's much better at telling our story."

"I guess she's the romantic one then, hey?" She winked.

In an attempt to appear nonchalant, he shrugged.

"According to my sources, Julie's known as a flirt. Does that bother you?"

Damping down his irritation, he smiled tightly at her but refused to respond.

"I suppose it must—she's a very attractive woman." The reporter sounded smug. "It stands to reason your girlfriend will draw an awful lot of male interest."

"Yes, except she's just as beautiful on the inside too. She's also compassionate and generous, with a huge heart."

"So it *does* bother you?"

Jack glowered. He wasn't about to feed her any more ammunition. "I'm sorry," he said, "but this interview is over. There's someplace else I need to be."

***

In the past, this would've been Julie's dream—a group of good-looking men all giving her their undivided attention. Tonight, she wasn't feeling it.

"Would you sing for us, Julie?"

"Yeah, listening to you on the radio was amazing, but watching the gorgeous Julie Rolland perform live would be even more awesome."

"It would make tonight a Halloween to remember for a long time to come."

The appreciative comments continued to flow from her various admirers, yet her gaze kept wandering to the door. Why was Jack taking so long? Surely that reporter had enough information to write her piece already?

Just as she held up her hand to put an end to the grilling, Jack marched into sight, his agitated expression causing a tightening in her chest.

What had happened?

Determined not to reveal anything personal about her relationship with Jack, Julie had done her best to sidestep difficult questions from that awful woman. She thought he'd be proud of her evasive answers—assuming he'd been able to witness them.

"Can I borrow you for a minute?" Jack grasped her hand, his expression hard.

"Sure." Giving the disappointed men a quick wave over her shoulder, she let him drag her away toward the far side of the room. He was on a mission.

"Don't get me wrong," she said, "I'm grateful for the rescue, but—"

Her pulse accelerated. They were headed straight for Kevin, who currently displayed a thunderous facial expression. Any normal person would've been deterred from approaching. Yet Jack carried on.

"Jack?" She touched his shoulder to get his attention. "What's going on?"

"I have a bone to pick," he said, his tone decidedly chilly, his stride unbroken while his focus remained solely on his destination.

"Did I do something wrong?" When he didn't answer, she added, "If I did, I apologize."

Finally, he spared her a brief look, and his expression softened, along with his tone. "You have nothing to apologize for." His gaze returned to their boss, now only a few feet away. "On the other hand, he has," Jack said, his voice steely.

Oh no! Causing a scene was a terrible idea. If Kevin took offense—whatever the issue—he could easily drop them from the label. The novelty of being a recording artist, with one song released, hadn't worn off yet.

If Julie had her way, it never would.

Accounting work paid the bills, kept a roof over her head, but it didn't satisfy her creative side—singing did. Pretending the rest of the world didn't exist and blocking out her past shameful behavior while she sang —that diminished her guilt, made her feel like a different person. If only she'd had the foresight to change her name before signing that contract, then she really could've been someone else.

"*Mr*. Taylor, I'd like a word." Julie flinched at Jack's authoritative tone and formal address.

After momentarily lifting his dark eyebrows, Kevin addressed the person he'd been conversing with. "Excuse me for a moment, would you?"

The man nodded curtly and left.

Jack gestured to a side door not too far away from them. "Preferably someplace private."

Julie wiped her brow as they entered the interview room, then peeked at Jack. Mouth in a thin line, his jaw twitched while he held her hand tightly.

Afraid to let go in case she ducked?

Well, he was right to worry.

"I'm not sure what's on your mind, Jack," Kevin said smoothly, peering between them with pride shining in his eyes, "but I wanted to say well done. You both handled that reporter like pros. I know I sprung it on you without warning, but I needed you to get a feel of what it'd be like to be put on the spot."

"About that." Jack's tone was fierce, his expression unchanged as he waggled a finger at Kevin. "If Julie and I are *ever* made to do interviews separately again, I assure you, there will be hell to pay. We're the Jays, a team, a couple, therefore a package deal. Wherever Julie goes, I go and vice versa."

Julie's stomach knotted into a giant ball listening to Jack's strong words of admonishment. Had he taken it a step too far? His tenacity was admirable, showing her a side of him she'd never seen, but... They should've discussed this before he railroaded Kevin with his demands. Not that she disagreed with him. A team? Yes. A band? Yes. A couple? She frowned.

Not exactly.

Although Kevin's expression was grim and surprise and anger registered in his eyes, he didn't respond.

"Do I need to remind you about our most recent conversation, Kevin?" Jack's lowered tone was even more threatening than before. "You know, where I had to correct your assumptions?"

Huh? What was he talking about?

Julie opened her mouth to ask, but it seemed Jack hadn't finished talking.

"If those facts are discovered, your credibility and honesty will be called in to question, and that'll reflect as badly on the Jays as it will on you. I know you don't want that any more than we do."

The understanding that flickered in Kevin's eyes and his suitably contrite look lessened Julie's anxiety. Still, she remained confused as to what he'd been assuming.

"You're right, I wasn't thinking, and I apologize. It'll never happen again." And just like that, Kevin Taylor capitulated.

At the same time, Julie's respect for Jack grew—he'd been right to address the issue, to play her protector.

"Good." Turning to her with a devilish smile, Jack's voice contained a hint of playfulness. "Now, Kevin, if you don't mind, we're going to hit the dance floor one last time before we take to the stage."

Another chance to be in Jack's arms?

Julie grinned. She sure loved the sound of that!

Chapter Thirteen

Jack's body hummed with nervous excitement as he buttoned up the cuffs of his black paisley shirt. Thoughts of Julie had consumed him all day. Now, the countdown to having her close enough to hold in his arms had turned into minutes instead of hours.

Last night on their way home from the party, they'd compared interview notes and discovered their fans would still believe they were a couple. Knowing no harm had been done, Jack had suggested a celebratory dinner at Gino's. Julie had readily agreed.

"Jack?" Charlie's voice startled him. "I have bad news," she said. Dark smudges showed under his sister's puffy eyes, and her lips were down-turned.

A sinking feeling hit his stomach.

"Peter's cold isn't just a cold. His temperature's over a hundred, and he has flat red spots below his hairline."

"That doesn't sound good." Jack's gaze skittered to his bedroom alarm clock, and his pulse accelerated. He needed to leave in five minutes, or he'd be late for his date. Selfishly, he didn't want to stand Julie up, but Charlie looked a little too worried for his liking.

"My guess is Peter has measles."

Jack's pulse slowed a beat. Not so bad, then.

"I'm sorry to hear that," he said. "From what I can remember, you'll need to keep his temperature down, make sure he rests and drinks plenty of water."

Walking over to his bedside cabinet, he slipped his

cell and wallet into his pocket and turned back around. If he hurried, he'd still make it on time.

Charlie stood like a statue in his bedroom, her eyes pleading.

Surely she didn't expect him to stay home too?

No chance. He'd have to put his foot down. His promise to Mark was one thing, but staying just to keep her company was another.

"Charlie, what's wrong?" he asked, suppressing a sigh. "You know if you're worried about anything, you can call me. I'll keep my phone on, and I promise I won't be out late tonight."

'It's not that, Jack." Her hands started to twist.

Reaching out to cover them, he asked, "What is it?"

She lifted her chin. "I've never had measles, and I believe Peter's extremely contagious right now. I'm sure you'll agree I can't afford to get sick."

The fight left him just like that. Charlie was right. When he'd gotten measles, their mom had kept him in quarantine for several days while he had a rash and a fever. His sister had luckily escaped infection.

To get it as an adult wouldn't be advisable.

Blaming Charlie for not giving Peter the second dose of the MMR vaccine wouldn't accomplish anything either. Jack had understood her reasoning a year ago, but now he questioned that decision. Sure, the little man had reacted badly to the injection, but he'd been fine, and Dr. Danvers Senior had assured them they needn't worry about the second, top-up vaccine.

"I'll tell Julie I can't make it and let David know I won't be back at work until Monday."

"Thanks, Jack. I don't know—"

"What you'd do without me," he said, cutting her off mid-sentence. "Yeah, I know. It's okay, Charlie. I love you."

David completely understood.

Julie wasn't so forgiving; Jack heard it in her voice. "It's alright. Now I can order my favorite pizza and watch a movie I've been dying to see. I hope Peter gets better soon."

"Thanks for understanding. I really am sorry. If he's better by Friday, maybe we can go out then?"

"I've already told Brad I'll go with him to the pub."

Stumped by her admission, Jack didn't know what to say, so he kept quiet.

"If I need to take my car into the studio on Saturday, just let me know, okay?" Julie then said before ending the call abruptly.

Wow. He scrubbed a hand over his stubbled face. If that conversation was anything to go by, the next few days were going to be the longest of his life.

***

Annoyed that her little act of defiance wasn't having quite the desired effect, Julie ran her sweaty palms down the smooth fabric of her avocado print swing dress. Accompanying Brad to the pub, wearing the exact outfit she'd bought for her dinner date with Jack, felt wrong.

Even if the date would've been fake.

They weren't really a couple. She wasn't Jack's girlfriend; she was nothing more than a partner in his band—a friend. No more, no less. Yet, if she were being honest, she really, really wanted to be Jack's girlfriend. For real.

She tried to muster a smile anyway, then remembered she hadn't heard from him since his text last night: ***Peter's fever finally came down. Huge relief, but he's not out the woods yet.***

Whatever that had meant.

She'd replied: ***Wishing him a speedy recovery. See you Saturday?***

Jack: ***Fingers crossed, if not b4.***

Julie: ***Ok.***

She'd left it like that.

It didn't matter if Jack didn't come tonight. She didn't expect him to. Besides, Brad would look after her.

After grabbing drinks from the bar, they headed to the Peterson's reserved table—handy, given the place was often so busy that tables were like gold.

Brad sat right next to her on the bench seat. He was

all about appearances; no surprises there. Neither were the unfriendly female faces staring back at her from around the table. She groaned inwardly. None of the regular gang had been able to make it.

It was going to be a long night.

Taking a larger sip of her gin and tonic than was strictly necessary, she closed her eyes and thought about the last few days.

She'd gotten through the long lonely hours by pouring herself into her day job and, in her free time, writing songs about unrequited love. Songs she never planned on showing to anyone. If nothing else, they'd provided a creative channel. It's not like she had a girlfriend she could confide in. The closest she'd ever had to a best friend was in junior high when Elizabeth, Lizzy—as Julie had affectionately nicknamed her—had joined her school.

She and Lizzy had sat together in every class, shared their lunches, and even enjoyed sleepovers. But it hadn't lasted long. One year on, Lizzy's dad—a computer programmer who relied on contract work—had uprooted his entire family to London, England, for a better opportunity.

Julie had been distraught, as had her friend. They'd kept in contact online for a while, but eventually Lizzy fell in love, married, and had a baby. They still exchanged greeting cards, but Lizzy's news had dwindled with each passing year.

With a deep sigh, Julie opened her eyes and caught movement in the far corner of the pub. A man wearing what appeared to be a black leather jacket and fitted blue jeans was walking quickly toward the exit.

Jack?

It couldn't be. The man was going in the wrong direction. Plus, Jack hadn't said he'd be coming tonight, so obviously it was just her mind playing tricks on her.

Feeling the weight of Brad's arm on her shoulders, she suddenly realized he was leaning across her, speaking with the person on her right.

Her heart sped up. If it *was* Jack, he might've thought

Brad was kissing her!

But, no, it definitely wasn't him. Because he'd have let her know he was coming and not just showed up.

The next morning, Julie pulled up alongside Jack's truck in the studio parking garage and frowned. Why hadn't he called or texted? They could've shared a ride to the studio session, then afterward gone straight to lunch, making up for Wednesday's missed dinner. Assuming he still wanted to take her out...on a date. Not that he'd called it that. But come on? Dinner out? A date, right?

Perhaps Charlotte hadn't given him any notice that she didn't need his help with Peter anymore. The little guy must be better by now. That must be it. Whatever the reason, she was happy Jack was back. Recording without him had been lonely and not nearly as productive.

Butterflies swooped in her stomach as she reached the recording booth's solid outer door. Dragging in a fortifying breath, she pushed it open and took a moment to soak up the sight of the man who dominated her dreams.

Jack had his headphones on, his expression intense. It seemed he'd been rehearsing for a while. She approached slowly, her spirits dipping further.

How long *had* he been here?

Not wanting to startle him, she touched his shoulder lightly. His head whipped around, and he yanked off his headphones.

"Julie!" he said, but nothing followed. No smile, no words.

A crater-sized hole formed in her stomach, and she cleared her throat. "So, Peter's better?" she asked, knowing the answer.

"Yes."

She pinned on a smile. "That's good."

Jack peered over at the booth where Kevin had just joined Carl. Julie did the same and waved at them.

"I guess we'd better get on with it. After all, our fans are expecting an album from us." Jack stuck his headphones back on. His let's-get-back-to-business attitude made her heart constrict.

What had she done to deserve his cold shoulder?

It wasn't her who'd canceled their dinner date and not kept in touch about their plans this morning. He was always the one warning her about appearances. And now, strangely, he was about to blow everything.

So, pretending nothing was wrong, Julie muddled through the session until Kevin left halfway through. Then she removed her headphones, retrieved her phone from the music stand, and said, "Let's take a break."

"I suppose I could do with another coffee," Jack muttered, his expression grim.

They collected their drinks from the bar counter in the studio's café area, and when she found a secluded table in the corner, Jack joined her.

Reluctantly, if his huge sigh was any indication.

While they sipped their coffee, he assessed her with a fixed stare. Shifting uncomfortably under the scrutiny, she wondered if he'd be forthcoming about his latest bone of contention.

Crossing his arms, Jack leaned back against the booth seating. "What?"

"What?!" She narrowed her eyes. "Exactly. I'd like to know what's bothering you, Jack."

He shrugged.

Exasperated, she blew out a long breath. "Just when I think we're making progress, it's like suddenly the switch is turned back, and we go back to square one."

"I feel the same." His hard tone was so unlike him. "Just when I think you and I are heading in the same direction, *you* veer off in a completely different one."

Shaking her head, she frowned deeply. "Okay, now I'm really confused. I haven't seen you since Tuesday night, so what exactly did I do to make you say that?"

Running his hand over his head, he squeezed his eyes shut for a few seconds and held the back of his neck. "I saw you last night."

"What do you mean? Where?"

"At the pub."

"But you weren't even there." She blinked twice. "I saw someone who looked like you, but he left."

"I thought I'd surprise you." Folding his arms again, Jack's prosecuting gaze remained steady.

The blood drained from her face when the realization hit, and her mouth formed an 'O.' "You think you saw Brad kissing me?" she whispered.

"I don't *think*, Julie, I *saw* you two kissing."

Her heart raced. He didn't believe that, did he?

Gripping his forearm, she forced her voice not to tremble. "Brad didn't kiss me, Jack. You have to believe me. In typical Brad style, he leaned across me to talk to the person on my other side. You must've arrived at exactly that moment and misunderstood the situation."

She released Jack's arm but didn't break eye contact. Disbelief flittered across his face, but he kept quiet.

"Wow, I thought you knew me better than that!" she said. "When have I *ever* expressed any interest in Brad?"

Aware of the aggression in her voice, she lessened it before continuing, "He's just a coworker who happens to be the boss's son and therefore requires some delicate handling. I can't afford to get on his wrong side, Jack. I may know David a little more than some employees, but if it's my word against Brad's, David will always take his son's side. And where would that leave me?"

She should've been angry and disappointed that he'd even imagine she'd kiss another man. But it was her fault. She'd been the one to institute the no kissing rule. Who knew where they'd be if she hadn't?

"I'm so sorry, Julie." Jack's expression softened as an apologetic smile formed on his lips. He gathered her hands in his. "You're right," he said. "Looks can be deceiving. I should've trusted you and stayed. I won't repeat that mistake. Forgive me, please?"

***

As Jack waited for Julie's response, the knot growing in his stomach didn't ease until a small smile lifted her kissable lips. Except, even if she forgave him, he'd still only have her as a friend.

"I forgive you," she said softly.

He squeezed her hands lightly. "Your kindness amazes me. Thank you."

She withdrew her hands, uncertainty filling her eyes. Jack braced himself, sensing a 'but' coming.

"There's something I need to clear up."

"What's that?" He examined her face for any hint of what she might be thinking but found none.

"We agreed to be friends, to keep things professional between us."

"Yes?"

"I was wrong."

"I don't follow."

Slipping off her seat, Julie scooted over to his side. The sweet smell of jasmine captured his senses, causing his pulse to spike. He shifted sideways to face her on the booth seat, and she smiled at him.

"What are you doing?" he asked.

Leaning closer, she cupped his cheek. She was so close, his heart hammered in his chest. If he reached forward an inch or two, he could kiss her.

"I don't want to be just friends anymore," she murmured, her eyes sparkling. "I don't think I can be. Fighting my feelings... it's way too hard."

Jack froze, swallowed, and let her words sink in. "Ditto." His voice almost cracked on the word.

"Oh, good." She giggled, her hand sliding to the back of his neck. Delicious sensations moved through him as she eased her fingers through his hair. Enraptured, he could barely breathe, and his gaze dipped to her mouth.

Would she let him kiss her?

But he held back, not wanting to break his promise. Though each agonizing second that passed only increased his desire to press his lips to hers.

When she finally brushed her lips briefly against his, the world around them faded. A second later, her eyes closed, and tiny tingles raced over his lips as their mouths reconnected. He snaked his hand around her waist, resting it on the small of her back. Then taking charge, he moved his lips over hers, tasting every soft section and reveling in her response. She matched him with equal intensity, her sigh of contentment spurring him on. Coaxing her closer, he deepened the kiss.

After a while, he broke away and grinned.

"Wow," he said.

"Ditto."

They both laughed.

"Is this wise?" he asked, becoming serious once more. "I mean, sure, Kevin wants us together. But, if we're a couple for real? It's not like if things go south we can part ways hoping to never see each other again."

"Trust me," she said, "I understand the risks, Jack, and I didn't make this decision lightly. I'm prepared to take that chance. A relationship with you is worth it."

Julie's confidence in them, in him, lightened the pressure bearing down on his shoulders.

"I'll admit it's become harder and harder for me to keep things purely professional," he confessed, his fingertips grazing her upper arm, eliciting goosebumps on her ivory skin. "The closer we've become, the more I've gotten to know you, the deeper my feelings have become. You're an incredible woman," he said, his voice gravelly. "Sometimes, I wonder why you haven't been snapped up before now."

Her hug was unexpected, but he welcomed it, returned it eagerly even. Never wanting to let her go, he marveled at how perfectly she fit in his arms.

Eventually, she leaned back and looked him straight in the eye. "You want the honest truth?"

"Always."

"I've been waiting for *you*, Jack Carrington."

He frowned. She had to be kidding!

"You don't believe me," she said, inching away on the seat, and he immediately mourned the loss of her warmth.

"No, I—"

"The first time I laid eyes on you, Mr. Carrington," she interrupted, "my heart stopped beating. After that, I tried not to spend even the smallest moment focused on you because my heart literally hurt every time I did.

Don't you know, you're kind of amazing? Kind-hearted and handsome, too." She shook her head slightly before fixing him with a look of determination. "When you started dating Alex, I thought she was the luckiest woman on earth. I was so jealous."

His eyebrows darted upward. "But you never flirted with me!"

"You noticed?"

"How could I not? I thought it was because you didn't like me at all."

"I liked you way too much! *That* was the problem. Ignoring you, as much as possible, was my way of coping."

That explained some things—one in particular—a memory as clear as the sky on a cloud-free day. "Do you remember last Christmas at Steven's?"

"Of course."

Heat suffused his face. "I wanted to kiss you so badly under the mistletoe."

"So did I. But I couldn't let it happen. You had a girlfriend; it wouldn't have been right."

"I wasn't thinking about Alex at the time, just that I had a chance to kiss you 'legitimately' if you like. But you said you didn't care for tradition and walked away. I was so disappointed."

"One of the hardest decisions I've ever had to make."

Leaning forward, he pressed a fleeting kiss against her warm lips. "You truly do amaze me, Julie Rolland," he breathed before drawing back.

"The feeling's mutual, Jack Carrington."

He linked their fingers. "So, we're a couple, both professionally and personally?"

"Yes." Her quick reply made his heart soar.

"Though, may I suggest," he said slowly, "that we keep our personal relationship to ourselves?"

Her forehead wrinkled. "What do you mean?"

"Well, professionally, there's going to be plenty of attention on us as the Jays. I'd rather our personal life wasn't under the spotlight too. At least, not until we've secured our place in the entertainment industry. And besides..." He laid another heated kiss on her lips. "Our kisses are our business."

"I agree," she said, sounding out of breath—the way he felt.

After tracing her bottom lip with his thumb, he forced himself to look away from her tempting mouth. "I also don't think our friends need to know about us just yet. We need time for our relationship to grow." He massaged his temple. "Are you okay with that?"

For a moment, her expression was contemplative, and his heartbeat took off like a rocket. What if she didn't agree?

"What about Charlotte?"

"She's the only one I will tell. If you're okay with that?"

"More than okay." Julie smiled widely, then rewarded him with a quick kiss that stole his breath away. "We'd better get back," she said while he fought to remember where he was and what he was meant to be doing.

Thankfully, the rest of the recording session went like clockwork.

At last, they were a couple, and Jack prayed they'd finally reached a turning point in their relationship. From here on out, it could only get better, right? Their careers and, even more importantly, their happiness depended on it.

Chapter Fourteen

"I wouldn't mind a hot chocolate. If it's not too late?"

Jack concentrated on backing his truck out of the studio parking space and didn't answer Julie. They'd just wrapped up recording another song, and he should've felt happy. Instead—

"I'm not going to see you until Friday," Julie moaned.

Well, she wasn't the only miserable one. Two whole days was a long time!

Back in the studio, given Charlie's last-minute plans to celebrate after Mark's unexpected arrival earlier, Jack had asked Julie, "What are you doing tomorrow for Thanksgiving?"

"I already have plans."

Her response had felt like a slap in the face. One Jack hadn't seen coming. "Oh. I see."

She didn't have any family with which to make plans, so... Who?

"I assume you're celebrating with Zac," he'd surmised.

"No. My foster family." An emotion—irritation?—had flickered in her eyes. "They invited me months ago."

Jealous of some family he'd never met, Jack had quickly buried his disappointment. He'd been looking forward to sharing some of his traditions with her; Thanksgiving would've been the start. And Christmas? Well, he hadn't dared ask about her plans for *that* holiday.

"I didn't realize you still saw your foster family."

"I don't, not really, but their children have been scattered all over the globe for a couple years. So this is the first time we'll all be together to catch up on each other's lives." Lifting a palm to his cheek, Julie had peered at him sadly. "I *am* sorry. I would've loved to share this first holiday with you."

Yeah, well, that wasn't happening.

Shifting into drive, Jack navigated the turns until he'd exited the studio garage and was heading down the street.

Julie's hand brushed over his arm. "Forty-eight hours of dreaming about being in your arms, Jack. Dreaming of your magic lips on mine, rather than the real thing. I'm not sure I can manage."

Casting her a sideways glance, he chuckled. She was actually pouting!

"Has anyone ever told you it's hard to stay mad at you?" he asked.

Her brows rose. "You're mad at me?"

"Not anymore."

"I don't know why you were in the first place." Huffing, she stared out the truck's side window, no doubt marveling at the glittering festive displays of the department stores as they flashed by.

Jack crept his hand onto her thigh and rested it there, palm up, fingers splayed. A moment later, she accepted the invitation, sliding her hand into his with a sly smile.

He grinned. "Two hot chocolates coming up."

After finding an open restaurant and placing their order, they collected their drinks from the pick-up point and sat at a small, round table. The dim overhead lighting helped them to keep a low profile. Thankfully—other than the one incident at Kevin's masked party—they hadn't been approached for an autograph again, though Kevin had warned it was only a matter of time.

Hopefully, that wasn't today.

Jack sampled his hot chocolate while Julie blew steam off the top of hers, her eyes fixed on him. "Charlotte must be pleased to have her husband home," she said.

"Sure." He licked some cream off his top lip.

"Charlie's thrilled, even though Mark's only staying through the holiday weekend."

"What exactly does Mark do?"

"He's the Program Director for a charity that builds homes for the underprivileged in South Africa."

"Wow, that's admirable. I didn't realize."

Undoubtedly, the cogs in her brain were spinning furiously as she sipped her hot chocolate, working out how Mark could possibly support a family of five.

Settling back into his seat, Jack savored his drink and waited for the inevitable questions—there usually were when it came to his sister's marriage.

"Don't you think Mark's missing out, you know, on seeing his children grow up?" Julie's voice was full of judgment.

"Of course!" He sat up straight and folded his arms, his gaze hardening. "It's really hard for Mark. Charlie video calls him every day and gets the kids to talk to him as much as possible. Amy's great, but the boys sometimes complain. They're not fans of speaking to a screen."

"I bet; they're so young." Julie fiddled with the handle of her mug before meeting his eyes. "I imagine the distance causes a bit of strain in their marriage."

"Not really." He took a deep breath. "Charlie's a wonderful mother and wife, Julie."

She frowned, opening her mouth as if to argue.

He beat her to it. "My sister takes everything in her stride. I know she wishes Mark could be there when things get tough, but she has me at least. A poor substitute, I know, but—"

"You're not a poor substitute! On the contrary, Charlotte's very lucky to have you. But..." Julie shook her head. "I couldn't live like that."

"It takes a special kind of person," he said gently.

Glowering at him, she crossed her arms.

"Hey." Desperate to ease her mind, his hand shot out to rest on her arm. "It's not that you're not special. You are." He offered an encouraging smile.

"Thanks," she said, squeezing his hand.

"You know what I mean, though, right?"

She blinked.

"Some people *can* keep faith in each other, despite the distance. For others, it's just too difficult."

Steven had done that to Melanie once, and it had temporarily ended their relationship. Their situation had been unique, but still.

"I know I wouldn't want to *ever* live apart from the woman I loved," Jack added.

Various emotions played out on Julie's face— confusion, concern, and maybe even longing.

Did she have hope for them the way he did? How could he convince her? Perhaps she needed more information?

"Actually, they won't be separated forever," he said. "Mark's contract ends in March, and he'll be coming home permanently."

"Oh." Julie's eyes brightened, and she released a pent-up breath.

He leaned forward, cupping her cheek with his palm. Slowly, his fingers caressed the skin behind her ear. "Do you know, Mark sends Charlie a letter every week? And she sends him one too."

"Like romantic love notes?" The breathiness in her voice made his pulse race.

"Yes, according to Charlie." Enticed by Julie's scent— reminding him of freshly picked flowers—Jack inched closer as her eyes darkened to the color of seaweed.

"That's so sweet," she whispered.

Their lips touched briefly. When he eased back, she groaned, probably wishing—like him—that the table wasn't between them. This just wasn't the place.

"You're not going to tell me they were high school sweethearts, are you?" she asked.

"They were."

"No way!" She swatted his arm playfully. "Seriously?"

He nodded, a smile splitting his face.

"Wow. I really admire them, and I admire you for always being there to help your sister out. Not many brothers would make what I'd term a major sacrifice for

ONLY FOREVER

their sisters."

His lips flattened. She thought what he did for his sister was a sacrifice?

"What? Don't you agree? You're basically putting your life on hold so you can be your sister's go-to while her husband's away?"

"You have a problem with my family commitment." He phrased it as a statement.

"No." She shook her head slowly. "I just said I admire you, didn't I?"

"Fine," he said gruffly, though he wasn't convinced.

Reaching over, Julie traced his jawline. Her smooth fingertips against his rough skin generated sparks. "I'm not going anywhere, Jack," she said. "And I want you to know, I'll always stand by you."

Her words and attitude seemed sincere.

Now he just had to believe it.

***

It was early Friday evening when a firm rap on Julie's apartment door had her heartbeat kicking up a notch.

She swung open the door.

"Jack," she said, her hungry gaze roaming his length. The fitted dark blue jeans and black grandad top—its three buttons unfastened—did nothing to disguise his athletic body. And, as if that sight didn't get her blood pumping faster than normal, his perfectly chiseled jaw and dreamy green eyes just accelerated it further.

It felt like a lifetime since she'd last seen him, not forty-eight hours. Thanksgiving with the Andersons had been amazing, but she'd missed him.

"Hi." He laughed, motioning behind her. "Are you going to let me in? Or just stand there with your mouth hanging open?"

Feeling her cheeks heat, she closed her mouth and stood aside, shutting the door behind him. She was barely able to catch her breath before his arms circled her waist, and his lips were eagerly claiming hers. The minty taste of toothpaste vied with the smell of his woodsy aftershave.

A few seconds later, she eased back to whisper, "Hi,"

131

against his lips. Then, before she could say another word, he retook control of her mouth. Their kiss quickly grew in intensity, and all coherent thought fled.

Of their own accord, Julie's hands lifted the hem of Jack's shirt, her errant fingers wandering over his six-pack and up onto his rock-hard chest. She felt rather than heard his sharp intake of breath and immediately dropped her hands to his waist.

Jack grabbed her hands, breaking the heavenly kiss, and leaned his forehead on hers. While she struggled to control her breathing, he kept his eyes closed. "Julie," he murmured huskily, "we need to stop."

"Why? Don't you want me, Jack?"

His eyes flew open, revealing his dilated pupils. "Oh, trust me, I do. I just have no intention of going there."

Rejection was a new experience and one she didn't particularly care for. It hurt.

When she tried to tug her hands free, he held on tightly. "Oh no, you don't."

One hand after the other, he pressed a warm kiss to each knuckle. The simple gesture did things to her insides she couldn't describe. Afterward, when she stared into his eyes, she could've sworn she saw love.

Huh, like she knew what that looked like! Clearly, she was mistaking lust for love.

She peered at his chest and tried not to think about the feel of his solid muscles under her fingertips. Nor about where she wished they could be right now. Trying to block out that vision, she squeezed her eyes shut as disappointment took root.

"Julie?" Jack's index finger forced her chin up while the concern in his voice broke into her desirous thoughts.

She opened her eyes slowly.

"What's wrong?"

"You're not like the men in my past. They'd never have passed up the opportunity to be with me."

"You're right. I'm not. I intend to cherish the special woman you are by respecting you."

She frowned. What did *that* mean? He wouldn't sleep

with her because she was *special.* That made no sense.

He tapped the fourth finger of her left hand. "Until I put a gold band there, I won't make love to you."

It took a few seconds to process his words.

He was thinking of marriage?

They'd only been dating three weeks. Was it possible his intentions had changed that quickly? He'd said it wasn't on his radar.

Honestly, marrying Jack would be her dream, but... could she dare think that such a wonderful man, who pretty much had a family already, would actually welcome her into his family?

And what did he mean by 'make love?' Didn't he mean sleep with her?

After planting a fleeting kiss on her lips, he released her hands. "Are you ready?" he asked softly. "We *do* need to go. Otherwise, we'll be late."

With her mind spinning, she somehow managed to concentrate on retrieving her coat and purse.

"I'm ready," she said.

Physically that was true. Mentally and emotionally? She wasn't so sure.

***

Jack stole a glance at his passenger and noted the absentminded tracing of her wrist tattoo.

Ever since he'd stopped the direction their kiss had been barreling toward, Julie had become withdrawn. Which, unfortunately, didn't bode well for them or a night out with their friends.

Neither did the somber mood in his truck.

"You're not worried about letting our team down tonight, are you?" he teased, trying to lighten the atmosphere and get her to relax.

"What?" She peered at him with a furrowed brow. "Oh, you mean bowling? I mean, I'm rubbish at it, but as long as you don't plan on winning..." she trailed off, her gaze drifting away, her grim expression remaining.

"Maybe we should split up then."

Her eyes widened in surprise. "What?"

"I meant divide ourselves between the teams, silly."

He chuckled. "We wouldn't want anyone guessing we're a couple now, would we?"

A worried look flittered over her face, and he instantly regretted his teasing.

"I'm kidding, Julie." Reaching over, he laced his fingers through hers. "I couldn't care less who wins. I'm just glad I get to spend tonight with you."

She raised a questioning brow.

"Earlier tonight, I thought I'd be asked to look after the kids so Charlie and Mark could be here."

"Huh?" Julie pulled her hand away. "I thought Mark's parents agreed to babysit? Charlotte wouldn't expect *you* to, would she? Just so she could come out with *your* friends."

"No, of course not. Mark's dad has just gone through chemo, and because Daniel looked like he might be running a temperature, they didn't want to risk passing on anything to Mark's parents."

"Oh, I'm sorry. I didn't know."

"It's okay. Daniel's fine, so everything worked out like it was supposed to."

"I guess so."

Suddenly, Julie smiled wide, and her eyes danced. "Actually," she said, "Melanie's suggestion of bowling was an excellent one." Entranced, Jack couldn't look away from her. Thankfully, a stoplight had caught them. "This way, I get to be with my boyfriend, who I wasn't expecting to see until Monday morning."

"First of all, I like hearing you call me your boyfriend —you never referred to Zac as that."

"Because he wasn't."

"I know that *now*." He chuckled, sending her a sidelong smirk. "Let me finish. Secondly, have you forgotten something?"

She looked at him curiously.

"Ben's christening on Sunday?"

"Oh, gosh, I still need to buy a gift!"

Jack frowned. "Sorry, I didn't think. Charlie kindly sorted mine. We can easily add your name to the card—"

She cut him off. "That's so kind, but you'd better not. I

think I'll enjoy shopping for the little guy."

"Maybe we should rethink this not telling everyone about us," he said. "It would certainly make things a lot less complicated."

"No, let's stick to our plan. The others knowing about our relationship isn't going to make it feel more real. I already know it is."

"Okay."

Jack found an empty space in the bowling alley's parking lot and killed the engine. Julie undid her belt and reached for the door handle.

"Wait," he said, and she glanced back.

He beckoned her over, and when she moved into his waiting arms, anticipation danced in her eyes. Her palm landed on his chest, and she probably felt his racing heart. Not that he minded.

Outside, the lighting was sub-standard. If he kissed her, would she mind re-applying her cherry lipstick for the third time? He didn't have to wonder long—her attention went straight to his lips, confirming she had the same idea. Dipping his head, he planted a short, passionate kiss on her mouth.

"Not that I'm complaining, but what was that for?" she asked softly.

He brushed his thumb over her swollen bottom lip, loving the way she shivered at his touch. "Well," he said, staring into her desire-filled eyes, "for the next few hours, I'm not even going to be able to hold your hand, let alone kiss you, so I thought I'd store up some reserves."

"Good thinking. Except, I'm not sure your stash is sufficient."

A second later, Julie was kissing him like there was no tomorrow, and he forgot all about what had just happened at her place. Instead, he lost himself in the moment. Slipping one hand into her silky hair, he caressed her lower back with the other. All he could think was that he never wanted to leave this truck or, more specifically, the comfort of her arms. Being with Julie felt like home.

When headlights from another vehicle shone directly at them, they flew apart then laughed at their guilty reaction.

Julie checked her watch. "We'd better go."

"I guess."

Jack's phone buzzed with a message, and he groaned. "I almost forgot. I promised Charlie I'd wait out front for them, but they're running a little late. Do you mind going in alone?"

She winked. "As a one-time only?"

His stomach clenched with self-reproach. Why was he even considering making Julie enter on her own?

For all he knew, Alex was already inside. Given Zac would be coming too, things could get mighty awkward if Alex decided to get territorial. The last thing he wanted was for Julie to feel left out or ostracized.

Julie's hand covered his as he fumbled with his cell, trying to text Charlie to meet them inside. "Don't stress about me, Jack; I'll be fine." Then, wearing a resigned expression, she added, "You forget, I'm used to being alone."

Her easy acceptance almost broke his heart.

Maybe his suggestion of keeping their relationship a secret until they had time for it to develop wasn't such a good idea after all.

Chapter Fifteen

"Ben MacAlistar's the sweetest baby I've ever met."

Jack smiled at Julie's blissful expression as he pulled out of the church parking lot and into the late Sunday afternoon traffic. "He *is* rather cute."

While the road ahead cleared, he reflected on the christening service and added, "And, I have to admit, baby Ben was perfectly behaved, just like his big sister Sophie."

"Yeah, Steven and Melanie are lucky to have two such beautiful children together." Julie sounded wistful, and her smile waned. "Would you ever want a child of your own one day?" she asked, running her fingers lightly up and down his thigh.

He sucked in a breath. Was that a trick question? Her touch made it almost impossible to think logically, but eventually, he came up with an answer. "Assuming I'd found the right woman."

"Right woman?"

Covering her errant hand with his, he halted her assault on his senses and retrieved his rational thoughts. "Yes." He nodded firmly. "If that's what she wanted."

After another stretch of silence, he realized Julie hadn't commented, and her hand no longer warmed his leg.

He spared her a glance. "Julie?"

"What?" she snapped before turning to look at some gray industrial buildings on their route.

Shocked by her cold tone and indifference, he pulled over when he could and flicked on his hazard lights.

"Why have you stopped?"

Releasing his seat belt, Jack slid over the leather seat and took Julie's beautiful, puzzled face in his hands. He peered deeply into her eyes. "Would it freak you out if I said I think you might be the right woman?"

"N-no."

"Honestly, with Alex, the thought of having children didn't appeal. Caring for Charlie's three was plenty. But I do remember once looking over at you when we were all talking about kids and seeing mini Julies." He smiled slowly. "Would you believe me if I told you my heart skipped a beat right then?"

A ghost of a smile appeared on her lips. "Really?"

He nodded.

"Oh, Jack," she whispered, her eyes filling with liquid. "That's the sweetest thing anyone's ever said to me."

Lowering his mouth to hers, he kissed her tenderly, softly, and with as much passion as he could without completely losing control.

When the kiss ended, and he opened his eyes, she was staring at him, an expectant look in her pretty green eyes. "I really hope I'm the right woman for you," she said.

He stroked her cheek. "Honey, every minute I spend with you, every time I kiss you, I become more certain."

She giggled, her voice returning to normal. "Did you just call me, honey?"

Easing away from her, he pretended to look ticked off. "Way to ruin a romantic moment."

She leaned over and brought her lips tantalizing close to his. "You can call me honey any time you like," she said in a husky voice. Then, after planting another enticing kiss on his mouth, she shifted back into her seat. "Now, are you going to take me home or not?"

Jack checked his watch. "How about I take you to dinner instead? If I remember correctly, I believe I owe you a date."

"That sounds perfect."

Her sexy smile made him want to pull her into his arms and do more than just kiss her.

**

The Christmas lights and decorations shone more brightly in the center of New Haven than they did on the outskirts. Like a full moon on a dark night, they reminded Julie of the holidays around the corner. The heady feeling she'd had, only moments ago, when Jack referred to her as 'the one' fled at the thought of Christmas and where she'd be spending it.

After they parked in a lot behind High Street, Jack led her to the entrance of a Spanish restaurant she'd never visited before. It looked pretty busy.

"Are we going to be able to get a table?"

"Fingers crossed. It's not usually open to the public on a Sunday night, but I saw an 'OPEN' sign when we drove past."

Inside, the place was buzzing. The host gave them a welcoming smile, grabbed two menus, and motioned for them to follow her to a small table near the back.

Julie had a look around. The place had modern, sleek furnishings and was decorated in muted tones giving it a clean feeling. Festive decorations added sparkle.

The host handed out the cards and lit the candle. "Your server will be with you shortly."

Julie chose the fish from the limited menu, while Jack swiftly set his aside.

Smoothing the white linen serviette on her lap, she raised her eyes past the simple white candle and discovered his narrowed gaze on her.

"You seem rather pensive," he said, pouring them each a glass of water from the jug provided. "Everything okay?"

"Mmm. Just thinking."

"About?"

"You two ready to order?" A man wearing smart black pants and a white shirt with a bow tie stood beside them, his finger hovering over an iPad.

Once they'd ordered, the man left, and Jack lifted his glass in a toast and smiled. "To us and our future together."

"To us." She clinked her glass against his.

"So, about Christmas...I'm guessing you already have plans?"

She blinked.

Was that a statement or a question? She'd go with the former and save him any potential embarrassment. "Considering it's only a month away, that would be a reasonable assumption."

"Right," he said, a flicker of disappointment in his eyes. "Charlie and I are making plans based on Mark being home, but we never know until the last minute. As far as the children know, he'll be away." Julie raised a brow. "It's easier to manage their expectations that way."

"I see." She nodded. "It must be hard for them, not having their father around. I never knew mine, so there was never any hope of seeing him at Christmas time or otherwise."

Jack's warm hand covered hers, and he squeezed her fingers. "Holidays must be difficult. I know how that feels. That's why I'm so grateful for Charlie and Mark."

Carefully extracting her hand, Julie slipped it into her lap. "You're very blessed to have a sibling and a family. Especially at this time of the year. Being alone when everyone else is celebrating..."

Moisture clouded her vision, and she shifted her attention to a nearby table where another couple was being seated. Their shiny rings confirmed they'd be together for Christmas.

Would that ever be her?

"The cod for you, ma'am, and the beef for you, sir."

Their server interrupted Julie's negative thoughts, bringing a welcome distraction. She glanced down at her plate, enticed by the smell of garlic and sage. Small, stubby, finger-shaped potatoes surrounded a piece of succulent-looking white fish. There was no way she'd eat the slimy skin, but the chickpeas and cauliflower looked delicious.

She studied Jack's plate; his meager portion of grilled

tenderloin covered in a dark sauce—probably red wine— looked tasty and smelled beefy, but it made her think of the generous portions they'd enjoyed at his friend's restaurant.

"You know, I would've happily gone back to Gino's," she said.

Chuckling, Jack waved a hand around the room. "What and miss out on this fine-dining experience?"

"It *is* lovely, and the dishes *are* beautifully presented. I just hope you have enough to eat." She pointed to his plate. "I think Italian might've been a little more filling."

"Oh, don't you worry about me, I intend to have the biggest dessert on the menu, and if that doesn't fill me, I'm inviting myself to yours for your scrumptious scrambled eggs on toast."

Julie laughed. "How do you know my eggs are scrumptious?"

"How could they not be? Everything you cook is amazing." He said it so matter-of-factly that she couldn't help but grin.

After their plates were collected and they were given dessert menus, Julie asked for a cappuccino straight away. Jack handed back the menu card. "I'll just have a scoop each of hazelnut-chocolate, crème brûlée, and passion fruit ice cream, please."

"That's not like you." She angled her head. "Nothing else grabs your fancy?"

"Yep, but not the dessert," he smirked.

Heat rose to her cheeks. "Jack."

"I wanted some hot chocolate fudge cake," he said, quite serious. "But it's probably a good thing they don't serve it here. I've already experienced the best one ever."

"I never knew you were such a flatterer."

"Oh, honey, you don't know the half of it." His green eyes twinkled mischievously.

When the coffee arrived, Julie immediately took a sip then had to wipe froth off her top lip.

"So," Jack said after she set her cup down. "What exactly are your plans for Christmas? Are you spending them with your foster parents?"

"No."

"With who then?"

She scowled. "You don't think I have other friends to spend the holiday with?"

"I happen to know you spend all your time either at work or with me. So, unless you're talking about Brad, I'm confused."

"There'll be three of us, actually." It was tough keeping a straight face, given Jack's intense scrutiny. Somehow, she managed.

"I can't decide whether I want to throttle you or kiss you." He sounded exasperated.

She giggled. "Personally, I'd prefer a kiss."

"Excuse me?" A woman with makeup plastered on her young face stared at Jack. She wore a form-fitting black dress that barely made it past her mid-thigh, and if her neckline was any lower, she'd be sued for indecent exposure.

Julie snickered. Okay, maybe that was a little harsh, but really?

"Are you Jack Carrington? Of the Jays?" The woman's voice dripped with honey.

Jack nodded and was confronted with a piece of paper that looked suspiciously like it came from the dinner menu.

"Would you give me your autograph, please? I absolutely love 'The Face Behind the Mask.' I've been playing it on repeat ever since I heard it on the radio. You have an amazing voice."

Taking the pen and paper, Jack signed his name, then gave the woman a pointed look and gestured to Julie. "Would you like Julie Rolland's signature too?"

Tearing her eyes from Jack, the woman glanced at Julie before addressing him again. "Yeah, that'd be good. My boyfriend loves her. Says she has the voice of an angel and a figure to go with it."

Realizing what she'd said, the woman quickly covered her mouth. "I probably shouldn't have said that."

"No, it's okay. Your boyfriend's quite right." Grinning,

Jack pushed the paper over to Julie with a wink.

Doing her best to hide her heated face, Julie dipped her head low and scribbled her signature for the female fan.

"Thank you *so* much," the woman gushed, retrieving her scrap of paper like it was worth a million dollars. "I just want to say, Mr. Carrington, you're even hotter in person." Blushing furiously, she then made a quick getaway—well, as fast as she could on six-inch heels!

"That was surreal." Julie grinned at Jack. "Our first autographs."

His expression matched hers. "Unexpected, for sure."

"She's right, you know."

"About what?"

"You are hotter in person."

"Is that so?"

His gaze darkened as she nodded. With any luck, her cheeks weren't quite as red as the woman who'd just left.

Finishing his ice cream in record time, Jack then pushed to his feet, and with a protective hand on Julie's lower back, steered her toward the front of the restaurant. "You never did tell me which three people you're spending Christmas with," he said, his voice gruff.

"Oh." She sighed. "Me, myself, and I."

Chapter Sixteen

Jack linked his arm with Julie's and navigated the narrow sidewalk to the parking lot. Tightening his scarf against the cold night air, he was thankful he'd parked his truck only a short distance from where they'd eaten dinner.

Was Julie seriously spending Christmas alone?

No. She had to be joking.

Reaching his truck, he cast her a sideways look. "Did you notice the curious looks we got leaving the restaurant?"

Julie turned to face him. "I did."

"Do you think they knew who we were?"

"Yes, or they probably had a suspicion. That skimpily dressed young woman drooling all over you might've given it away," she said wryly.

He let loose a laugh. "Jealous much?"

"Oh, definitely. I mean, didn't you notice how pretty she was? I particularly loved her dress sense, totally sophisticated." Julie didn't even try to hide her sarcasm.

"Now now. Be nice."

"I'm sorry." She shook her head. "If I thought you'd actually be interested in someone like her, I might be a little worried, but..." Her voice trailed off.

"I get it. So long as the person showing interest in me pales in comparison to the fabulous Julie Rolland, you're good?" he teased, opening the passenger-side door.

"You make me sound full of myself."

He stared at her adorable pouting lips and sobered. "Never," he said. "Honey, you're the most unpretentious person I've ever met."

Needing to force his gaze away, he grabbed the seat belt to buckle her in but then caught a whiff of her signature jasmine scent. Next thing, his heart was thudding in his chest, compelling him to lift his eyes to her dilated pupils. Awareness buzzed between them, and resistance was futile; she was irresistible, and so were her lips. Julie returned his kiss with such vigor it sent a bolt of desire through him. He parted her lips with his tongue and deepened the kiss. After that, her intensity matched his until she nudged his chest.

"Jack," she murmured. "We should stop."

"Okay."

Willing his heart rate to slow down, he took a moment to catch his breath. Then, after planting a chaste kiss on her cheek, he closed the door and rounded the back of the truck, pausing when he spotted a bunch of people in the distance.

From the looks of it, they were taking photos, or worse, recording with their phones. Uneasy, he jumped into his seat and started the engine. He backed out of the parking space, tires squealing.

"W-what's wrong?" Julie asked.

"Hang on, I'll explain in a minute."

He drove toward the parking lot's exit where his suspicions were confirmed—the small gathering *was* recording everything. Hopefully, whatever grainy videos or photos they managed to capture would be of no interest to the media.

"T-those people weren't recording us, were they?" Julie's voice held an undertone of panic.

"They were, but I don't think they'll have gotten any worthwhile footage. We were too far away, and the lighting was terrible." Even so, his gut still twisted unpleasantly.

Julie stayed quiet.

"Honey, we knew this day would come. Now that it

has, we're going to have to be a little more careful about what we do in public."

"Yeah. Especially if we don't want our friends to know about us just yet, right?" There was a weird, sharp edge to her tone. He couldn't tell if she was upset or not, so he let it slide.

"At least we know Kevin won't be concerned. He'll just say any publicity is good publicity."

Julie groaned.

Hoping to distract her and ease the tension in her shoulders, he switched on the radio. Mariah Carey's "All I Want for Christmas" was playing. Impossible to ignore the upbeat song, Julie began harmonizing along with the melody. Jack joined in.

Later, after he parked outside her apartment block and cut the engine, he turned to find her smiling at him. "I like seeing you smile. If you're happy, I'm happy."

"Well, *you* make me happy." Her earnest expression warmed him to his toes.

Was it too soon to tell her that he loved her? Probably. Instead, he smiled. "Ditto." Lifting her palm to his lips, he peppered it with kisses. "Now about those scrambled eggs."

She threw back her head and laughed. Some women sounded like witches cackling, Julie's laughter he likened to an instrument—beautiful and melodious. He needed to make her laugh more often.

"So...would you like to come up?" A seductive smile played on her lips, and his heart skipped a beat at her unspoken invitation.

When he raised his eyebrows, she laughed again. "For some eggs à la Julie?"

He squashed down his irrational disappointment. After all, he'd set the boundaries, not Julie. "I thought you'd never ask."

***

Mindful of Jack, perched on the other side of the kitchen island, Julie switched off the heat and dished the fluffy eggs onto warm toast.

After sliding the plate over to him, she waved her

hand with a flourish and bowed low. "Enjoy."

His deep, throaty laugh warmed her insides.

"I will."

He seasoned his food and took a bite.

"Mmm, so good." Pinning her with a pleading look, he asked, "Any chance you'd move in with me?"

Giggling, she leaned over the cold stone surface and shoved him playfully. "Don't push your luck, Mr. Carrington." She pointed at her ring finger. "Remember what you said about this?"

"Silly, I meant to cook for me." He smirked.

"Uh-huh."

Seeing him shovel giant mouthfuls of her food into his mouth filled her with joy.

"You know I live in a pretty big house, right?" he said when he'd eaten every last bit.

She straightened. "I do."

"So you could have your own bedroom and bathroom suite and save on rent."

Oh, he wasn't kidding!

"That sounds enticing, but no thanks. And anyway, I don't think your sister would take too kindly to that suggestion."

"Honey, Charlie wouldn't object. She'd never stand in the way of my happiness. She loves me too much."

Fighting the uncomfortable grip around her chest, Julie turned around to boil the kettle. "Would you like coffee or tea? I'm having herbal."

"Coffee," he said, bringing his plate over to the sink. "That was amazing. Thank you." Their eyes met, and her heartbeat sped up.

Worried she'd drown in the glorious depths of those green orbs, she busied herself sorting her mint tea before moving across to the coffee maker.

"So, who *are* you spending Christmas with?"

Right. She hadn't clarified her answer.

"Um." Throwing an espresso shot into a mug of hot milk, she stirred it, then passed it to Jack without making direct eye contact. "Let's sit."

Sinking gradually onto the double sofa's comfortable

seating, Julie took care not to spill her drink. The cushions moved slightly as Jack filled the space next to her.

"Julie?"

She glanced at him. "Mmm?"

"Christmas—where *will* you be?" Exasperation laced his voice.

Her gaze honed in on the corner of her open plan living area where she'd envisioned a small Christmas tree. If she was going to spend the holidays alone, she'd better make an effort to make her place look more festive. "By myself," she finally admitted.

Jack set his coffee down with a thud. "So you weren't kidding?"

"Nope." She sipped her tea until he pried her mug from her hands. "Hey!" she complained, "I was enjoying that!"

Grasping her hands in his, he looked at her intently. "Join us on Christmas day."

"But—"

"Come as early as you like, dress up, wear pajamas, I don't care. Don't bring gifts, just yourself and, if you feel like helping with cooking lunch, I'd definitely appreciate it. Charlie's not a bad cook, but I do prefer my turkey not totally dry." He grimaced. "The kids tend to get over-excited, given the holiday, so they may rope you into playing games with them—it's fine if you say no."

"I don't—"

"Mark may or may not be there, but if he isn't, you mustn't let it bother you. I'll warn you now, though; I plan on kissing you in front of my sister." His brow furrowed briefly. "Though probably not when the kids are around. Amy's a bit opinionated, and I'd rather not have to explain why I like kissing you." He winked. "Even if it's in my own home."

She opened her mouth again, but he put a finger on it and kept talking. "We'll probably go for a walk after lunch, then put on a kid's movie. We can watch, or not. The choice will be yours. Once the sun sets, I want to show you the stars. Alone." The hint of a challenge entered his eyes. "We'll see how much you remember from when Zac tried to teach you."

Julie waited a full second before chuckling out loud. "Are you finished?"

"Are you coming?" he countered.

"Yes."

"Good."

After pressing a quick kiss to each palm, Jack released her hands and returned her tea. Sighing, she leaned back against the sofa and closed her eyes, her muscles no longer taut.

"I hope that's a contented sigh."

"It is."

They sat in comfortable silence for a few minutes, Jack's arm around her shoulders, his fingers gently caressing her arm.

"I've been thinking." His voice broke the silence. "Things will probably get crazier soon, especially with our song being played on the radio a lot. So explaining why we're holding hands in public or staring into each other's eyes might become trickier."

She gave a slow nod. "Yeah."

"I know we agreed to wait until the Jays were more established, but we're in a good place, right?"

"I think so."

"Personally, I don't think anything's going to change just because we tell our friends we're dating. It's likely on social media now, anyway."

"So, what's your plan?" she asked, her mug halfway to her mouth.

"Well, after our weekly meeting tomorrow, I'll speak to Steven, then he can tell Melanie. If you're okay with that?"

"Sure."

A thought occurred as she swallowed down her tea. "What about Alex, Jack? Won't she be a little surprised, possibly even put out when she hears?"

Jack's palm settled on her cheek, his touch spreading heat through her veins. "Honey, I have this feeling Alex will be the least surprised of them all."

Samantha J. Ball

"Why?"

"When we broke up, Alex hinted that I needed to find the person who turned my world upside down. The one who made the world and everyone in it fade away when we kissed. She said I'd figure it out, and she said it as if she knew."

"Knew what?"

"Who that person was, is—you."

Julie laughed, and his hand fell away.

"Okay, well, I'll believe it when I see it. Alex has never liked me, and I don't expect her to be any friendlier when she discovers I'm dating her ex."

"Honey, Alex and I are friends. I'm sure she'll be thrilled for me, for us."

"Fine." Suddenly she felt disagreeable, which was ridiculous considering Jack was dating her, not Alex. "You won't mind then if I tell Zac since he's *my* friend."

"Naturally." Jack rose from the sofa, taking the mugs with him.

Had she annoyed him by mentioning Zac?

Biting her lip, she stood when Jack returned, donning his coat. "You're leaving?"

"It's safest if I do." His smoky gaze snagged hers, his hands slipping over her hips and linking behind her back.

Her pulse skittered.

"It's late, and I have to be up super early to pick up this stunning woman I love...spending time with." A mocking half-smile claimed his mouth. "She's a stickler for punctuality."

She shoved him good-naturedly. "I've *never* complained, even when you do come a few minutes late."

"I'm teasing. But I do have to go." Leaning in close, he kissed her for all of one second. Feeling cheated, Julie reached up and pressed her lips to his. She moved her lips slowly over his, coaxing them open. Even knowing the dangerous ground she treaded, she was powerless to stop the ardent kiss.

A short while later, Jack's ragged breathing matched

hers as he stepped back, his hands disappearing into his pants pockets.

"I'm sorry," she said softly. "You have to go, and I'm not making it easy."

"No, you're not. But don't ever be sorry for showing me how you feel because I feel the same way."

Hope rose inside of her like a bubble. "You do?"

"Yes. Of course I want you, too." His voice was low and husky. "More than anything."

The bubble popped. How stupid was she, thinking Jack might actually be in love with her?

Chapter Seventeen

The story was about to break, and Julie didn't know how she felt. Excited, relieved, worried?

In all likelihood, Jack was speaking to Steven this very minute, telling him that he was dating Julie. Then Steven would pass the information on to Melanie, and after that, who knew how quickly Alex—Melanie's best friend—would hear the news.

Pointless worrying so much. They were only friends by association, not even friends, really. Except for Steven—he'd always had her back.

Bracing herself before entering the Administration office, Julie rubbed her sweaty palms over her skirt. A bunch of coworkers hung around her workspace, but they'd move soon enough.

She marched past them and sank onto her desk chair with a grateful sigh. Unfortunately, they continued to hover, their eyes pinned on her.

"Julie, do you think...?"

"Would you mind...?"

"I can't believe..."

"So, you and Mr. Carrington?"

They all spoke at the same time, making it almost impossible for Julie to keep track.

What was going on?

She clapped loudly, and the noise quietened down fast. Tamping down her frustration, she kept her tone neutral. "I'm sorry, but maybe don't all speak at once."

"It seems you're a celebrity now, Miss Rolland, after singing *one* song on the radio," Brianna muttered sarcastically before turning on her heel and striding away, leaving a group of women staring straight at Julie.

"We apologize," one woman said—what was her name again? Oh yes, Sandra. "She's just jealous that not only do you have the number one spot on the music charts, but you've also got the man."

Julie kept her lips sealed tight. She had no clue where they'd gotten their information, but it certainly wasn't Jack. He'd never do that to her.

"We're all wondering if you'd give us an autograph?" Sandra motioned to include everyone around her. "And Mr. Carrington's too?"

The women all held out pieces of paper and smiled encouragingly.

Laughter threatened to burst from her. She'd finally gotten to do what she'd always dreamed of—singing her own songs—and now, now her coworkers decided they wanted to know her.

Go figure.

If she was the spiteful type, she'd send them packing. But these people were fans, insincere or not. "Sure. I'll return them tomorrow." Faking a smile, she collected the papers and placed them in a pile on her desk.

The gathering disbanded, except for a few stragglers like Sandra.

"What's it like to be dating Mr. Carrington? I mean, you're so lucky, Julie. He's so hot. Is he a good kisser? I bet he is." Sandra's cheeks flushed while Julie wished a hole would open and swallow her up.

Was this what it felt like to have one's personal life in the spotlight? Well, it was none of their business! Clenching her teeth, she continued to smile. "Listen, I appreciate your support of the Jays' music, but my relationship with Mr. Carrington is my business, okay?"

"Sorry, we just thought..."

"I know. But the answer is still no."

Much later, stuck in the middle of a complicated email to a supplier, her cell buzzed silently on her desk.

Gritting her teeth, she waited until it almost went to voicemail, then answered quietly. "Hi."

"Hey, you busy?" Jack asked.

"Why?"

"I wanted to see how you were doing. How are you?"

She frowned. He never usually called to check up on her. "Fine."

"Honey, you don't sound fine. What's up?"

"Nothing."

"I'm not buying it. My guess is you've seen the news, and you're mad."

"I haven't and I'm not."

"Really? You could've fooled me."

"I've got work to do."

"Hey, we both know the boss." She heard the smile in his voice. "He'll cut you some slack. Talk to me for five minutes."

Why wouldn't he take the hint?

"That's not a good idea. I'll talk to you later." She cut the call. It didn't take long for Jack to call back. This time she let him leave a message.

Pulling up the local news site on her computer, she searched 'the Jays.' The grainy photograph was instantly recognizable, and a huge knot formed in the pit of her stomach. Under the picture was a short caption:

The Jays—Jack Carrington & Julie Rolland ... both off the market?

This was what Jack had called about! She was about to text him when she noticed three missed calls. The clock showed nearly midday already, so maybe she could take an early lunch and phone him instead?

Yep, that would work.

Only once she was on the sidewalk outside her office building did she hit Jack's speed dial. He answered after one ring. "So you're not ignoring me."

"I'm so sorry, Jack," she said, strolling toward Mary's. "If you knew what kind of morning I've had, you'd understand why there was no way I was going to have a personal conversation at my desk."

"Why didn't you just tell me that?"

"I tried, with one-word answers, but—" She groaned. "Will you trust me when I say I couldn't?"

She heard his deep sigh. "Okay."

"I saw the photo."

"Are you cross or mad?"

"You can't even see our faces! Sure, it's two people kissing, but the truck could belong to anyone. I don't know how they could even print it!" She caught the raised eyebrows of a man heading toward her and realized she'd been speaking a little too loudly.

"I know and I'm sorry." Jack's soothing voice comforted her almost as much as his embrace would've. "I guess they're desperate for news."

She lowered her voice. "I think we need to lay low for a while."

"That's gonna be a little difficult, don't you think? We see each other every day." His cheeky voice held a smile.

Why wasn't he more upset?

"You know what I mean, Jack!"

"Yeah, I know. Listen, honey, I spoke to Steven."

"It didn't go well, did it? Is that why you kept calling earlier?"

"No, and you couldn't be more wrong. Steven's exact words were, 'It's about time, man!'"

"Oh. Okay."

"You don't sound pleased."

"Steven's my friend, so it makes sense he'd want me to be happy. Honestly, I'm more worried about Melanie's reaction."

"Hey, don't worry about Mel, or Alex, or anyone else for that matter. What matters most is what I think of you, and you're the most incredible woman I've ever met. Every day with you is as special as you are."

Stopping to lean against a wall, Julie closed her eyes and breathed deeply. She'd been a little in love with Jack ever since she'd first laid eyes on him, and she'd been falling harder ever since. Now it was full-blown love, and there was no escape.

Lately, everything he said hinted at a future. But what if she was wrong and he didn't feel the same way?

Sure, he wanted her body. Yet, if that's all he wanted, he'd have taken her to bed already.

"Julie?" Jack broke into her thoughts. "You okay?"

"Can I ask you something?"

"Anything."

"Do you love—?" Her heart skipped a beat as indecision flowed through her. "Sushi?"

"What? No. Why?"

"Um. I..." She chuckled nervously. "I can't imagine kissing a man who loves raw fish."

He laughed. "Lucky for you, I don't."

A subject change was in order before things got any weirder. "I need your autograph later. About twenty times over."

"Why?"

"Our latest fans, my coworkers, bombarded me with requests earlier. They also think you're hot and wanted to know if you're a good kisser."

"You're kidding!"

She stifled a giggle at his outrage. "No. I'm quite serious."

"What did you tell them?"

"That your kisses are the best in the world and that I've got dibs."

***

Jack waited for Julie just inside the entrance of the Peterson building, his hands shoved in his pockets. He wasn't exactly keeping a low profile, but he'd scanned the immediate area outside, checking no press were loitering. Of course, you could never be sure there wasn't someone wielding a long-range camera. But the Jays weren't famous. Yet.

He chuckled at the absurd thought.

Earlier, while he'd been working, he'd tried not to think about Julie's words. Now, about to confront her face to face, it was a different story.

Had she seriously told the whole accounting department about his kisses?

When he finally set eyes on her, his heart rate accelerated. She rode the escalator toward him, a stunning vision in a short, purple formfitting dress. The closer she came, the easier it was to see the excitement on her beautiful face. His heart sang—she couldn't wait to see him either.

She glided off the last moving step and immediately turned in the opposite direction, away from him and the exit.

Where was she going? To be fair, she wasn't expecting to see him until she reached his truck parked in its usual spot around the corner.

After striding toward the giant Christmas tree in the center of the lobby, Julie disappeared for a moment before coming back into view with a man Jack didn't recognize. The stranger kissed her and then wrapped her in his arms.

Who the *heck* was that? An ex-lover?

With his pulse racing, Jack rushed out of the revolving doors and jumped into his truck.

Julie hadn't mentioned meeting anyone today, and he'd met all her friends, right? Because they were his friends too. The man wasn't one of her foster family's sons either; they both had blond hair. This man had been dark-haired. So who was he?

An ache formed in his chest—Julie was keeping secrets. And while the urge to leave was strong, they had a standing arrangement. Maybe he could text saying he wasn't feeling well? He lifted his phone as the passenger door swung open, and Julie hopped in, smiling.

Too late.

"I'm sorry I kept you waiting. I had a surprise phone call just before I left my desk." She didn't sound guilty, more like cheerful.

"No problem," he said, starting the engine. Julie's belt clicked into place as he signaled to pull out into the traffic.

"Have I ever mentioned Lizzy?"

"No."

"I didn't think so. Well, Lizzy was my best friend in

eleventh grade. Then, for her senior year, her family moved to London and Hong Kong after. We tried keeping in touch regularly, but..." She trailed off.

Refusing to look at her, Jack kept his eyes firmly on the road.

"Anyway, Lizzy went to study in Australia and fell in love with William. They got married four years ago. I was invited to the wedding, but the timing was awful. I'd just started at Peterson's and couldn't take leave."

What did this have to do with anything? If her trip down memory lane had been about a man, he'd understand. Instead, a myriad of questions came to mind, but he kept quiet. He'd been foolish believing she'd be honest with him.

"The amazing thing is," she continued, seemingly unperturbed by his silence, "they moved here a few weeks ago. It took Lizzy a while to track me down, so when she called saying she was downstairs, I raced to meet her even though I knew you were waiting too. I didn't want to miss the opportunity to reconnect."

He looked at her then and found her peering at him with a questioning gaze. He ignored it.

"Seeing Lizzy after so long was surreal."

"I bet," he said through clenched teeth.

"And I finally got to meet William and their children."

The man was her friend's husband! Jack should've felt relieved, but Julie had never mentioned these people before, and they were obviously important to her.

What other secrets did she have?

She placed a hand over his, creating tiny sparks along his skin. "Jack?"

Choosing to concentrate on driving, he barely glanced her way. "Mmm?"

"Why don't you seem happy for me? You've basically said nothing. What's wrong?" At the genuine concern in her tone, he felt a smidgen of remorse for not being fair. She hadn't known her friend would be visiting, and from everything she'd said, she hadn't had time to share the news either.

He forced a smile. "I'm glad you saw your friend. I

just wish..." He tightened his grip on the wheel, and her hand fell away.

"Wish what?"

"Nothing."

What was he doing? Communication was vital in any relationship, and he was about to blow it. Making a hasty decision, he made a right turn and found a place to park.

"What's going on?" Julie asked.

"Hang on a second." Undoing his belt, he fired Kevin a quick text then pushed on his door handle. "We need to talk," he said over his shoulder.

"Haven't we been doing that, or rather I've been talking," she said sulkily before he hopped out the truck and rounded the hood to open the passenger-side door.

Releasing her belt, he held out his hand. "Grab your coat and come with me." He led her down the sidewalk until they came to a path hidden from the road. Ducking onto it, away from prying eyes, he pulled her into his arms and kissed her unreservedly.

They were both breathless when they broke apart.

Julie quirked a brow. "Not that I'm complaining, but I thought you wanted to talk.

"I did, I do, but I wanted to kiss you more."

"O-kay."

He ran his thumb along her lower lip and leaned down to pepper it with soft kisses. Moaning, she drew his head down for another deep kiss.

Jack was more than happy to oblige.

Eventually, though, he eased back from her delectable mouth before he completely lost it. Wrapping his hands around her waist, he held her close and looked her straight in the eye. "Honey, I'm sorry I wasn't more excited to hear your news. It's just...I'd decided to meet you inside today and—"

"Oh." She shook her head. "I didn't know."

"Well, imagine my surprise when you headed toward me and then suddenly disappeared from sight just to reappear in a stranger's arms. I let jealousy get the better of me." He scratched his chin. "Unreasonable, I know. It's just, I'm kinda hurt you never told me about Lizzy. Especially since she seems to be someone very special to you."

She opened her mouth, but he silenced her with a finger on her lips. "What else don't I know about you?"

"Nothing I can think of. I promise you, Jack, I'd never intentionally keep anything from you. You have to trust me if this relationship is going to work," she said softly.

"Will you forgive me for being an idiot?"

Smiling, she threw her arms around his neck. "Of course."

Closing his eyes, he breathed in her familiar floral scent. "Honey, I love—" His eyes flew open, and he floundered. She was staring at him so expectantly that heat crept up his neck. "Uh, that you don't hold grudges...that you forgive so easily."

"You're easy to forgive." She smiled seductively. "And I love...that you admit when you're wrong and that you're willing to communicate."

"Oh, honey." He pressed his lips to hers, her heated response sending sparks of desire throughout his body, igniting the flame he'd had to douse only yesterday. Deepening the kiss, he tasted her, savored her, and lost himself in her sweetness. Only a shiver, passing through her body, helped him rein in his hunger and enabled him to drag his lips away.

He laid his forehead against hers. "We'd better get to the studio," he murmured, giving her temple a quick kiss. "I told Kevin we'd be a little late. That meant five or so minutes, not fifteen."

She giggled. "I guess we'd better go then."

They headed back to the truck in the relative dark, with only the moon illuminating their path. Once they'd taken their seats inside, he cast her a sideways look. "I assume you're planning on seeing Lizzy and her husband again."

"Yep. Since we aren't performing on Saturday night, I invited them over for dinner."

Plugging in his seat belt, Jack shifted into reverse and slung his arm along the top of the seat. When he caught

Julie's joyful gaze, he dropped his arm onto her shoulders and gave her arm a squeeze. "Well, I've no doubt you'll enjoy catching up with them."

"You make it sound like you won't be there," she said, her tone teasing.

"I didn't know I would be."

She laughed, threading her fingers through his and snuggling closer. "Of course you're coming! How could I not introduce my hot boyfriend to my oldest friend?"

Chapter Eighteen

Adjusting his microphone stand, Jack's gaze roamed over the large crowd of country music lovers at College Street Music Hall. Excluding the balcony seats, the theater venue seated over two thousand.

A lot of people. A lot of pressure.

Bright lights made it difficult to identify any one particular face, yet their combined excitement created a buzz that energized him.

Tonight, the Jays were the headliners' supporting act —a far cry from the free performance at last night's karaoke bar. They also planned on performing another original song during their set, one which would be aired on the radio directly afterward.

"Good evening, New Haven!" Jack beamed at the audience. "It's great to be with you tonight."

A cheer went up, easing the slight tension in his shoulders. He turned to Julie, his eyes skimming the maroon satin dress Kevin had chosen for her. Short and sexy, it hugged her curves in all the right places. The whole outfit was sensational, overlaid with matching colored lace to just above the knees, and she wore it with black kitten heel boots.

"This is Julie Rolland," he said while Julie peered at him with sparkling eyes and smiled warmly.

"And he's Jack Carrington."

"Together, we're the Jays," they said in unison.

The ensuing response was so enthusiastic it took a

while for the noise to subside.

"We're going to start with a song we released a few weeks ago, 'Face Behind the Mask.'" His statement was followed by even louder cheers, as well as screaming.

Boy, these are some serious fans!

He shot Julie a rehearsed look. She nodded subtly, and he motioned for the band to begin playing.

One original song and three covers later, Jack wiped his brow with the back of his hand. The vibe felt right. He glanced at Julie for confirmation and found an excited, possibly half-nervous smile gracing her lips.

"Right folks, you've been incredible." Keeping his expression solemn, Jack tapped his mouth three times with his index finger. "Now, we could carry on with covers—"

Shouts of 'yes' and 'go on' came from all across the auditorium.

He grinned. "Or we could treat you guys to something new... something you'd be the first to hear," he said.

Huge shouts of encouragement echoed in the massive space, along with a few piercing whistles. Julie laughed with him, then took over.

"Obviously, Christmas is just around the corner, and I'm sure, like us—" she shared a tender look with him "—you'll want to celebrate the festive season with your family and loved ones. Many will be waiting for servicemen, or others like them, to return home. So, that's what this song's all about. We've called it 'Come Home to Me.'" She smiled slowly as if to let it sink in. "Tell us if you like it. Okay?"

Again the response was so overwhelming Jack almost missed his cue when the piano intro began. His throat felt uncomfortable during the first few bars until he witnessed the fan's grins, then the tightening eased, and he settled into the music.

For the final verse and chorus, Julie stood right in front of him, so close he could smell her lavender perfume and see the tiny concentration lines on her forehead. Itching to reach out and hold her, his heart thudded in his chest. He sang on autopilot, completely lost in her soft yet intense gaze.

When the last note finally faded, the thunderous applause went on for a full minute, or so it felt. The whole time he couldn't take his eyes off Julie.

Afterward, a chant began.

At first, he couldn't figure it out. Then he heard the word they repeated, and his stomach dropped.

"Kiss. Kiss."

Well, this is awkward.

Just before the show, Kevin had pulled him aside. "I've been thinking, Jack. Up to now, the Jays have been portrayed as a couple."

"Correct." Jack hadn't liked the feeling that a but was coming.

"But...it'd be better to keep the public guessing about your relationship. I reckon we'll get more mileage out of media speculation. Everyone will be wondering if you're an item or not."

"Why?"

"Well, romantics will love the idea of you two possibly being together; men will dream of a chance with Julie, and women will like the idea of dating a handsome music artist."

"So no kissing Julie in public?"

"Basically, yes."

"You *do* know I'm in love with her, don't you?" Jack had practically growled at Kevin. "That she considers us a couple? Because we are."

"What you do in your downtime is no one's business, Jack. While you're representing the label? Different story." Kevin's expression had become adamant. "Oh, and don't mention this conversation to Julie. The less she thinks she's being manipulated, the better."

So what now?

The crowd was still expecting a kiss, and Julie was waiting too, her expression open and inviting. The last thing he wanted to do was disappoint anyone.

More importantly, he didn't want to hurt Julie.

Her eyelids slipped closed as he leaned in, and by sheer willpower, he avoided her delectable mouth.

Instead, he brushed her cheek with his lips. The crowd went wild, and Julie's eyes filled with confusion.

A surge of anger rose in him, the exhilaration from moments ago disappearing quicker than a drop of water in the desert. He debated saying something to Julie. Realized he couldn't. And blamed Kevin.

Slowly, he faced the excited fans. "Sorry, folks. Our time's up. Thanks for being a fantastic audience. We look forward to playing again for you very soon." Blocking out their response, he spun back to Julie, his stomach clenching at the sight of her narrowed gaze and pursed lips.

She marched off the stage amid shouts of "Encore" and "Don't leave." Distressed, he followed her into the private corridor.

"Julie, wait!" he called, but she did the opposite; she hurried. Eventually, he caught up with her right before she reached her dressing room. She glared at him briefly over her shoulder, then promptly entered the room and slammed the door in his face.

***

Hunched over the makeup table, Julie dug her elbows into the hard surface. So what if Jack didn't want to kiss her in front of all their fans?

It was his choice.

Fighting to suppress the tears welling up in her eyes, she lifted her head and stared angrily at her reflection in the mirror. Why had she reacted like that?

She let out a juddering sigh. Jack was right—public figures or not, they didn't need to have their personal lives on display. Besides, she'd said they needed to lay low. He'd just been honoring her request.

The door handle gave a telltale squeak, and she turned immediately, but the door stayed closed, the handle hovering at half-mast.

Julie held her breath.

Would Jack risk entering?

Should she go to him?

They had originally planned to freshen up, then meet in their specially reserved seats for the main event, but now she just wanted to apologize. She half rose from her seat then, hearing Jack's heavy footsteps retreating, she realized her indecision had cost her.

Willing her racing heart to return to normal, she sunk to her seat and attacked her long, slightly curly locks with a brush. After adjusting the diamond clips, she patted on another smattering of face powder, then skimmed her lips with brownish-crimson lipstick to match her dress.

She checked her appearance—it would have to do.

The door swung open behind her, shutting just as quickly. With a smile of regret on her lips, she spun in her seat.

"Oh," she said, coming face to face with a complete stranger. Casually dressed in ripped jeans and a tight T-shirt, the attractive, dark-haired young man didn't appear to be staff. Yet he stood just inside the door with his hands behind him, staring at or, rather, ogling her.

A junior manager sent here to escort her to her seat?

"I thought...never mind." Julie shifted uncomfortably in her seat, her face heating from his silent perusal. "Did Mr. Taylor send you?"

He shook his head, looking confused.

"So why are you here? Who are you?"

"I'm..." He took a couple steps forward.

Jumping to her feet, she held out her hands in a defensive gesture. "Stay there, please."

His eyes returned to hers, but he ignored her plea, slowly closing the distance between them.

Julie's heart rate picked up, and she glanced at the door. No way could she get there. So instead, she retreated as far as she could from the advancing man, stopping when her back slammed into the sharp edge of her dressing table. She stifled a curse and grimaced.

"I had to meet you, Julie. You have the most amazing voice I've ever heard, and you're even more stunning up close." The intruder extended his left hand in greeting.

Somehow managing a tremulous smile, she shook his sweaty hand then tried to let go. Except he held on and threaded his fingers through hers.

"Hey!" she said, her erratic pulse beating in her throat. "Let go!" But he inched closer, his dilated eyes focused on her mouth.

"Just let me taste those luscious lips of yours."

"No!" She shoved her free hand against his solid chest, but he didn't budge. Instead, he grabbed her hand and raised it to his lips, and once he'd kissed her knuckles, it was a real struggle not to react to the unpleasant dampness that remained on her skin.

"Come on, Julie. One little peck. No one has to know."

She threw back her head, but he was stronger, more determined, and he pulled her roughly to him. No matter how hard she tried, she couldn't dodge his lips. Then, before she knew what was happening, the man was dragged away, and Jack's thunderous face appeared in her line of vision. "What the heck?!" he demanded.

"He was kissing me without permission!"

"Julie wanted me to kiss her. I was only obliging."

She cringed at the man's sugary voice.

"Yeah, right, and I'm the president." Jack's sarcastic tone was hard to miss.

Frozen, she watched as Jack pulled his cell from his back pocket while holding onto the man's arm. "I'm going to call security to escort you off the premises," he growled. "And, if you ever come within six feet of Miss Rolland again, I'll personally press harassment charges. Do you understand?"

Before Jack could speak to security, the hostage broke free and rushed out the door, proclaiming his innocence as he went.

She rushed into Jack's outstretched arms. "Oh, Jack, he was so strong! I couldn't stop him. If you hadn't come when you did..." A shudder ran through her, and Jack responded by tightening his arms around her.

"I'm so sorry, honey." He pressed a kiss to the side of her head. "I thought you needed space. I shouldn't have left you alone." He leaned back, their eyes connecting. His were full of concern and regret, not anger like she expected. "Good thing I decided we needed to talk, sooner rather than later," he said softly.

"It's me who needs to apologize, not you. I reacted badly. Immaturely. I should never have questioned your actions. I know you wouldn't do anything to hurt me intentionally."

"Darn right about that." This time his growl was huskier than the maddened snarl of earlier, and his smiling eyes, along with his gentle tone, wiped away her guilt. "Apology accepted."

She smiled up at him as his mouth hovered over hers. "You okay with me kissing you, Miss Rolland?" he whispered, his breath tickling her skin, sending tingles up her spine.

"Hurry up already, Mr. Carrington."

***

After the show, the Jays met with the headliners and their support staff in the VIP lounge to celebrate. Jack must've given off a don't-come-too-close vibe by sticking to Julie's side like a Siamese twin. But every time a man so much as looked at her, he automatically tensed up.

Who wouldn't? Having a crazy fan near the woman he cared about, kissing her, or potentially worse, wasn't something he'd ever considered about this life.

Would Kevin arrange security if he asked? It's not like Jack could be with Julie 24/7, though the thought was rather appealing.

Julie squeezed his hand. "I have a question." Jolted out of his thoughts, Jack transferred his full attention to the gorgeous woman at his side. "Not here," she said in a low tone.

They found a relatively quiet corner where she then asked, "Is everything alright?"

"Why?"

"You're acting strange. People come to talk to me but end up leaving quickly." Her eyes narrowed. "Are you glaring at them and scaring them away?"

"I may be sending 'get lost' signals," he admitted sheepishly.

"Jack!" She swatted his arm. "Why would you do that? I'm fine. I still want to go and rinse my mouth out with salt water, but other than that, I'm fine. You don't need to protect me from every man around. They're not *all* trying to kiss me."

"That's what you think," he muttered as a bunch of people nearby laughed loudly.

Her head dipped closer to his. "What?"

"It's my duty to keep you safe."

She looked incredulous. "Since when?"

"You're my girlfriend, aren't you?"

"Am I?" she asked, a flirty smile on her lips.

"I don't want men hitting on you, Julie."

Looking him in the eye with an intensity that should've made him quake in his leather boots, she huffed. "Don't you think I can take care of myself? Because believe it or not, I've actually been doing it for the past twenty-five years. Quite successfully, I might add."

He didn't miss a beat. "And what would've happened if I hadn't come in when I did?" Her lips twisted, and her forehead puckered. "Exactly," he said triumphantly. "I don't even want to think about what that man might've done to you."

"I'd have bitten his tongue. Hard."

"And then? You make him mad, and he slams his fist into you. You fall backward, cracking your skull open against the marble counter, and I never see you again?"

She crossed her arms. "You're being overly dramatic."

"Maybe, maybe not." He expelled a frustrated breath. "I don't want to take that chance, do you?"

After regarding him for a second, she shook her head.

His chest puffed up. *Finally, some agreement!*

"Though just to be clear," Julie said, her voice steely, "I don't need you or anyone else to be my protector or bodyguard."

She stalked away, leaving him with no doubt she meant every word.

Chapter Nineteen

After drying the breakfast dishes, Julie shook out the red and white plaid kitchen towel and hooked it under the countertop.

If only she could shake out her neck and shoulder muscles as easily.

Sighing deeply, she snagged her favorite coffee cup from the bamboo mug tree. Her thoughts ran to yesterday—Christmas. The day, spent with Jack and his family, had brought with it mixed emotions. Ones she still wasn't quite sure how to deal with after everything she'd learned.

Celebrating with them had revealed the lack in her own life and shown her the potential—from the exuberance of Charlotte's three children while opening their gifts, to sharing a delicious roast turkey with all the trimmings, to ending the evening stargazing in Jack's arms.

All memorable moments.

All extremely desirable.

All a reminder of what she'd desperately craved ever since her mom had died—a real family.

Pressing the long shot on her coffee maker, she stared at the liquid streaming into the stoneware mug and recalled yesterday's conversation with Jack's sister.

They'd been fixing a bunch of hot drinks in Jack's kitchen when Charlotte glanced her way. "I have to say, Julie, when Jack insisted you join us today, I wasn't sure it was the right thing to do."

What was she supposed to say to that?

Ignoring the tightening in her chest, Julie focused on waiting for the tea kettle to boil.

"We're a close-knit family, as I'm sure you've gathered."

Julie nodded, spinning the handles of an empty teacup first one way then the other.

"I didn't want my children confused about a near-stranger celebrating the holiday with us, especially when their father couldn't be here this year."

"I understand." She hadn't, really. Instead, she set the steaming cup down on the tray then caught Charlotte's surprisingly open and warm expression.

"The thing is Julie, the way Jack is around you, seeing you interact so beautifully with my children, with kindness and thoughtfulness, well, I've changed my mind. Jack was right to invite you; you're a big part of his life, and I'm glad he felt he could share you with us. I can see you make him very happy."

A lump formed in her throat, and all she managed was a small smile.

Charlotte then picked up the tray full of assorted refreshments, only to drop a bombshell a second later. "You should know two things about my brother: Jack's a man of his word, and his family will *always* come first," she said, her tone completely earnest.

Now, just thinking about those words made Julie's heart ache. Ultimately, although she'd been included in Jack's Christmas celebrations, she understood she wasn't his family, and family was the most important thing to him.

Her last foster family, The Andersons, were as close to a family as she'd ever had, but it wasn't the same. They'd already had four kids of their own when she joined them. One day, she wanted to come first in someone's life. She wanted to be that person's most treasured someone.

With Jack, that was never going to be the case.

Nestling her steaming coffee in her hands, Julie sank

onto the comfy sofa and dredged up a happy memory from last night—stargazing with Jack. An experienced observer, he'd shown her so much more in the beautiful night sky than she'd ever seen before. Wrapped in his strong arms, he'd kept her warm while pointing out each and every star or constellation he recognized without bringing out his telescope.

At one point, he'd swiveled to look directly at her, his look so intense, she'd thought he'd been about to say something significant. But he'd swallowed, shifted his attention to the patio decking, and said something like, "I'm so glad we could spend this day together. It wouldn't have been the same otherwise."

Afterward, feeling cheated by his fleeting kiss, the crucial moment had passed, and she'd been grateful for not blurting out the words on the tip of her tongue.

Now, she congratulated herself on her restraint. Confessing her feelings would've been a grave mistake.

She took a tentative sip of her coffee and let out a soft moan. *Perfect*. After another satisfying taste, she closed her eyes and re-lived Jack's goodnight.

Outside her front door, she'd stood close enough to witness the darkening of his pale green eyes, and her heart had raced. He'd dipped his head, his warm lips caressing hers, and the desire she felt—always just a hair's breadth away—whenever she was in his vicinity, was awakened. Their ardent kiss ended way too soon, with both of them breathing heavily.

Wrapping her arms around his waist, she'd peered up into his smoky gaze. Then when he'd opened his mouth to speak, she'd held her breath, guessing it was what she'd been waiting to hear. Except...he'd given his head a quick shake and remained quiet.

Once again, the moment had passed.

Now, raising her eyelids, Julie surveyed her small apartment. Her paradise. Not grand the way Jack's house was, but it was her space. A shiver ran through her, and she rubbed her arms. Great, the heat needed cranking again!

Oh, to be somewhere warm right now.

Hmm. Why couldn't she take a few vacation days and jet off to a sunny destination? She didn't have to be at the studio until early January and had no plans until New Year's Eve. Jack would surely spend the holidays with his niece and nephews, so this would be the perfect opportunity.

An hour later, she'd emailed her boss at Peterson's and booked a plane ticket and accommodation for the next four days—a beach corner studio overlooking the water and apparently only a minute's walk away. It sounded ideal.

Time was not her friend, though. Not when her plane was meant to leave for Miami in less than three hours!

While she packed furiously, she kept her phone nearby. Somewhere in between folding beachwear and finalizing toiletries, Jack texted: *Fancy joining us 4 ice skating & lunch? I can pick u up at 12.*

Julie: *I already have plans. Raincheck?*

Jack: *Sure, I'll miss u. Call u later?*

Her fingers hovered over the screen, wondering how to respond. If she told Jack she was taking a trip, he might try to dissuade her. Equally, she didn't want him worrying about her.

Catching sight of the time, she gulped. The cab was due in ten minutes! Scanning her bedroom for forgotten items, she spotted an unread novel lying on her bookshelf. No doubt she'd have plenty of time to read. She slipped the book, along with another, into her suitcase just as the doorbell chimed.

Post check-in and security at the airport, she bought a flat white and a chicken with mayo on seeded bread in one of the many stores. A cooked meal was off the table since her stomach was still feeling the effects of all the roast turkey and trimmings from the previous day.

Waiting to board, Julie watched a few music videos. It was only once she'd secured her seat belt and was peering out the small cabin window at the drizzle that it hit her—someone should know where she was going.

Her fingers flew over her phone screen. *Hey, Kevin, happy holidays. Flying to Miami. Back on New*

Year's Eve for party. Julie.

As she pressed Send, guilt assailed her. She could've been skating with Jack and his extended family about now. Battling on the ice was hard enough on her own, though. Imagine doing it in front of Charlotte and her kids. If Amy was anything like Melanie's daughter, Sophie, she'd be skating circles around Julie.

Maybe she'd dodged a bullet by not being available.

On the other hand, Jack's strong arms supporting her on the ice held plenty of appeal. How would she survive without him? Without his passionate kisses? Kisses that ignited such heat in her, she sometimes thought she'd spontaneously combust.

She may not be his family, but she ought to let him know her plans. It was the right thing to do.

Hey, Jack, she texted, *hope you're enjoying the ice. Decided I needed some sun, so flying to Miami. Will be back for Kevin's party. Have fun with your family xx*

Powering off her phone, she stuffed it into her purse and braced herself for take-off.

***

This was getting ridiculous!

Jack flung his phone across his bed and grabbed the back of his neck for a moment. He scrubbed his hands over his face. Where was she?

Yesterday, after skating and dinner, he'd called Julie, as promised. The call had gone straight to voicemail, so he'd left a message. Today he'd been calling and messaging all day.

Nothing.

Whatever plans she'd made for yesterday had possibly rolled over into today, but why not just text him? Why was her phone off?

Unless something had happened?

Jack's pulse quickened. That stalker from a couple of weeks back who'd kissed her—had he discovered her whereabouts and tried his luck again?

Pushing his fingers through his already disheveled hair, he retrieved his phone and tried Julie once more.

Still nothing.

He searched out his sister and found her folding clothes into a neat pile in the laundry room. "Charlie?"

"What's up?"

"I'm taking a drive to Julie's. I need to make sure everything's okay. That she's okay."

"Alright, but I'm sure she's fine." Charlie picked up a T-shirt and shook it out. "She probably put her phone on silent and forgot to switch it back. I've done it way too many times. Drives Mark mad." She glanced at him before pairing two pink socks. "Or maybe her battery ran out, and she couldn't find her charger. That's also happened to me before. Well, to be honest, it was Amy's fault." Charlie chuckled. "She decided to use it for her pretend store."

"Whatever." He scowled. Clearly, she wasn't taking his predicament seriously.

The door buzzer at Julie's apartment building went unanswered, yet her car was in its usual space.

Maybe she'd been picked up by Lizzy? Or...

The idea of anything sinister happening to Julie was unthinkable. He had to believe she was okay.

Hoping another resident would arrive and let him inside the building, Jack waited in his truck for half an hour, but to no avail. In the end, he went home feeling even more worried. If only he'd insisted on getting a neighbor's number!

By Thursday morning, Jack was tempted to call the police and report Julie missing. He didn't; instead, he explored other avenues. Wishing he had Lizzy's number was fruitless, so he contacted Zac, then Steven. When no joy came from either of those conversations, he phoned Kevin as a last resort.

"Jack, what a surprise! I trust you had a good Christmas?"

"I did. Listen, sorry to bother you, but Julie's been MIA for a few days. I wondered if you knew anything?"

"Sure, she sent a text, uh, on Tuesday morning, if I remember correctly. Said she was flying to Miami and would be back on New Year's Eve for the label's party."

"Oh." Relief flooded Jack briefly until worry and confusion stepped in. Why hadn't she let him know? It didn't make sense that she'd take a trip without a word. Why disappear when they had a few commitment-free days and could've spent quality time together?

Unless she hadn't enjoyed Christmas day?

No, from all appearances, she'd loved her time with his family and later, looking at the stars with him. Her goodnight kiss had certainly left him desperate for more. Every muscle in his body had gone weak from just her touch. It had taken every ounce of willpower to walk away from her place and not invite himself in for the night.

"Quite frankly, I'm shocked she didn't give you the details." Kevin's deep voice interrupted his wayward thoughts.

"Join the club." Hopefully the hurt he was feeling wasn't apparent in his gruff voice.

"Everything alright between you two? Did our recent conversation somehow interfere with your relationship? I had hoped it wouldn't."

"Honestly, I figured it would too, but either Julie hasn't noticed, or she's ignoring it. In private, things haven't changed. At least, I didn't think they had." Jack frowned. "Maybe I was wrong."

"Don't forget. I've organized transport for eight o'clock sharp on Sunday."

"Yeah, I'll be ready."

He'd been looking forward to the party. A memorable setting and occasion, he'd planned on telling Julie how he felt.

Now he wasn't sure it was the right time to offer his heart or declare his undying love.

Chapter Twenty

Emerging from a restless sleep at the crack of dawn, Jack reached for his phone. December 31.

Finally!

He released a heavy sigh.

The days since Christmas had been the longest of his life. Working with Charlie to distract her kids from their father's notable absence hadn't been awful; they'd had fun together. Yet he still missed Julie like crazy. Going from seeing her daily to going cold turkey? Not great.

It did make him acknowledge a fact—he loved Julie absolutely. And, clearly, he'd never experienced real romantic love before. Sure, he'd fancied himself in love with Melanie, then believed he was in love with Alex, but this was different. His mind constantly drifted to Julie, and his heart ached just thinking of her.

He squeezed his eyes shut. Did she miss him at all?

Just yesterday, Charlie had set her steely eyes on him. "I see your gloomy expression when you don't think anyone's looking, Jack. You'd better cheer up. My kids might be young, but they're sure gonna figure out something's up. Especially Amy. I'm amazed she hasn't already picked up on your fake enthusiasm."

After that, he'd tried to hide his feelings better.

With a groan, he jumped out of bed and grabbed his workout clothes. A ten-mile run would refresh his mind.

Sadly, his plan didn't quite work out. For the last mile, Julie's angelic voice pumping through his AirPods achieved the exact opposite of relaxing his tense muscles. All he wanted now was to hold her close and never let her go. Tired and sweaty, he returned home to indulge in a long soak in the bathtub.

Much later, feeling a little dehydrated, despite the gallon of liquid he'd downed after his run, he padded barefoot through his wing of the house to the kitchen.

Amy was perched at the island, lost in her drawing book, and on the dining table sat a stack of steaming buttermilk pancakes. He lifted one from the plate and took a large bite, his stomach rumbling as he peeked at the kitchen clock—five o'clock. Charlie must be tending to the boys.

Swallowing the last bite, he crossed to the island and peered over his niece's shoulder. The dark page contained various brightly-colored fireworks.

"Great use of color, Amy," he said, ruffling her hair. "I'm guessing you enjoyed the display?"

She grinned up at him, her eyes sparkling. "Yeah, you should've seen them, Uncle Jack, they were so big and loud and amazing! It was totally awesome!"

A few hours ago, Charlie and Melanie had taken all the kids to their own New Year's Eve celebrations—clearly the inspiration for Amy's picture.

"Sophie and I had so much fun," Amy continued, barely taking a breath between sentences. "We made noisemakers *and* masks, which we kept on when we danced. Did you know there was a real DJ?"

Amy's palpable excitement almost rubbed off on him until he remembered why he'd stayed home, alone. He hadn't wanted to go without Julie. Was she even back in New Haven yet? The party was in three hours, and he'd heard nothing. She was cutting it fine.

"Uncle Jack?"

Temporarily confused, he frowned at Amy. Then remembering her question, he nodded quickly. "Yes, your mom mentioned the DJ planned on playing all the latest hits so you kids could dance until you dropped."

"We didn't fall down!" She giggled. "That's just silly."

"Amy?" Charlie's voice came from the TV room.

"Would you like to watch a movie with the boys?"

Slamming her book shut, Amy hopped off her chair, her face somber. "I know you're missing Miss Julie; we do too. Maybe next year she can see the fireworks with us. I bet she'd love that."

Would Julie even be in his life this time next year?

Jack had no clue.

Even so, he gave his perceptive niece a half-smile. "I bet you're right."

"I am." After hugging him tightly, she dashed out the room, shouting, "I'm coming, Mommy."

Jack was about to take a sip of his coffee when Charlie appeared in the kitchen doorway. She pointed at his mug. "Mind if I join you for one of those?"

"Of course." He sorted her drink, then sat opposite her at the table.

"Thanks. The kids are finally quiet and camped out in front of a Disney movie they've seen a hundred times." Despite the tiredness in her eyes, she chuckled.

"Why am I not surprised?"

"I take it you survived on your own while we were gone?"

"Believe it or not, I can take care of myself."

"I know. I just wish you'd have come with us. It was an incredible experience, and the kids had such fun. Plus, the time would've gone faster for you, and the outing would've taken your mind off your problems."

"Julie's not a problem," he huffed.

"You know what I mean."

Avoiding her worried gaze, he spun his mug. A minor spill made him stop.

"You'll see her soon, Jack. Then you can find out what's going on." Charlie's gentle tone made him look at her. "She won't have a choice but to talk to you, in the car at least."

"Is that supposed to be comforting?"

"It's hard, I know. But wouldn't you rather find out now how she feels about you?"

An alert sounded on his cell. Julie.

What the?

Samantha J. Ball

"Is it Julie? What does it say?" Charlie peered at him anxiously.

He showed her the message. "She must've sent it Tuesday, but it only got delivered now because she switched her phone on again. Which means she's home."

"And she *did* try to tell you she was leaving."

Jack flipped his phone over so he couldn't see the screen. Anger seeped into his voice. "Doesn't explain why she left in the first place, though, does it?"

"Hey." Charlie tugged on his arm, forcing him to focus on her. "I'm sure she had her reasons. Maybe she wanted time to herself. Maybe she figured you'd want to spend time with us without her around."

"Why on earth would she think that?"

A guilty look flittered across her face.

"What did you say to her, Charlie?" he growled.

"I told her family would always come first for you. But I—"

"You what?" Standing abruptly, he began to pace.

"Thinking about it now, I realize she must've misunderstood me."

Blood boiling, he marched toward his sister and pointed his finger at her chest. "My girlfriend deserted me for the holidays. Because of you!"

"I'm so sorry, Jack," Charlie murmured, her eyes shimmering.

"It doesn't matter. What's done is done." He couldn't bring himself to apologize for his outburst.

Not yet.

Instead, he stalked out of the kitchen toward his bedroom. Head in his hands, he sank to his bed, his jaw clenching. Things were finally starting to make sense— why Julie needed convincing to stay and watch the stars on Christmas day and the reason for her impromptu trip to Miami the following day. She knew he'd try to change her mind about 'being in the way,' hence the late text just before she flew. Also, her phone had been off, supposedly giving him time and space with his family.

True, he *had* promised to look after Mark's family in

his absence, but, family or not, he wanted Julie with him. Always.

The sooner he cleared things up, the better. Julie had to know she was the most important person in his life. Heck, he wanted to spend every day with her and had every intention of putting a ring on her finger.

As soon as the timing was right.

Unless...

Unless she didn't feel the same way?

***

After one turbulent flight and a rather hair-raising cab ride home, Julie finally reached her apartment and switched on her phone. Missed call alerts and pinging messages bombarded her—all Jack's. 'Honey, call me please!' and 'Why aren't you answering your phone?' certainly painted a picture of how desperate he'd been.

She waited to see whether he'd responded to her text about her spontaneous trip.

Nothing.

She checked more thoroughly, her brow furrowing. From Tuesday onwards, only radio silence. So much for thinking she was doing the right thing. Still, she needed to hear Jack's voice. Set to click on his name, she backtracked, apprehension tightening her gut. If he'd wanted to talk, he would've texted or called.

The lack of contact spoke volumes.

Needing to get ready for the party, Julie put on her game face. She'd see him soon enough.

Butterflies danced heavily in her stomach as she smoothed body butter over her newly bronzed skin. Kevin would expect her and Jack to play the happy couple. But, considering the past few days, she doubted that would happen easily tonight. A few practice smiles in the full-length mirror couldn't convince her.

Fingers crossed, others could and would be fooled.

Sliding on her skin-tone tights, she again pondered Jack's recent withdrawn behavior in public. Their private time hadn't been affected at all, so something else was going on.

She just couldn't put a finger on it.

Pulling the navy sleeveless maxi dress over her head, Julie examined herself in the mirror. The cross-over bodice with the V neck fit snugly, and the leg split to her thigh was sure to get tongues wagging. Good thing she'd made this purchase some time ago; otherwise, she'd be wearing something Jack and everyone else had seen before.

Kevin's driver was due any moment, so with her makeup applied satisfactorily and her hair straightened and styled in a simple side parting, she slipped on her heels and went to grab her coat and phone.

The doorbell buzzed, and she ran to the intercom. "I'm coming down," she said breathlessly, reaching for the door handle. Another buzz stopped her. She pressed the button again. "Yes?"

"It's Jack. I'm coming up."

Heart racing, she let him into the building, then opened the door to await his arrival. It wasn't long before he appeared in a black tux, his face unshaven and his strawberry-blond hair wonderfully gel-free.

"Hey," she said around the lump in her throat.

"Wow." His intense blue eyes locked on to hers. "You look incredible."

Glancing down at her dress, her sweaty hands skimmed her hips. "Thanks, so do you." She smiled nervously as various emotions—none of which she could identify—crossed his face.

"You ready to go?" He asked, his tone neutral, his gaze slightly averted.

None of the questions, 'what were you thinking?' or 'why didn't you discuss your plans with me first?' came.

She didn't know whether to sigh in relief or be concerned.

"I-I am. Yes," she said instead, stepping across the threshold and inhaling his familiar woodsy scent. He smelled so good it was hard not to reach out and touch him. But his stiff demeanor ensured she kept her distance as she walked beside him the whole way to the waiting limousine.

Jack followed her into the luxury vehicle and left a

generous gap between them on the seat. Julie wrung her hands in her lap during the slightly awkward silence before the engine hummed to life.

Finally, his eyes met hers. "So, did you enjoy Miami?"

"Yes. Uh, no."

"Which is it?"

She blinked. "Honestly? I missed you."

"You never called."

"I'm sorry. I thought you understood." She fiddled with the clasp on her evening purse. "I wanted to give you time alone with your family, without me underfoot."

"Why would you think that?"

"Because your family means everything to you."

He appeared puzzled. "Julie, you're like family to me."

"I am?"

"Why else would I include you in our Christmas? I've never asked a girlfriend to join in the holidays before. I thought you knew that."

"Not even Alex?"

He shook his head. "It didn't feel right."

'I see."

Leaning forward slightly, his warm hand covered hers, his fingers sending tiny electric sparks along her skin as he caressed her knuckles. "I don't think you do."

He stared at her lips for a moment, then cupped her chin. She sucked in a breath.

"Not telling me about your trip? That hurt. When Kevin told me where you were, I was stunned, especially since I only got your text today."

"What?"

"Yep." His eyes never left her face. "And that's when everything clicked—you didn't want me to stop you."

"No, I didn't."

"Well, you were right. I would've begged you to stay."

Unable to take his intense scrutiny any longer, she pulled her hand away and peered at her lap. Her mind raced; her heart galloped. If she'd only talked to him before. Was it too late to repair the damage?

Next to her, Jack shifted away.

Peeking at his downcast expression, her heart

constricted. Tears threatened to fall, but she squeezed them back into place. This rift was her fault, and she needed to face the consequences. She touched his sleeve lightly. "Jack, I'm so sorry. I made a mistake. But Charlotte—"

"Leave my sister out of this!"

Startled by the anger in his voice, she flinched and drew back her hand.

"This misunderstanding might've been caused by Charlie, but you didn't even bother to confront me about it. You just made up your own mind." He blew out a long breath while mussing his hair with his hand. "If this relationship is ever going to work," he said, his tone softer, "we need to trust each other, have each other's backs. And honesty is paramount."

He was right...yet he hadn't mentioned love.

"I agree." She met his eyes briefly. "But it's not that simple."

***

After five whole days apart and with the scent of jasmine lingering in the air, Jack didn't want to question why it wasn't exactly *that simple*. Every time he looked at Julie in that sexy dress, he had to fight his physical desires. All he wanted was to drag her into his arms and kiss her senseless. It was fast becoming a losing battle.

Forcing a deep breath, he crossed his arms. "Oh, it's very simple, Julie. Either you want to be with me, or you don't."

The limo stopped abruptly, and seconds later, the door swung open to reveal the driver. "You ready, Mr. Carrington? Miss Rolland?"

Huffing in frustration, Jack nodded.

A flash, right in his eyes when they stepped onto the sidewalk, alerted him to the media's presence. Directly ahead of them, reporters and photographers were hanging around the building. Thankfully, excited fans were secured behind thick barrier ropes on either side of the path leading up to the entrance.

"Julie," someone called out. "You look terrific. How was your trip to sunny Miami?

Intending to ignore any unsolicited questions, Jack moved forward, but Julie remained rooted to her spot. When he glanced back at her, he saw her wide smile.

"It was great, thanks," she answered the man while waving at another fan.

"Why didn't Jack go to Miami? Was there trouble in paradise? Have you kissed and made up?" someone else asked.

Feeling the blood drain from his face, Jack knew he had to take control of the situation before things got out of hand.

"We don't—" Julie began.

"Have anything to say," he finished, reaching back to grab her hand and tug her forward.

He led her quickly up the short flight of stairs into the party venue, marveling that she didn't stumble in her high heels. Behind him, more questions were flung in their direction.

Once they were safely inside the building, Julie yanked her hand from his. "What's your problem, Jack?" she demanded. "Why didn't you want me to set them straight?"

"You wanted to tell them I wasn't invited? To let them know things are not rosy in paradise or that I haven't kissed you for five days, and your lips are driving me to distraction?"

Before Julie could answer, another couple arrived. Reacting fast, Jack steered her behind a pillar and into a quiet corridor. He checked they weren't about to be followed, then spun around to face her and found her closer than expected.

"I'm driving you to distraction, am I?"

Julie's velvety voice and sexy body, mere inches away, were the last straw. In one swift movement, Jack's arms circled her waist, and his mouth crashed down onto hers. Lips, warm and willing, met his, tasting just like strawberries.

This woman! Did she know what she did to him?

With a soft moan, Julie's fingers slid through his hair to the back of his neck. Her hand held him firmly in place as if she didn't want him to stop. Parting her lips with his tongue, Jack deepened the kiss. Then, coming to his senses a short while later, he slowed the intensity of the kiss and brushed his lips swiftly over hers a few times.

Struggling to get his breathing back to normal, he stared into her dazed eyes, eventually whispering, "Oh, honey, I missed you so much."

"I believe you." Her voice was just as quiet, and her seductive smile made him instantly want to kiss her again.

Her fingers traced his jawline, then settled on his cheek. "And I'd much rather stay right here in your arms. But... I don't think we should keep Kevin waiting, though. Do you?"

He pressed a kiss on the soft skin near her ear, then pulled back to see her face. "No, but this conversation isn't over either. I still have things I need to say to you, things you need to hear before we say goodnight or goodbye."

Chapter Twenty-One

Whoever Kevin employed for events like this sure knew how to throw a party. White chiffon drapes hung from ornate silver rails along the walls while occasional tables, scattered on the outer edge of the room, displayed revolving glitter balls. Tiny mirrors covered them, reflecting the disco lights.

Julie's gaze drifted upward to the banquet hall's vaulted ceiling. Too bad the twinkling star decorations did nothing to calm her wound-up-tighter-than-a-cotton-reel stomach. It would take more than a fake night sky to help it unravel.

Soft jazz music played through giant speakers while waiters offered flutes of champagne from silver trays to small groups of men and women in tailored tuxes and beautiful evening dresses.

No one heard Julie's stomach rumble, not even Jack, who stood beside her chatting with a stylish, gray-haired couple. Shifting her attention to what was easily a twenty-foot table on one end of the enormous room, Julie eyed the delectable selection of hors d'oeuvres.

Would Jack notice if she slipped away?

She peeked at his attractive profile. The brief smile he offered as he glanced her way was reason enough to stay put. If only he'd hold her hand, or put his arm around her waist, then she'd feel less like a spare part.

Ever since they'd entered the party venue and immediately spotted Kevin, Jack hadn't touched her. If not for the kiss in the lobby, she'd have thought he was no longer interested.

He *had* stuck to her side, though. And every so often, when a man leered at her, Jack effectively emitted a 'take a hike, buddy' aura that sent them in a different direction.

Fast.

Of all the faces around her, Julie settled on a familiar one—Kevin's. The perfect host, he'd been traveling from one group of guests to another. Now within shouting distance, he was talking to a pretty blonde. The woman laughed, and he grinned, his eyes locking onto Julie's. A determined look replaced his broad smile, and he touched the woman's arm briefly, then strolled over.

Julie stiffened, then felt Jack's hand brush her lower back and stay there. Why the sudden possessiveness?

Curious, she eyeballed him.

He shrugged, giving her a soft smile instead—one that melted her insides. The words he'd left her with, hours before, the ones she'd been trying so hard not to dwell on, 'things I need to say to you, things you need to hear before we say goodnight or goodbye,' were cryptic and distressing.

Saying goodbye wasn't an option, not unless, thinking she didn't want to be with him, he planned on dropping the label and ending his contract.

"How was Miami, Julie?" Kevin's pointed question startled her. He peered between her and Jack as if his words had a possible double meaning.

She went for the safest answer. "Hot?"

"I don't suppose you noticed your photograph being taken while you were out sunning yourself on South beach? Or in the SLS nightclub? Or strolling down Lincoln Road?"

"N-no," she said, a little nauseous at the thought of being watched totally unawares. "I didn't think anyone knew who I was, especially not there."

"I hate to break it to you, but you're a stunning woman with an equally stunning voice. Any music industry reporter with an ounce of commitment to their job is going to know about you. Never mind the groupies who want to be involved in every part of your life— they'll follow you, even as far as Miami."

"What?" She gulped, shock reverberating through her at the suggestion.

"That man who accosted you in your dressing room at College Street Music Hall? Remember him?" Kevin's voice was hard, his eyes steely.

"You've got to be kidding me!" Jack sounded livid. "I thought you'd organized security for her?"

"Security?" Julie glared at Jack, her shoulders tensing. "I can't believe you told him about that! I said I didn't need a bodyguard."

"Clearly, you did. You do." Kevin's tone had a note of finality about it, his serious expression unbending. "Jack had the good sense to request one. If I hadn't agreed, who knows what would've happened to you in Miami."

Maybe they were right. But she hated relying on anyone else and feeling defenseless. She'd been on her own for so long, she'd forgotten how to accept help. It still didn't make her feel any better about them going behind her back. Huffing, she crossed her arms over her chest. "Fine. I guess I should say thank you for caring."

"You're welcome." Kevin's voice softened a little. "I need to protect my investment, and Jack here?" He patted Jack's back. "Well, he just wants you safe."

Looking at Kevin, she forced a smile. "Good to know I'm valuable to someone."

The lights dimmed, and the music cranked up.

"Listen, the dancing's about to begin, and..." Kevin's gaze shifted over Julie's shoulder. "I'm being beckoned."

"Don't mind us." Jack waved him off.

After a curt nod, Kevin departed, leaving Julie alone with Jack. Then as couples began swaying to the beat around them, she discovered they were standing in the middle of the dance floor.

"Dance with me?" Raised brows accompanied Jack's question.

"You sure? Because dancing could involve physical

contact, and I'm not entirely sure why, but you've been avoiding that all evening, except for..." She didn't need to remind him about the passionate kiss. Her blush did that all on its own.

Firm hands landed on her hips, tugged her nearer. "Honey, just dance with me. You know you want to," he coaxed, the smile on his lips widening into the kind that killed all resistance. "I promise I'll explain everything later."

"Okay." Sighing, she linked her fingers behind his neck and rested her head on his chest. With his muscular arms cocooning her, her need to feel safe was satisfied.

For now.

***

Forty minutes later, a love song blasted through the speakers as Jack stalked onto the dance floor.

"Excuse me," he said, tapping the shoulder of the guy who was holding Julie a little too closely. How many men had she danced with after their one dance? A dozen?

"I need a word with Julie."

"Can't you wait, man? The song's nearly done."

"No, I can't."

Julie extracted herself, giving her dancing companion an apologetic look. "Thanks for dancing with me, Tony."

Not waiting to see if she followed, Jack marched toward the far side of the hall and out onto the glass-enclosed balcony.

Earlier, annoyed with yet another male fawning over his girlfriend, Jack had checked out the spot for viewing the midnight fireworks display. Now currently deserted, they had five, maybe ten minutes before their privacy was invaded.

As he admired the city lights, his nostrils filled with Julie's floral fragrance.

"Beautiful," she breathed from beside him.

He glanced at her profile. "Not as beautiful as you."

"You wanted to talk," she said, her tone no longer whimsical.

He faced her fully. "About Kevin. He didn't want me to tell you, so I didn't, but I'm no longer comfortable keeping anything from you."

Her scowl deepened. "What is it?"

"Our boss decided, for publicity purposes, that we should keep the public guessing about our relationship. His idea was—romantics would put us together anyway, and the unattached would think we were available." He chuckled humorlessly. "Win, win, right?"

"Hardly."

"I know, but I didn't know what else to tell him."

"Tell him we're not playing games. You said it: either I want to be with you or I don't. The same principle should apply wherever we are, in public or in private."

How was she so wise? And five years younger too. No wonder Kevin wanted to keep her in the dark. But did he really think she was that naive or stupid?

Julie was right; he needed to put his foot down and not allow anyone, even Kevin, to manipulate them.

"You're right. I'm sorry. From now on, Kevin talks to us both, or not at all. I love what we do together, but I don't want to compromise my morals or appear to be something I'm not, just for the label's benefit."

"Exactly." Her head bobbed up and down. "So no more withholding physical contact and pretending I'm not your girlfriend."

"No." He stepped closer and gathered her hands in his, his heart rate accelerating. "Besides, not being able to touch you has been driving me wild."

"Good." A bright, teasing smile lit up her face as she squeezed his fingers.

"So, honey, the question remains. Do you want to be with me or not?"

"Seriously? Of course I want to be with you!" she said adamantly, yet uncertainty entered her eyes, and his breath caught in his throat.

"It's just—"

Brushing his fingertips over her cheek, he cut her off. "Before you say anything else, know this—you're the most important person in my life. I can't imagine it without you, and when I'm not with you, I feel like a part of me is missing. All I can think about is you. I love you, Julie."

She peered out over the balcony and spoke quietly, a hint of sadness in her voice. "I've never been in love before, Jack. Never known what it's like to be truly loved either."

What was she trying to say?

Turning back to him, she wore a thoughtful look. "I think my mother loved me in her own way, but she didn't know how to communicate it, so I guess I missed out on what love looked and felt like."

She closed her eyes for a moment, then slid her palm up to his chest and covered his heart—the one still thundering in his chest.

"What I'm trying to say is—" Her intense gaze met his, and he swallowed hard. "It took me a while to figure out my feelings. In Miami, even one day alone was like being trapped on a desert island by myself. I hated it. The only reason I went to the beach, shopped, and went clubbing was in a vain attempt not to think about you."

"So it didn't work?"

"No, it didn't."

Not knowing what Julie would say next was absolute torture. His dry mouth was a testament to it.

Leaning in, she brushed her lips over his cheek. "Jack, you mean everything to me," she whispered.

"Does that mean...?"

"I love you, too."

Jack's heart soared, and he couldn't contain his goofy grin. "Honey, I'm officially the happiest man alive. I'd hoped you felt the same way, even thought you might, but then..." He didn't know how to finish the sentence.

"I know." She frowned slightly. "I left, and it made you doubt everything."

"Exactly."

Rumblings of conversation forced him back to the reason they were there in the first place.

"Look," he said, gently moving Julie so her back was to him, the riveting view in front of them.

Encircling her waist, he covered her hands with his and bent his head until his lips were near her ear. "I think the countdown is about to begin. You'll want to see this."

Ten, nine, eight...three, two, one!

Soaring vermillion, amber, and emerald flares burst into replicas of Amy's art as the night sky lit up in a kaleidoscope of colors. The fireworks' explosive sounds were nothing compared to the beautiful light trails blazing across the once-clear canvas.

At another sudden bang, Julie shuddered in his arms, and Jack tightened his grip automatically.

She turned her head and mouthed, "You okay?"

Nodding, he flashed her a smile. After scrutinizing him for another second, she smiled too, then her attention returned to the fantastic display.

During a short break in the demonstration, he nuzzled her neck. She giggled and shifted away, spinning around. Her rosy cheeks and sparkling eyes made her glow.

"I forgot to say Happy New Year," he said softly as he admired her lovely face.

"Oh, me too! Happy New Year. I gotta say, I'm excited to see what twenty eighteen brings."

"Well, I have a feeling it'll be an incredible year for us, and I can't wait to spend it with the woman I love."

"Who's this lucky woman?" she asked, her tone playful. "Me?"

"You," he replied, just before his lips descended to claim hers.

The fireworks resumed, drowning out everything else, and Jack decided it was the perfect time to concentrate all his efforts on thoroughly kissing the woman he loved —the one who loved him back.

Chapter Twenty-Two

Six weeks later

"Can you come over, right now? Something terrible's happened."

Julie replayed Jack's words in her head as she raced toward his house, thankful for the relatively deserted Sunday afternoon streets.

What *had* happened?

Was it one of the kids? Or Charlotte?

Grogginess clouded her mind. Maybe cranking up her car's heating hadn't been the wisest idea. She cracked open the window and breathed in the ice-cold air. She sighed; it didn't make her feel any better.

Everything had seemed perfect three days ago— Valentine's Day. The Jays' third song, "Love Me Every Day," had shot to number one on release. To celebrate, she and Jack had eaten at the best oyster bar in New Haven and ended up signing a few autographs—a small price to pay considering their success.

Ever since New Year's Eve, their relationship had grown stronger. Strong enough that Julie had begun visualizing their future together. The unexpected news of Mark coming home today, for good—two weeks earlier than planned—placed that perfect future within reach. Jack had even mentioned skipping town for the weekend, just the two of them since Charlotte wouldn't need him with Mark around.

So why did it feel like everything was set to fall apart?

Given the five centimeters of forecasted snow, dark clouds, now visible through the windscreen, had her wondering if an overnight bag would've been prudent. Except, after Jack's cryptic, urgent call, there'd been no time for packing.

The first flakes began falling as she rang his doorbell. She sighed longingly. Soon the bare trees and shrubs in the front yard would be coated in a white dusting, painting a beautiful winter wonderland outside. Behind her, the door swung open.

Turning, she gasped at the sight of Jack's deeply furrowed brow. "What happened?"

He raised his arms wordlessly, and Julie stepped willingly into them. "Thanks for coming," he whispered against her hair, holding her tight.

"What happened?" she repeated, leaning back slightly to see him. "What's so terrible?"

"Mark's dead."

"W-what? No, that can't be!" Julie couldn't have been more surprised if someone had physically punched her in the gut. The anguish in Jack's eyes told her it was true. "How?" she asked.

"A box truck hit him head-on while he was traveling from JFK. He died instantly." Jack spoke mechanically as if he didn't quite believe what he was saying.

"Oh, Jack, I'm *so* sorry," she said, hugging him again. "Charlotte must be inconsolable."

"She is."

"What about the kids? Do they know?"

He shook his head. "They didn't know he was coming home today, remember?"

"Of course."

Jack had warned her that he and Charlotte hadn't told the kids about Mark's early return because often his plans changed last minute. He'd given examples.

"One time, a burst water pipe caused a flood, so Mark showed up two days late. Another time, a part of the building Mark's team had just finished caught fire canceling his vacation entirely."

Cupping Jack's cheek with her right hand, Julie asked quietly, "How did you explain Charlotte's grief?"

"I haven't. When the call came in, they were watching a movie. It's almost finished." He pointed aimlessly toward the TV room. "Charlie's in bed. I told her I'd feed the kids and put them to sleep. I'll tell them she's not feeling very well and has a headache."

"I bet that's true."

He nodded.

"Okay, well, put me to work. I can make dinner."

"Honey, I didn't ask you here to work." He gave her a weak excuse for a smile. "I wanted your company."

She studied him. With his lackluster eyes and pale skin, he looked like a lost boy still in shock. "You say the sweetest things. But I'm happy to help."

"All right." He blinked. "Charlie prepared a pot roast earlier, so that's sorted. Can you get Amy ready for bed later and read her a princess story? I don't think I can look her in the eye and not have my heart break for her. Amy's bond with her dad..." He swallowed. "I think I can manage the boys."

"No problem. I'm here for you, whatever you need."

Over the next fourteen days, Julie almost regretted her promise. It was hard supporting Jack and Charlotte when she wasn't a family member, but she did her best.

On the day of Mark's funeral, she spent a minute chatting to her old school friend, Lizzy, who'd offered to help serve food. Around them, guests enjoyed the post-funeral refreshments—a welcome change after an hour of sitting on a wooden pew in the poorly heated church.

"Generous of you to cater." Lizzy held an empty tray in one hand. "Your canapés went down a treat."

"Thanks. My way of contributing." Julie's lame attempt at a smile fell flat, and she sighed deeply.

The hardest part of the day was over. Charlotte, who'd just begun to get a handle on her emotions, had sobbed uncontrollably in the church. The meltdown had necessitated her physical removal from the service by Jack, and a full ten minutes had passed before they'd returned.

Julie's gaze roamed the church hall. Woven hanging baskets filled with fresh lilies added natural beauty to the otherwise stark, white-washed walls and gray stone floor. A crowd of about eighty were scattered in groups, some chatting, others looking more somber. With no clue who most of the guests were, she assumed they were either Mark's family or coworkers.

"A lot of people showed up to pay their respects. Interesting for a man who wasn't around much the past three years."

Bristling at Lizzy's incredulous tone, Julie felt it necessary to enlighten her. "Considering Mark worked for a charity organization, it's not *that* surprising. He built homes for the poorest in Africa, so it wasn't like he deserted his family."

"Oh!" Lizzy's eyes widened. "I'm sorry, I didn't know. I thought he preferred being an absentee father."

Julie patted her arm. "It's okay. I also thought it was extremely selfish of him, you know, to work abroad. But when I learned of his actual mission, I had a change of heart. And besides, his job wasn't exactly general knowledge."

"Well, Mark Scott just went up in my regard." Lizzy gave a firm nod as if to emphasize her revised opinion.

"Lizzy!" William, Lizzy's frazzled-looking husband, called from across the room.

"Sorry, I'd better go rescue William," Lizzy said with a frown. "Our eldest can be a handful." Then, after exchanging a brief smile with Julie, hope lit her eyes. "See you soon?"

"When my routine returns, you'll be the first to know."

"Hey, Julie!" A deep, familiar voice redirected Julie's attention to the approaching couple—Zac, who wore a relaxed expression, and his girlfriend Alex, who didn't.

"Zac! It's good to see you." Julie stepped straight into his warm embrace while glancing over his shoulder at Alex. The woman wasn't scowling, so that was progress.

When Julie moved back from Zac, she offered Alex a small smile. "Thanks for coming," she said, "I know Jack appreciates your support."

"Of course." Alex's friendly tone and reciprocal smile were unexpected.

"I feel just awful for Charlotte," Zac said. "It's terrible losing a grandparent, never mind a husband, and so young? I can't imagine how that must feel." He fixed an adoring look on Alex and drew her to his side. She smiled just as sappily back at him.

"Jack's lucky to have you, Julie," Alex said kindly. "Not many women would put up with his situation the way it was, nor the way it's likely to be, going forward. I know I couldn't."

What exactly did *that* mean?

Yes, it was unusual for Jack to have his sister living with him when she was married with children, but considering the circumstances, it made sense. Besides, the fixed arrangement was about to come to an end—as far as Julie understood—since Mark had been on his way home to stay for good. Charlotte had even been excited about viewing houses online.

That wouldn't be happening now, though. Instead, Charlotte would be staying in the house until Mark's estate was settled. Maybe for up to a year.

Was that what Alex was referring to?

No matter. She loved Jack, and if she had to wait for Charlotte to move out before he could think about settling down, then so be it. She'd give him the space he needed. She wasn't going anywhere.

"Alex is right." Zac smiled sympathetically. "The circumstances certainly aren't easy."

A light touch on Julie's arm had her eyes swinging back to her boyfriend's ex. "Listen, if you ever need to talk...about...well you know, Jack or anything, let me know. Okay?"

Wow. Was Alex seriously offering to be her friend? To bond over Jack? The genuine concern in her voice and the display of camaraderie made Julie want to look for the hidden camera. She mentally shook away the ridiculous thought.

"Um, sure. Thanks, Alex."

"Let's catch up over coffee soon," Zac said, squeezing Julie's wrist.

"Any time, Zac."

The couple walked off, and Julie's gaze flittered over the faces in her immediate vicinity. Disappointment tightened her gut when she didn't see Jack. Never mind, he was dealing with more important things.

Someone just needed to remind her heart.

***

Stuck in the far corner of the church hall with Charlie by his side, Jack shoved his hands into his black pants pockets and silently blew out a long breath. He'd had enough unwanted attention today to last a lifetime. Sure, his brother-in-law was gone, but it was his sister who felt the loss more acutely. She'd lost the love of her life, the father of her children. Jack couldn't begin to imagine how he'd feel if he lost Julie.

Nope, not happening.

He slid a sideways glance at Charlie. Despite her puffy eyes and slumped shoulders, she still managed to crack an occasional smile. Once while Steven relayed a story about his son's bath time escapades, and again when Melanie cut in with an anecdote about their eight-year-old daughter, Sophie.

Jack watched as Julie strolled over to where Sophie was trying to rope Amy into a game. His niece was shaking her head, so Julie crouched down and wrapped her arm around the little girl's shoulder. She peered from one girl to the other. "What would you say to us girls taking a walk outside? Seeing what treasures we can find to show to your moms?"

"What sorts of treasures?" Amy's tone held a smidgen of interest, despite the grim set of her mouth.

Julie smiled encouragingly. "We won't know until we venture out."

"I'm in." Sophie took her best friend's hand. "*Please* come too, Amy."

"Okay."

Gathering a small hand in each of hers, Julie led the girls toward the side door. As she passed Jack, their eyes met.

"Thank you," he mouthed.

Instead of dropping the girls' hands and wrapping her arms around him—something he desperately wanted and needed—Julie squared her shoulders, nodded, and kept on walking with the children.

Jack tracked their progress to the side door that led to the church's garden. Once again, his girlfriend was helping selflessly. These past two weeks had been tough for his family, yet she'd been amazing through it all.

Tomorrow, the kids were returning to school, and he was expected back at Peterson's. For several nights, he'd tossed and turned, trying to figure out the foreseeable future. The thing was, he'd promised Mark he'd take care of Charlie, and he would.

A few years ago, his brother-in-law, rather than opening an architectural firm in New Haven, had chosen to help build homes in third-world countries. At the time, it meant Mark couldn't buy a family home, but at least he'd been fulfilling his dream of helping others—an incredibly noble cause.

Mark's admirable undertaking was the reason Jack had promised Mark he'd personally take care of his wife and kids. Many assumed Mark had been shirking his responsibilities while in Africa, but to Jack, the man had shown true compassion, caring for others less fortunate than himself. And Charlie, knowing it wouldn't be forever, had supported her husband completely.

After making an enormous difference to the future of the underprivileged, Mark had chosen to return home permanently. Sadly, that plan hadn't worked out the way everyone hoped. Now there was a great big, gaping hole in the Scott family.

Scrubbing his hand over his face, Jack decided he needed another coffee.

Preferably a strong one.

"Mind if I leave Charlie in your capable hands, Mel?" he asked, during a short break in the conversation.

"Of course. We're not leaving yet, not as long as Julie's entertaining the girls. She's been a star."

"Thanks. I'll let her know you admire her babysitting skills. She'd like to know she's appreciated."

"Oh, trust me, Jack," Charlie cut in, "we couldn't have gotten through this awful time without her. Your girlfriend's a keeper, so you'd better not do anything to lose her. You hear me?"

"I hear you," he said, waving off her warning as he headed toward the refreshments table. It was funny how people changed their attitudes about Julie once they got to know her caring and compassionate side.

Honestly, Kevin had also been great, agreeing to time off for the Jays so Jack could sort out the funeral arrangements. Nevertheless, time marched on, and their next song, "Because Of You," needed to be recorded soon. Only a month remained to its release date—April 4, just after Easter.

Break time was surely over.

A recent conversation with Julie came to mind. They'd reached the end of another evening where she'd helped him cook, feed, and bathe the kids. Hesitating at his front door, she'd scratched her head.

"What's up?" he'd asked.

"We need to talk about when you think we'll be able to hit the studio again. You know the label expects us to fulfill the terms and conditions of our contract, and as it stands, we're behind."

"This isn't the time," he'd responded gruffly. "I've got more important things to worry about, like Amy not eating and the boys constantly playing up."

"I understand." She'd pressed a kiss to his cheek, said goodnight, and walked out the door.

Now every time he put Charlie first, Jack battled guilty feelings. He couldn't remember the last time he'd been alone with Julie for more than a few minutes. And even now, he had no idea when he'd get to spend quality time with the woman he loved. Neglecting her wasn't fair to either of them.

"Hey, Jack." Kevin appeared in his line of vision, his hand outstretched. "You doing okay?"

"Yeah, thanks for coming." Forcing a polite smile, he

shook Kevin's hand. "I appreciate your understanding, given the circumstances. My sister's grateful too."

Kevin patted his back. "It's important to be there for a sibling when they've lost a loved one. But equally, at some stage, you have to return to your normal life."

Normal? Impossible. His life was never going to be the same again. Mark would never be returning.

"You must realize your period of grace is over."

Jack stiffened, his gaze shooting to his boss's stoic expression. "Sorry, what?"

"Well, with the funeral behind you, I assume you're returning to work tomorrow?"

"I am."

"As I expected. I guess I'll see you and Julie back in the studio then. Your next release is in a month. I'm sure you understand the time constraints?"

"Yep." The invisible band around his chest tightened. The thing was, though, he had no intention of stepping foot in that studio. Not until he knew for sure his sister could cope without him. And that wasn't going to happen any time soon.

They'd talked about hiring part-time help, but Charlie wouldn't entertain the idea. "Leaving my children in the care of a stranger isn't something I can even think about just yet," she'd told him when he'd addressed the issue.

Frankly, the last thing Jack wanted to do was push his sister into a situation she wasn't absolutely comfortable with. Not after everything she'd gone through.

That left him between a rock and a hard place. A situation he wasn't keen on acknowledging. Which didn't make it any less real.

Chapter Twenty-Three

Jack didn't make it to the morning studio session the day after the funeral. Somehow, instead of the event helping everyone come to terms with Mark's death, it had the opposite effect. No one managed to sleep very well. Consequently, Jack went into work late, drank copious cups of coffee, and eventually headed home around four o'clock.

Before he left work, he texted Julie to say he wouldn't see her in the studio. As much as he wanted to, he just didn't have the energy.

Later, after supervising the boys' bath time, Jack sat with them while they listened to an audiobook in their bedroom. With an important decision to make, it didn't take long for his mind to wander. Whatever he decided would affect his future as a recording artist and possibly his future with Julie. So, no pressure.

His promise to Mark had been for a defined period, agreed because Mark had planned on resuming his family responsibilities. Similarly, Jack had agreed to the Scotts living in his house because it made sense to have his temporary wards close by.

Was he now supposed to leave his sister to fend for herself? Was it expected that she'd return to work to provide for her children on her own?

Mark's life insurance was minimal, while Charlie's savings, by virtue of Jack buying out her half of the house when their parents died, was sizable but not nearly enough to live on for more than a couple years. And that was without buying her own home.

No, he'd have to continue being the father figure to Mark's kids and the male support Charlie needed. At least until she moved on with another life partner.

Assuming she was even able to entertain the idea.

Timewise, if he couldn't commit one hundred percent to the Jays, then stepping down from the recording contract was the only solution.

But how would that affect Julie? He couldn't even begin to imagine.

Right from the outset, Kevin had made it clear—he only wanted a duo act. Would he make an exception?

The fans loved Julie, so her as a solo artist was entirely feasible, and besides, she had more talent than anyone he'd ever known. Kevin would be crazy not to capitalize on the Jays' success and keep Julie on, albeit alone.

Seemed he'd made his decision.

An ache started in his chest and spread to every last part of him. With his family depending on him, he needed to maintain a semblance of control.

Inhaling deeply, he let out a juddering sigh.

"Uncle Jack?"

Peter's voice drew Jack's attention, and he noted the narrator had gone quiet. "Time for lights out," he told the boys.

Groaning, they gave him pleading looks. "Just one more story, please?"

"Sorry, Peter, you know eight o'clock bedtime's not negotiable."

"What's ne-go-shable mean?"

Jack ruffled four-year-old Daniel's short hair. "It means it cannot be changed."

"Okay."

The sadness in Daniel's expression tugged at Jack's heart. Giving in wasn't an option, but he sure found it hard.

Charlie always said, "The key to happy, well-adjusted children is routine. Change it, and you double your work as a parent."

Switching off the Bluetooth speaker, Jack hugged them goodnight and pressed a kiss to each young head. They were so precious, and he was incredibly grateful to Charlie and Mark for bringing them into the world. It was a privilege to mold them into the men they would be one day, and he was ready for the challenge. He'd made a promise, and he intended to keep it.

The following day, he approached the studio boss's office with hesitant steps and butterflies in his stomach. The door was open, so he knocked firmly on the hard wood, then poked his head inside. "Hey, Kevin. You got a minute?"

"Jack?" A flicker of annoyance crossed Kevin's face. "This is rather unexpected." Rising from behind his gray antique desk, he then skirted it to grip Jack's hand. "After leaving Julie in the lurch yesterday and not making your early session this morning, I thought you'd be giving the studio a complete miss today."

"Is now not a good time?" Jack cleared the gravel from his throat before adding, "I could come back later, I guess, but I do have a pressing matter to discuss."

Kevin motioned to the more comfortable-looking wingback chairs in the far corner of the spacious office. "All right. Let's sit."

Countless music awards decorated the wall above the furniture while bright light streamed in through the large picture window nearby. The cozy setting seemed like a good place to quit the band, though, once Julie found out, she'd be devastated.

Where would that leave them as a couple?

He didn't want to guess.

This decision he'd made would undoubtedly test their relationship to the limit, but hopefully, they'd survive; otherwise, he was making the biggest mistake of his life.

Pressing his palms to his pants, Jack nodded, then crossed the plush maroon carpet. He took a seat opposite Kevin, whose concerned blue-gray eyes stared at him intently. "What brings you here, Jack?"

Was the pounding in his chest audible? He hoped not.

"The day you offered me the recording contract was one of the best days of my life," he said, with as much confidence as he could muster. "And working with you and Carl, and of course Julie, has been an incredible experience—"

"I don't like the sound of where this is going," Kevin interrupted, his expression thunderous. "Tell me you're *not* here to give up on everything you've worked so hard for over the past eight months?"

Jack had expected no less of a strong reaction. However, he'd made up his mind.

He recalled his last conversation with Mark a couple of days before his death. "I'm so excited to be coming home," Mark had said, the phone line static-free for a change. "I'm eager to be in New Haven. To spend the rest of my life looking after my beautiful wife and our gorgeous kids. I'll finally get to be the hands-on husband Charlie deserves and the father my children need."

"Well, you should see the glow on Charlie's face, Mark. She can't wait to see you, knowing you'll be home to stay. Although, we haven't told the children the good news yet."

"A wise decision. I know Charlie would understand if something delayed the project finishing, but the kids, especially Amy, well, they'd be devastated if my return got pushed back."

'Exactly.'

"I'm so grateful for all your support, Jack. You've taken great care of my family, but would you mind keeping your promise a little longer? Until my family is safe in my arms? I'd really appreciate it."

"I promise. However long it takes for you to get home, I'll be here for them."

Now it was time for him to keep his word. He couldn't...no, wouldn't break it, just so he could selfishly live his own life.

"I'm sorry, Kevin," Jack said. "I really am, but my responsibilities changed with my brother-in-law's death, and I'm no longer in the position to honor our contract."

Kevin scowled. "Don't tell me you've suddenly become your sister's guardian? I understand it's tough for her, but is there nobody else who can help?"

"No, there isn't. Charlie needs me."

"What about Julie?" Frustration seeped through in Kevin's raised voice. "Doesn't she need you? I thought you loved her."

"I do!" he blurted.

"You realize if you quit, her contract becomes void, and it finishes her? Frankly, your decision is imprudent. Does Julie know what you're doing?"

Burying his anger as best he could, Jack kept his tone low. "I *have* given it a lot of thought, and no, I haven't told her yet. I needed to know whether there was any possibility of you taking her on as a solo artist first."

Kevin let out a shocked laugh. "You've got to be kidding! The terms of your signing were crystal clear. A duo act or nothing. I'm not suddenly going to change my mind just because you've decided your sister needs mollycoddling."

Jack opened his mouth to argue, but Kevin's glower was enough to shut him up.

"If you're determined to ruin your life, never mind Julie's, over some sense of duty to a sibling, then I'll release you *and* Julie from your contracts." Kevin stood abruptly. "But just so you know, I'm not happy, Jack. I think you're being extremely short-sighted."

While Jack attempted to process everything, Kevin stalked back to his desk and dropped into his chair. "This meeting is over," he said, slamming his hands on the wooden surface.

Pain, which had begun when Kevin first showed his anger, grew in Jack's chest. How could his boss possibly understand without knowing the whole story? But he wasn't about to enlighten him. Even though Mark had died, in Jack's mind, the promise still stood. And he wasn't about to break his word or tell anyone the reasons for standing by his word. Whatever happened with Julie, well, he'd just have to deal with the consequences.

***

Julie strolled through the studio's main entrance, humming a melody that had been circling in her head all morning. Spending the afternoon recording music rather than punching numbers at Peterson's was a no-brainer as far as she was concerned.

"Julie? I thought I heard your sweet voice."

Peering over her shoulder, she spotted Kevin coming out of his office. Something about his furrowed brow and clenched jaw didn't exactly gel with his kind words. Yet, even as knots formed in her stomach, she plastered on a smile. "Hey, Kevin. I've got this new song in my head, so I figured I'd get it down before Carl and I do some work on the track later."

Kevin's jaw twitched suspiciously, and Julie's smile slipped. "Is that a problem? I can come back later."

"Have you spoken to Jack today?"

"No. I thought I'd give him space to catch up on some much-needed rest. Besides, a few extra days on my own won't be the end of the world. Jack's a fast learner. He can catch up."

She thought back to yesterday morning and the text she'd woken up to—the one from Jack: ***Sorry, honey, skipping a.m. session. No one slept last night. Funeral made Mark's death real 4 kids & so final 4 Charlie.***

At the funeral, Kevin had given Julie the impression the Jays' schedule would be back on track by now, and Jack had implied as much after his fleeting kiss goodbye, accompanied by his, "See you tomorrow."

Alone in the studio, Julie had worried.

Eventually, she'd asked Carl, "Is it okay that Jack's not here? Kevin's awfully anxious to get this track ready."

"Don't worry about him," Carl had replied. "He's always controlling like that. Not too happy about anything rocking the boat. Trust me, I've been doing this for a very long time, and you and Jack work together like fire and dry wood—quickly and efficiently. You're hot together."

By the time Julie had left for the office, they'd only managed to get down the first verse. It *had* taken longer without Jack making the process smoother. Even when he wasn't singing with her, his presence usually grounded her and helped her focus. Strangely, the fact he wasn't physically there, well, *that* had been the distraction.

The crater in the pit of her stomach deepened when his second text came in around four o'clock: ***Hey, I'm exhausted. Going straight home. Sorry, don't think I'll make studio time tomorrow either. Talk soon.***

Trying not to be upset, Julie had sent a casual reply: ***Shall I bring mac 'n' cheese & meatloaf by after work?***

Jack: ***We're ordering in. Raincheck?***

When *would* she see him again? Julie had no clue.

"That won't be necessary, Julie."

Kevin's comment pulled her back to the present, to the studio's corridor and her boss's stoic expression. How long had she been woolgathering? She couldn't even remember what they'd been talking about.

She frowned as a few people wandered past. "I don't understand."

Kevin glanced over her shoulder then looked back at her, his gaze troubled. "Do you mind coming into my office for a few minutes?"

"Uh, sure."

Suddenly, she wasn't feeling sure at all, and the coffee she'd downed on her journey from the office threatened to re-surface.

What was going on?

A short while later, Julie sat across from Kevin in his enormous office, her fingers linked tightly in her lap. He gave her a small smile, one that most definitely did not reach his eyes. "Jack visited me earlier," he said.

"He did? Why?"

"There's no easy way to say this, so I'll just cut to the chase. He wanted out."

"Of the band? From his contract?"

Kevin nodded a few times.

Struggling to breathe, Julie put her face in her hands and swallowed hard.

"I tried to tell him he was letting you as well as the label down, but he was adamant," Kevin said gently.

Julie looked up. "But—" She shook her head. "I-I can't believe it. That means the Jays can't continue since our contract is no longer valid."

"I'm so sorry, Julie." The genuine remorse in Kevin's voice should've brought her a measure of consolation; instead, anger boiled up inside. Just like that, her dream was over because Jack had gone against his word and decided to quit! Without even discussing it!

"What time did he drop this bombshell?" she asked while her purse buzzed beside her. She ignored it.

"Less than an hour ago."

So, with enough time to talk to her first.

Her phone buzzed again. Wow, someone wasn't letting up!

Jack?

Snatching her phone from her purse, she saw the notifications—all from him. Four missed calls and one text: ***Honey, please call. We need 2 talk.***

Pity... It was a bit late for that.

Chapter Twenty-Four

Jack burst into the Administration office, his eyes honing in on Julie's unoccupied desk. Heart pounding in his chest, he scanned the crowded room. Where was she? The ladies' room? Or in an unplanned meeting?

Brianna strode toward him, and he steeled himself. "Mr. Carrington, how lovely to see you," she said, her voice unnaturally sweet and a knowing smile on her face.

"Hello, Brianna."

She rested a cold hand on his arm and fluttered her false eyelashes at him. "I'm guessing you're here to see Julie."

"I am."

He took a half-step back, forcing her hand to drop. Unperturbed, her smile widened.

"She's not here," she said. "Is there anything *I* can help you with?"

Jack narrowed his eyes at the woman's persistence, then made full use of his I'm-your-superior tone. "Do you happen to know where she might be?"

"Uh, she left early, Mr. Carrington." Brianna gave him a sly look. "I'm surprised she didn't let you know."

Wow, the horrid woman just loved to stir up trouble! No wonder Julie wasn't a fan.

"When *did* she leave?" he asked.

"I believe just over thirty minutes ago."

"Did she say where she was going?" He tried not to

show his impatience or sound too exasperated, but the exchange sure felt like searching for a green toy dinosaur in super long grass—fruitless.

Puffing out her chest, Brianna shook her head. "Whoever she was going to meet sure had her smiling. She left the office humming."

"Thanks for the help," he muttered sarcastically.

Confident Brianna was messing with him and trying to make him jealous, he turned on his heel and stormed out the office. As he headed to the elevator, he pulled out his cell and called Julie. It went straight to voicemail.

"Fantastic," he grunted.

Hopping into his truck, he slammed the door and started the engine. Eventually, she'd have to return home. Right? She might even be there already.

Barely obeying the speed limit, he raced to her place, trying her cell as he went. He desperately needed to assure her that although the band was over, it didn't mean they had to be.

No luck.

After pulling up to Julie's apartment block, it took three failed buzzer attempts before another resident kindly let him into the building. He didn't bother with the elevator. Instead, he leaped up the four flights of stairs and repeatedly banged on her front door.

Unsurprisingly, he got no response.

The dread in the pit of his stomach grew. If Kevin had gotten to Julie first, who knew how she might have reacted? He shot her a text: **Honey, please call. We need 2 talk.**

Slumping to the floor, he wrapped his arms around his legs and leaned his chin on his knees.

The elevator finally pinged, hours later, or so it felt, and Julie stepped into view. She was staring at her phone, her long hair hiding her face.

Jack jumped to his feet. "Julie!"

Her head shot up, and she immediately slowed her pace. Stormy eyes matched her angry expression. "How could you, Jack?"

His heart plummeted; Kevin *had* gotten to her first. Not a cursing man, he muttered an expletive.

"If you let me explain—" was all he managed to say before she cut him off.

"Why bother? What you've done can't be undone."

"Please?"

Skirting past him with lightning speed, she unlocked her door. Then turning halfway around, she glared at him for a long second. "Just tell me one thing. Did you mean anything you ever said?"

Her question pressed on his heart like an elephant stamping on a flower. How could she doubt his words or the way he felt about her?

"I love you, Julie."

"Really?"

The disappointment all over her gorgeous face tore at his insides.

She gave a humorless laugh. "Well, you have a funny way of showing it."

When he took a step forward to stand right in front of her—so close he was tempted to reach out and tuck a stray hair behind her ear—she flinched. "I *need* you to understand why I did what I did," he pleaded.

"Why? So you can justify your actions?" Crossing her arms, she shook her head. "No, Jack, I understand plenty. It's just taken me longer than it should have. Alex was slower, mind you."

His voice rose a notch. "What's Alex got to do with this?"

"She happened to see things as they really were. But me? I've only just got it."

"Honey, what are you talking about?"

She shoved her index finger in his chest. "Don't *honey* me. You said I was the most important person in your life. You lied. If it were true, we wouldn't be having this conversation, and you wouldn't have quit the band without so much as a word or even a hint!"

Before he could respond or think of moving, she stalked into her apartment.

Expecting the inevitable door slam, she surprised him

by appearing at the threshold a moment later. Fierce determination shone in her eyes as she blinked away tears.

"Go back to your family, Jack," Julie said in a raspy voice. "Charlotte and her three adorable children need you." She squared her shoulders. "I don't."

Those were her last words before she slipped back into her apartment. And this time?

This time, she slammed the door.

***

Jack turned the key in the front door and paused. How had he made it home? He barely remembered leaving Julie's place, let alone driving home or dragging himself up the steps. It was a miracle he hadn't been involved in a traffic accident; the thought sent a shiver down his spine.

What he could recall, though, was the devastated look on Julie's face when she'd called him a liar. She hadn't broken up with him, so maybe, hopefully, she just needed time to process everything. Sighing deeply, he pushed the door open and entered the house.

"Jack, is that you?" Charlie called.

"Yes." He had no energy to answer in his usual sarcastic manner.

Dropping his keys in the bowl, he discarded his coat and shoes and padded through to the kitchen. Charlie was chopping vegetables—yams—if his sense of smell was working correctly.

She made eye contact, and her perpetual frown deepened. "What on earth happened? You look like you lost something valuable and precious."

Perching on the edge of a barstool, he leaned his forearms on the granite island and brushed his hands over his head. "I may have."

Setting her knife down, Charlie rounded the island to give him an awkward hug. Then as she straightened, she scrutinized him. "Talk to me."

"The Jays are over."

"What! Why?"

"I told Kevin I'm out, now Julie's mad at me."

Jack cast his eyes over to the window above the kitchen sink. Tall trees swayed gently at the back of the garden. The bright sunshine gave the illusion of warm temperatures though it was barely above freezing. He brought his eyes back to his sister's sympathetic gaze. "I'm not entirely sure I have a girlfriend anymore."

"Oh, Jack!" Charlie cradled his cheek. "I don't understand why you broke up the band, but I'm sure you had a very good reason. Julie loves you, so I can't imagine she'd be anything but supportive once she's had a chance to think things over."

Buzzing from his pocket had him hauling out his cell to read Julie's brief message, but whatever hope he'd had before evaporated instantly. He forced back tears while gripping the phone to his chest and then hung his head.

Charlie prized his phone away and gasped. "This is all my fault! I'm so sorry."

"How could you think that?"

"If I didn't depend on you so much, you wouldn't have given up what you were born to do. It's something you love and has made you incredibly happy. I can't think of any other explanation for you quitting the band. Am I right?"

About to deny it, Jack realized the promise he'd made to Mark needed to stay between them. Charlie didn't need to know his motivation for screwing up his professional and love life all in one.

He gave a reluctant nod, wishing he could explain.

Charlie pinned him with a piercing look. "Go back to Kevin," she said, her tone resolute. "Beg him to take you back. You and Julie. You two belong together, on that stage and in life."

The band around Jack's chest grew tighter. "It's not that simple, Charlie."

***

Julie crumpled to the floor, her back against the door. The tears she'd kept at bay since stepping off the elevator and finding Jack outside her apartment, finally flowed.

How dare he show his face after crushing her dream? He'd not only broken his word, he'd broken her trust too!

The relationship and protective role he shared with his sister was a step too far. While she'd been willing to overlook the unusual situation because she thought he loved her and considered her family, it was clear now from his actions that he would never put her first.

How could I have been so wrong?!

Uncontrollable sobs shook her body. She'd lost so much falling for Jack and being blinded by love.

So stupid!

When she could breathe again without it physically hurting her chest, she wiped her eyes with her coat sleeves and pushed to her feet.

In the kitchen, she dug out her favorite ice cream—Chunky Monkey—and scooped a large spoonful into her mouth. The frozen dessert numbed her tongue, but she didn't care. If only it could numb her feelings.

Eventually, reality trickled into her consciousness—no more recording contract or boyfriend. Jack probably assumed she needed time to cool off before she allowed him to explain why he'd ruined her life.

She huffed. He should be so lucky.

Setting aside the empty carton, she punched out a text: ***Just to be 100% clear. We. Are. Over.***

Grinning crazily, she pressed Send with a flourish, then burst into tears again. Except for Lizzy, she'd lost all her friends in an instant. There would be no more Thanksgiving dinners at the Danvers, no more pre-Christmas dinner parties at the MacAlistars, no more singing at the karaoke bar.

No more Jack.

Her heart ached from the cruelty of falling in love for the first time, thinking she'd found her soulmate, then having her heart so spectacularly broken. She should've known it was too good to be true.

After her past, she didn't deserve to be happy.

For the rest of the workweek, Julie called in sick. Facing the likes of Brianna when the news came out that the Jays were over was something she had no strength for, never mind the risk of bumping into Jack or Steven.

On Friday, hoping for a new start away from everything that reminded her of Jack, Julie prepared a resignation letter and updated her résumé. She spent a couple hours on her computer, made a handful of phone calls, and secured a few interviews for mid-March. Thankfully, all the firms were in Devon, far enough away from New Haven to not run into anyone she knew, yet close enough for Lizzy to visit.

The whole weekend, she stayed glued to the TV for any entertainment news while also endlessly reviewing the Jays' social media accounts. Amazingly, nothing about the duo disbanding emerged.

Then it hit her—Kevin was milking their three hit singles as much as possible before letting the public know. Or perhaps he was waiting for the original release date of "Because Of You" in April.

It would make sense for the label if she was right, but until she knew for sure, her stomach remained knotted.

When there was still no statement in the music industry news by late Sunday night, Julie breathed a sigh of relief. Tomorrow morning she'd return to work, the letter to Mr. Peterson in her purse. At the first sign of trouble, she'd seal the envelope and leave her notice of resignation with David's secretary.

Chapter Twenty-Five

Charlie stared at the device ringing in her hand. "I have to take this," she said and disappeared back inside the house, leaving Jack alone on the porch.

He fiddled with his jacket sleeves as an icy wind whipped around him. The middle of March *was* technically spring, but somehow winter lingered like an unwelcome guest. Presumably, tomorrow's predicted snow was already on its way.

How long would Charlie be? Should he start the truck and give the heating a chance to kick in?

The decision became moot when the front door clicked shut behind him, and he turned around.

Charlie stood biting her lower lip. "That was Mark's attorney, Mr. Ryan. He wanted to meet at two o'clock," she said slowly. "That would allow us an hour with him before we need to collect the children, and we can still fit in some chores beforehand. Does that work for you?"

"Of course."

With Kevin out of the picture, Jack had no other plans. David—currently his only employer—had taken one look at his face this morning and insisted on a private word in his office.

After catching a glimpse of himself in the massive mirror behind David's desk, Jack had sucked in a breath. Quickly averting his gaze from his unshaven state and the devastation in his eyes, he'd sunk into an armchair and focused on David's concerned face.

"I understand that with your brother-in-law's death, you've been dealing with a lot lately." David's kind tone settled on him like a warm blanket. "But I'm worried about you, Jack. Is there anything else going on?"

Aware he owed his boss an explanation, Jack recounted the other recent events in his personal life.

"I appreciate you trusting me with this. But can I give you some advice? You need time to recover from these major life changes. These things don't just magically come right. Healing from a broken heart? Well, I can't imagine the pain you must be in." David paused, his expression earnest. "I reckon you should take some time off work."

Jack started to shake his head, but David raised his hand to stop him. "Your mental health is paramount, so take however long you need. At the very least, the rest of the week."

So Jack had.

Now, coming back to the task at hand, he noted the first chore on Charlie's list involved driving to Julie's favorite grocery store.

His heart ached.

For months, he and Julie had seen each other every day. Who was looking after her now? Making sure she ate? Keeping *her* company?

A week had passed since she'd ended things, and already Jack missed her terribly. Missed the way he felt when she put her hand on his knee or when she simply smiled at him as though he meant the world to her. Missed the way she fit perfectly in his arms, and he particularly missed their spine-tingling kisses.

Charlie sighed. "I hope the sun stays out," she said, sounding anything but hopeful as he pulled into a spot near the store's entrance and switched off the engine. "It makes everything seem better."

The sadness in her voice instantly reminded him of where he was and what he was meant to be doing, and why he'd given up the love of his life—to support and comfort his sister.

He made a vow, then and there, not to wallow in his

own self-pity. Sure, he missed Julie with all his heart, but at least she was still alive. Mark was dead. He couldn't compare his situation with Charlie's.

"I'm sure it will," he said, giving her a one-armed hug.

Once the errands were completed, Jack navigated the Monday lunchtime traffic to their attorney's office. Caught at a stoplight en route, he glanced at Charlie staring vacantly through the truck's windshield, her hands twisting in her lap. He covered them with his own and squeezed tight. "Any idea what this meeting's about?"

She responded with a quick shake of her head.

"Why do I need to be there? Not that I mind going with you, obviously. I'm just confused, is all."

"You have something to do with Mark's will." She shrugged. "That's all I know."

"Okay. I guess we'll find out soon enough." The light went green, and he eased forward.

The next time he looked at Charlie, worry crumpled her forehead. "Hey, don't worry about it," he said. "This is probably just routine. All Mark's assets go to you. End of story."

Her eyebrows shot up. "What assets? Because, other than Mark's meager salary—which just about covered our living expenses and clothing—I already have access to his small amount of savings. That's about it, given my inheritance went into an account in my name. And save for the occasional emergency, it hasn't been touched since."

She let out a strangled sound, a half laugh, half cry. "Mark's life insurance isn't exactly a windfall, but it'll pay out enough to keep me going for a bit." Tears slipped from her eyes, and she wiped them away and sniffed. "Ultimately, I'm going to need to find a job."

Jack handed her a tissue from the glovebox.

"I'm sorry," she said, blowing her nose. "I just can't imagine why I need to do this."

"Five minutes, and you'll be closer to your answer."

At the prestigious law firm, Mr. Ryan's secretary escorted them into a large corner office and motioned for them to take a seat. "Mr. Ryan will be with you shortly."

The woman offered a sympathetic smile, then left.

They'd hardly gotten situated on the plush petrol-blue two-seater sofa when a tall, slim, gray-haired man in an expensive-looking black suit strolled into the room. He approached with his hand extended and a welcoming expression. "Mrs. Scott, Mr. Carrington, I'm very sorry for your loss."

Jack and Charlie rose to their feet and shook Mr. Ryan's hand. His strong, no-nonsense grip and relaxed manner eased the tension in Jack's shoulders.

"Thank you," Charlie said, a slight break in her voice.

Jack wrapped an arm around her waist and gave her a reassuring smile as the attorney walked over to his beautifully carved, wooden desk and picked up two envelopes.

He handed them one each. "To read in private—per Mark's instructions."

The envelope Jack held had his name scrawled across it in Mark's distinctively messy handwriting. His heart rate accelerated. *Why on earth?*

Unless Mark wanted to ensure their promise still stood?

Jack peeped at Charlie, staring at her envelope, her lips pressed together in a thin line. Reaching over, he touched her arm lightly, hoping it wouldn't tip her over the edge. She didn't look at him.

"Mrs. Scott?" Mr. Ryan said, gaining her attention. "Were you aware that your late husband came from an extremely wealthy family?"

"N-no." She cleared her throat, raising her voice so it came out stronger. "Mark hardly ever spoke of his family or his past. What I do know is that while he was growing up, his parents struggled financially."

"I'm not sure why he never told you, but his grandparents set up a trust fund worth millions, which he was to inherit when he turned thirty."

"What?" The color drained from Charlie's face, while Jack's chest felt like it'd been knocked with a hammer.

"Mrs. Scott, with Mark's passing, the trust fund automatically releases to his next of kin. According to his will, you're now a multi-millionaire."

***

Jack scrubbed a hand over his prickly jaw as the coffeemaker spluttered on the kitchen counter.

He still couldn't believe it—Mark, a trust fund baby!

Charlie had been relatively quiet the whole way home from their appointment and after collecting the kids from school/daycare. Most would have been thrilled to hear all their money problems were over; for Charlie, it just reiterated her loss.

When the brew finished, Jack doctored his sister's favorite drink with cream and sugar and went in search of her. He found her in the living room where, instead of admiring the view of the garden through the floor-to-ceiling glass, she was lounging on the corner sofa, her eyes closed. The pained expression on her face made it clear she wanted to be left alone.

"I'm here for you, Charlie, whatever you need," he whispered, pressing a gentle kiss to her temple. He set the steaming mug down on a side table and returned to the kitchen.

A few sips of his hazelnut-flavored coffee warmed him, so he slipped off his bomber jacket and laid it over the back of a barstool. He then padded over to the dining table, thinking that a bit of research on Mark's family wouldn't go amiss.

About to enter the passcode on his iPad, he remembered the letter still in his jacket pocket and retrieved it. He tore open the envelope, unfolded the page, and began to read...

Dear Jack,

I guess if you're reading this, then I'm dead. I'm sorry—I didn't mean to die. I can only imagine what Charlie's going through right now, never mind the kids. Most likely, you're being the incredible brother you've always been and are supporting her during this devastating time. For that, I thank you.

"Charlie's going to need me more than ever"—I bet that's what you're thinking. Right? I bet you've put your life plans on hold too. The recording contract Charlie and I were so proud of you for landing—have you given that up already? I'm going to go out on a limb and say yes.

And what about the amazing woman you've fallen in love with? Have you let Julie go too? If you've done these things because of me, you must know this: I am **not** *a happy dead person. (I mean it!)*

When I asked you to take care of Charlie and our children, it was only ever meant to be temporary. I hope you believe that. I knew that when my trust fund kicked in, I'd be home, and Charlie and I would want for nothing.

I'm sorry I never mentioned the money, but it was a stipulation I had to stick to or lose the whole lot. I couldn't even tell Charlie. Hopefully, in time, she'll forgive me. At least she can't leave me since I'm already gone. (Haha.)

Seriously though, you need to start living your life, Jack. My death shouldn't be the reason you continue caring for my family. Charlie can manage on her own. Just make sure she hires help **and** *finds her own house as soon as possible. You, my friend, are going to need your own space, especially when you and Julie start a family. I know you want to shout at me right now... something like, "Mark, there's no Julie. I lost her because I needed to be there for my sister."*

Well, that sucks!

Please... fight for the woman you love and marry her pronto. Like my Charlie, Julie's one in a million.

Oh, one last thing—that promise you made? I release you from it.

Mark

Despite the tears pricking his eyes, Jack chuckled. Mark always did have a sense of humor. Yet the man had to be kidding if he thought he would stop caring for his sister. He'd been doing it since he was a teenager, and he wasn't about to stop now. As much as he wanted to take Mark's advice and go get his woman, he didn't think it was possible.

"Jack!" Charlie shouted, startling him. "Come here now!"

"Okay, okay. I'm on my way."

Stuffing the letter under his iPad, he rushed to the living room. Charlie was glowering, her hands on her hips.

"What?" he asked, his chest tightening.

"Why didn't you tell me Mark made you promise to look after me?"

"He didn't."

She waved a sheet of paper in his face. "According to this, he did."

"Mark didn't *make* me do anything." Gathering Charlie's hands in his, Jack smiled, hoping it would show her he meant his words. "I willingly agreed, and it was my honor and privilege to do it."

Her scowl deepened. "I didn't need you to do that! You should never have promised Mark. That's why you gave up the Jays and why you've lost Julie too. Isn't it?"

"Charlie, it's okay."

She snatched her hands away and crossed her arms. "No, it's not. Besides, that promise is no longer valid. Mark's gone."

"It's more necessary now. More than ever."

"Absolutely not! Mark said you'd insist, and he said I needed to insist harder. So I am. I forbid you to stop putting your life on hold for me."

"What do you mean 'I forbid you?'" he growled.

"You need to talk to Kevin, get that contract reissued," she said. "You need to speak to Julie, remind her that you love her and that she's going to come first in your life, the way things should've been in the first place. If you don't do these things, Jack, I'm going to move very far away and leave you a lonely man."

He narrowed his eyes. "You wouldn't."

"Watch me." From the scary look on her face, she was serious.

"Why are you so sure Julie will take me back?"

"If you explain to her what an idiot you've been, making ridiculous promises which put you in a very awkward position, then yes, she'll take you back. She loves you too."

"Are you really sure, Charlie?" He didn't want to dare hope.

"As sure as I am that the sun will shine again."

Chapter Twenty-Six

Julie sighed. A week off work apparently wasn't long enough to mourn the loss of her singing career *and* her boyfriend. Not when tears threatened to fall whenever she felt Brianna's close scrutiny. It was getting harder to avoid the insufferable woman. Next week's interviews couldn't come soon enough. She would have to—

Kevin's name lighting up her cell broke her train of thought, and butterflies bounced in her stomach. The only logical explanation for his call was to warn her about the band's official break-up announcement. There was nothing else left to be said.

She debated letting it go to voicemail.

Except, no point.

The persistent man would just call her work phone next, and she'd have to answer. So she kept her voice devoid of emotion, convinced that her nightmare was about to start. "Hello, Kevin."

"Julie! How are you?" His warm tone took her by surprise. She could've sworn he was smiling.

"F-fine," she stuttered, faltering in her decision to remain detached.

"I'm sure you're not, but that's why I'm calling. Are you free for lunch? There's something I want to discuss with you. A proposition I think you might be interested in." Kevin sounded happy, which didn't make sense.

Had he changed his mind and decided to offer her a solo contract? What harm could it do to find out?

"Uh, okay. Sure."

Excitement bubbled up for a millisecond until Julie realized—if she was right, she'd be singing without Jack. With her heart shattering all over again, she barely registered Kevin's response. However, she caught the last bit.

"Gino's?" she squeaked, assaulted by memories of her time spent with Jack at the restaurant.

"I believe you know the place."

Her stomach dropped. Half of her wanted an excuse not to go; the other half was curious, and it won.

"I do."

***

Gino bustled about inside the Italian restaurant, chatting and gesticulating to his customers, a broad, contagious smile on his handsome face. Meanwhile, Julie hovered just outside the glass entrance, recalling her last visit with Jack. Her heart thumped in her chest like she'd just run a marathon, and she swiftly buried the memory—thinking about Jack wasn't an option.

Easier said than done.

After securing the top button of her cream silk shirt, she smoothed down her emerald skater skirt and pushed open the door. Strolling in, she immediately spotted Kevin. Seated at a small round table along the back wall, he was peering down at some paperwork, his lips twisting.

"Bella donna! 'ow lovely to see you!" Gino said, appearing in front of her. He kissed both her cheeks, then stepped back.

She smiled tremulously. "Hello, Gino. It's nice to see you too."

"Where's my Jack? Where you are, I expect 'im to follow."

Swallowing hard, Julie prayed her tears would stay put. "We're not together...anymore."

"What did 'e do to you? Tell me, and I'll 'ave words. That boy must know you're the right woman for 'im."

She shook her head, touched by his concern. "It's okay. I'm fine, thank you," she said, then noticed Kevin waving. "I have to go, Gino. Someone's waiting for me."

The restaurateur spun to scan the place, then scowled. "Is it the man at the back with the receding 'airline?" he asked, his voice low. "Is that who you're 'aving lunch with? Bella! Tell me 'e is not your new boyfriend? Good-looking, but —"

"No!" A laugh escaped Julie's lips, lately a foreign sound to her ears. "He *was* my boss. I think he wants me to work for him again."

Gino patted her shoulder. "Okay, bella. Good. Go then. I will send your waiter shortly."

"Thanks." She squeezed his hand, then, weary of catching her tiny heels in the thick pile of the navy carpet, she picked her way to the other side of the restaurant.

"Hey, Julie." Kevin shot her a welcoming smile as he vacated his seat. Was that a hint of mischief in his eyes?

She blinked. She must be reading him wrong.

"You look spectacular as always," he said, pulling out a chair for her.

"Thanks, Kevin. You look sharp, as usual."

Besides making him look powerful and influential, the handmade gray suit he wore also brought out the gray in his eyes, softening them.

They ordered drinks, then, never a man to waste time with small talk, he handed her a wad of paper. "Take a look and let me know what you think."

As she scanned the first page, the words slowly sunk in—a standard commercial music agreement between music artists and their record label...for three years.

Her pulse quickened. The label wanted her back!

While the thought did wonders for her ego, it still left a huge gaping hole in her heart. *What about Jack?*

Glancing up from the document, she barely noticed the waiters scurrying by with plates of pasta or the customers conversing at nearby tables.

"Keep reading," Kevin instructed smugly.

In a daze, Julie turned over the page, then gasped. Speed reading to the back page, she discovered two blank signature lines. Kevin had signed and dated his section with today's date, March 13, 2018.

Pity he'd gotten ahead of himself.

Closing the contract with more force than was necessary, she shoved it across the table, biting her lower lip to hold back her anger. "It's never going to work. You're wasting your time."

Kevin had the good grace to look a little ashamed. "I've kept quiet about Jack quitting and your subsequent departure, Julie," he said calmly. "To the world, the Jays are a duo about to release their next song. So I wanted to give you two time to work things out on your own."

"Wishful thinking on your part."

Julie gulped down her soda, suddenly craving a drink laced with something way stronger.

"We could've discussed this over the phone and saved us both a lot of time," she said, crossing her arms over her chest. "I would've told you Jack would never change his mind. And even if, by some small miracle, he did come back to the Jays, I wouldn't be interested in this contract."

"Ah," he said, nodding as understanding came. "You thought this would be a solo artist offer." He tapped the bundle of paper in front of him. "That was never the intention. I was very clear from the beginning."

"I know, but—"

He gave her a funny look. "There's no but."

"I guess there's nothing left to say then." She rose from her seat.

"What if I told you Jack said he'd made a terrible mistake and begged me to re-issue the Jays contract?"

Pursing her lips, she sat back down. "I wouldn't believe you."

"Well, he did."

She examined Kevin's expression for any hint of deception. Nothing.

"Why?" she asked. Jack's sister still needed him, now more than ever. And even if he'd figured out a way to continue with his music career and still be there for Charlotte, he'd betrayed Julie's trust and lied.

"He wants to make things right."

"I don't know, Kevin. Separating my personal and professional feelings would be hard. And who's to say in the future he won't decide the same thing again—that he can't possibly manage his commitment to the label *and* his sister?"

"He assured me there'll no longer be a conflict in his responsibilities."

"Really?" She frowned. "He's choosing his career over his family?"

"Yes. For good reason."

That didn't sound like Jack at all.

What had made him change his mind? As a loyal brother and uncle, his unfailing duty to his family was one of the many qualities she'd admired and loved about him. And also why she'd so desperately wanted to be part of his family. But, if Kevin was telling the truth and Jack was serious about this, then maybe she should set aside her doubts and her feelings for him and put her career first, too.

"Can I think about it?"

"I don't need to remind you time is of the essence. You and Jack were needed in that studio yesterday." Determination showed in the set of Kevin's jaw and the tight wrinkles on his forehead.

"I know, but it's a complicated decision. I'm not sure I can trust—"

Kevin's attention traveled to her right. He gave a brief nod, then motioned to someone with his hand. Shifting slightly in her seat, Julie glanced over her shoulder.

Her heart stuttered.

Jack stood three tables away, dressed like a model for a men's fashion line. He wore ripped black jeans and a brown leather bomber jacket over a snug-fitting white T-shirt. Regret filled his expression.

After drinking in the sight of him for longer than she should've, Julie whipped her head back to Kevin. "You didn't tell me he was going to be here," she muttered, feeling totally blindsided.

"I didn't think you'd come if I did."

She huffed in response. Why had she wasted her

time? If only Kevin had waited another week. By then, she'd have lined up a job in Devon and refused to meet him. Then she wouldn't be in this predicament.

Awareness hummed through her body as Jack's musky scent enveloped her. He'd obviously closed the distance and had to be standing right behind her.

Kevin stood, his gaze flitting from her to Jack and back again. "I'll give you two some privacy. Let me know what you decide? Soon, please."

The lump in her throat made it impossible to get a word out, so she nodded.

"Hey, honey." Jack's husky voice and warm hand on her shoulder sent tingles down her spine, but Julie refused to turn around.

In no time, he filled the vacant seat at her table and was leaning forward on his elbows, close enough to kiss her. His gorgeous eyes locked onto hers, and she found she couldn't look away even if she wanted to.

"You went behind my back again," she growled before retreating in her seat.

"Would you have come if I'd called and asked?"

"No." Her voice rose as her indignation grew. "No, I wouldn't have."

Hurt flickered in Jack's eyes, and unable to bear the pain she'd caused, she closed her own. *Oh, how I've missed him,* she thought.

She ached to feel his floppy hair in her fingers, to rub her palm over his stubbled jaw, and to feel his sexy mouth moving over hers.

But this would never work!

Pushing to her feet, she pulled her purse over her shoulder and snatched her jacket from the chair. "I'm not going to sign that contract, Jack. You had your chance. I'm not prepared to go through this all again when you change your mind."

"Wait!" Half off his seat, he stretched and grabbed her wrist. "Hear me out, please? If you don't like what I say, you can leave, and I won't bother you again."

Her brain told her to just go; her heart begged her to listen. Finally, her heart won, and she sank onto her seat.

"Two minutes," she said.

He flashed a grateful smile and started talking. "When Mark decided to work in Africa, he asked me to take care of Charlie and the kids. I said I would. He also made me promise not to tell her because he knew she'd be livid about our agreement." He smiled wryly. "She was, by the way, when she found out yesterday."

That explained a lot.

"I was happy to agree to Mark's terms; he was doing a job I respected," Jack said. "And besides that, it was a temporary arrangement. As such, it never crossed my mind to share the terms of our agreement with you."

Folding her arms, Julie scowled.

"I'm really sorry; I should've told you. There was one thing neither of us took into consideration, though." A small smile curved his lips.

"What? That he'd die before his time?" The minute the words flew from her mouth, she felt awful.

"No."

Cupping her cheek, Jack's warm fingers sent electric pulses all the way to her toes. His searching eyes held hers, and her heart picked up speed.

"That I'd fall in love with the most talented, beautiful, wonderful woman in the world." His soft words spoke straight to her heart, melting away the first layer of ice that had taken hold since his betrayal. "You became the most important person in the world to me, Julie."

She shook her head, and his hand slipped off.

Jack sighed deeply, his expression tortured. "I had to stick to my word," he said, "at least until Mark came home. So, I made it work. When he died, I decided I had to keep my promise, at least until Charlie was settled again, maybe even remarried. I tried but failed to figure out how it could possibly work, you know, being in the band and caring for Mark's family, while most importantly, spending time with you."

"We could've come up with a plan together."

Jack shook his head. "Honey, I was in an impossible situation. You—the one person I never wanted to hurt—

would have suffered the most." Sorrow, mixed with regret, crossed his face. "I couldn't do that to you. So I quit the band."

"I still wish you'd spoken to me first."

"You're right; I shouldn't have made that decision without you." Tears hovered in his eyes as he squeezed the bridge of his nose. "I can't tell you how sorry I am; I know I broke your trust." He gave her what could only be described as a pleading look. "Can you *ever* forgive me?"

***

Julie let out a huge sigh. "I don't know if I can."

Seconds passed. Jack had no clue how to proceed with the ball firmly in her court.

"Kevin mentioned your responsibilities regarding Charlie have changed," she said eventually. "How?"

Leaning back in his chair, Jack scrubbed his hands over his face. So she wasn't ready to forgive him. Fine. He could at least answer her. "Turns out my brother-in-law had a big secret. He was due to inherit a substantial trust fund when he turned thirty. Given his premature death, Charlie inherits the whole lot."

"Wow, that's incredible! But she's still got three young children. I'm curious, who will help her if you don't?"

"She's going to hire a nanny."

"Really?" Julie gave him a quizzical look. "How do you feel about that?"

"Relieved."

"That doesn't sound like you." She frowned. "What about your promise to Mark?"

Jack smirked. "He left me a strongly worded letter insisting I get my life in order."

"Is that right? And what exactly would that entail?"

"Getting back my band and my woman." He hoped his frank tone would tell her he wasn't joking despite the flippant sounding words.

"I see," she responded quietly, her gaze shifting over his shoulder.

Maybe he should've taken a more serious tone and demanded she give him a second chance?

Julie brought her focus back to him and angled her head. "Well...the band may be possible. But I don't know about the woman. She's not sure where she fits in anymore."

That was his cue.

Pulse racing, Jack dropped to one knee and reached into his jacket pocket. He pulled out a small black box and heard Julie's sharp intake of breath as he snapped open the lid.

Her hands flew to her mouth. "Jack! What are you doing?" she breathed, staring at the diamond ring lying in the red velvet cloth.

Struggling to get a read on her, his chest suddenly tightened. Sweat beaded on his forehead. Charlie had helped pick out the ring.

What if Julie hated it?

Or if she couldn't forgive him?

No. He had to take a chance. Clearing his throat, he waited for Julie to look at him. When she did, he saw wonder and hope in her eyes.

Afraid he'd lose his nerve otherwise, he mustered up the courage and spoke boldly. "Honey, I love you with my whole heart, and I can't imagine my life without you. For always and forever. You're my best friend. My soulmate. My very own family. Will you please make me the happiest man alive and marry me?"

Holding his breath as tears welled up in Julie's eyes, he wondered if this was too much, too soon.

"Oh, Jack!" She flung her arms around him, almost knocking him off balance.

Laughing at her exuberance, he thrust the hand holding the box out of her way and steadied them. "Does that mean—?"

He really needed to hear her say it.

"Yes!" she squealed, wearing the biggest smile he'd ever seen. She held out her left hand to him. "Of course I'll marry you!"

Unable to peel the grin off his face, Jack carefully slipped the ring onto Julie's finger. Then, as they admired the ring sparkling under the restaurant lights, the tension he hadn't known was in his neck and shoulders drained away.

"I love it, Jack." The happiness in his fiancée's voice was undeniable. "It's gorgeous."

"Not as stunningly gorgeous as you, though," he said, rising to his feet and bringing Julie along with him. He held her securely in his arms, loving the way she fit perfectly against his body. The way she wrapped her arms around his waist, holding on like she never wanted to let go.

"I love you so much," he murmured, his gaze dipping hungrily to her mouth.

"I love you too," Julie whispered, her warm breath tickling his lips. "Forever."

A long, tender kiss followed, full of promises for their future.

Reluctantly he eased away from her magical lips and shook his head, chuckling.

"Only forever?" he asked, his tone light and playful. When confusion dotted her pretty brow, he winked. "Honey, that'll never be long enough."

Chapter Twenty-Seven

Sixteen months later

Having imagined this day ever since Jack's proposal, Julie wore an impossible-to-wipe-off smile. She was waiting in the hotel's opulent bridal suite, eager to glide down the aisle in a dreamy white dress and stand next to the man who was her family.

The one who completed her.

And all because of Kevin—who'd hovered like a papa rooster—pandering to her every request.

A rather significant change from the austere man previously only worried about his bottom line.

She chuckled. Following Kevin's constant prompting, Jack had employed the best wedding planner money could buy. And just like that, the exclusive event had gone from a complete nightmare to absolute pleasure.

Still dazed by the whole experience, her thoughts rewound to a little over a year ago when the Jays' first album shot to number one overnight. Not only had it cemented the band's place in the music industry, but it had also rocketed Jack and Julie to instant fame. Their sudden success required full-time commitment, which necessitated their immediate resignations from their jobs at Peterson Construction. Moreover, the six-month tour—arranged by their record label to promote the Jays' album—sold out in minutes, making Kevin an absurdly wealthy and ecstatic man.

Childish giggles brought Julie back to the present as Amy and Sophie skipped into the room.

"Miss Julie, can we see the aquarium, please?" Sophie asked, dragging Amy toward the far corner of the suite.

"Of course." She laughed at her flower girls, adorable in their replica bridesmaids' dresses.

Next to arrive were Julie's actual bridesmaids—Lizzy and Charlotte. Striking in their peach maxi dresses, they both wore their hair in elaborate updos, and each held a white rose bouquet.

"You two look absolutely perfect, exactly as I'd envisioned," Julie gushed, her gaze flitting between them and settling on Charlotte. "And those chunky pearl necklaces?" she added, "I love them, Charlie. Nice touch."

Charlotte gave a tremulous smile, and Julie squeezed her hand.

"A more beautiful bride, I've yet to see," Lizzy said, motioning for her to twirl.

Julie complied, laughing as the dress swirled around her smooth legs, the soft fabric sweeping against her skin like a feather.

"Fabulous!" Lizzy laid a hand on her chest, her eyes twinkling with delight. "Jack's going to swoon."

Julie's heart fluttered. She couldn't wait to see Jack. It'd been lonely sleeping in a king bed without him for the first time in twelve months. Her cheeks flushed. She'd particularly missed his warm breath tickling her skin as he held her close. Not to mention his kisses.

Lizzy's eyebrows jumped suggestively. "You ready to walk down that hessian aisle to meet your man?"

Julie smacked her friend's arm playfully. "It's covered in gilded eucalyptus leaves, silly. What do *you* think?"

"I think you've been ready for this day for long enough."

"Quite right." Sighing happily, Julie caught sight of Charlotte dabbing her eyes and pulled her into a short, tight embrace. "You okay?" she asked.

"Y-yes. It's just... I'm thrilled that this is finally happening for you two. That Jack gets to spend his life with such an incredible woman."

"Aww, that means the world to me, Charlie. No one could ever replace Mark, but that doesn't mean you'll never find love again."

Charlotte's lips twisted.

"Hey." Julie grasped her forearms lightly and smiled gently. "You *will* get another chance at a happily-ever-after. You're a fantastic mom, but I know there's a man out there who'll treasure you and love you as much as you deserve."

"Without a doubt," Lizzy chirped in.

A wobbly smile lifted Charlotte's lips. "Thanks."

"So, ladies?" Lizzy's usual perky manner got their attention. "Shall we get this show on the road?"

***

Jack folded his hands together and glanced sideways at Steven, but the best man's attention was on who occupied two front-row chairs—his wife, Melanie, and their toddler son, Ben.

Other seated guests chatted animatedly, their heads periodically swiveling toward the entrance, no doubt wondering if the ceremony was about to start. Didn't they know a change in music would be the signal?

Chuckling to himself, Jack's gaze roamed over the sprawling hotel buildings where they'd spent the past two nights. The clear blue sky sat above a spectacular mountainous background in a breathtaking setting.

Earlier, he'd awoken to the amazing sounds of birds chirping and waves crashing below his suite's window, but he'd still missed the most essential part of the whole incredible scene—Julie.

Thankfully, a one-time arrangement, had it also felt strange to her, waking up alone?

One side of his mouth lifted. He couldn't wait to see her in the dress she'd been fantasizing over for the longest time. Unbidden, his mind traveled another path that ended with him happily helping her out of that dress.

Jack smirked. All in good time.

First, he had other things to enjoy—their vows,

photographs, and the wedding reception.

In a cluster of bushes nearby, he glimpsed a security guard scanning the skies with powerful binoculars. The no-fly zone Kevin had set up made him laugh. Only licensed private jets were authorized to land on the secluded island, so getting their guests here had been quite an operation.

A slow smile slipped over his lips.

Steven gave him the beady eye. "Why do you look so relaxed, man?"

Jack laughed. "Am I supposed to be quaking in my boots, wondering if my w...woman is going to pitch?"

"Don't all grooms worry?"

"You've forgotten, I've already seen Julie on this island. So unless she plans on swimming off into the sea, her flight out of here is a helicopter. And that's scheduled to leave much, much later," he said smugly.

"So you're leaving on a helicopter, not a jet plane. Awesome."

Grinning, Jack shrugged. "Yep. Kevin insisted. Said we needed to make a 'grand' exit."

"That it will be. Does Julie know?"

"Of course."

Steven frowned, crossing his arms. "At least tell me your honeymoon destination is a surprise."

"Naturally."

"Just checking." Steven rubbed his chin. "You seem way too calm about everything, and Melanie said the same thing about Julie."

"We love each other, man. We're going to spend the rest of our lives together. What's there to panic about?"

***

When the wedding march started playing, Julie slipped her arm into the crook of Kevin's and smiled brightly at him. "Here we go."

He led her forward with slow, measured steps, sweat beading across his brow.

Poor man—he'd gone to so much trouble to make this day perfect.

"Kevin?"

He looked at her, his expression softening.

"Thanks for everything you've done," she said earnestly. "If it weren't for your belief in our talent and support throughout the good and the bad times, we wouldn't be here."

He patted her hand, his facial muscles finally relaxing. "You and Jack are worth every bit of my time and effort. I wanted you to remember this day for the rest of your lives." He shot her a cheeky grin. "Never mind the bucketload of cash the magazines were willing to pay for a photo from the celebrity wedding of the year."

Julie let out a laugh just as Lizzy and Charlotte stepped into position to follow the ten-year-old flower girls already breezing down the aisle. Ahead stood the raised wooden platform where they would exchange vows. Soft white fabric was draped over the traditional arch, while tiny clusters of peach and ivory flowers, with hints of green leaves, pinned the cloth in place. She sighed. Such a romantic sight. Yet, the vision of the best-looking man on the island drew her in the most.

Not that she was biased at all.

Dressed in his custom-designed black tux, Jack stood tall, his loving gaze fixed exclusively on her. Focusing on nothing but those sparkling eyes and his magnetic smile, Julie desperately desired to be in his arms and have his lips on hers. Subconsciously, she picked up her pace.

A warm hand restrained her. "Whoa! Slow down," Kevin whispered, "he's not going anywhere."

"Sorry," she muttered, slowing her steps to match the beat.

After what felt like a hundred more steps, Kevin adjusted her veil, kissed her cheek, and placed her hand in Jack's. He gave Jack a stern look. "Don't you ever hurt or disappoint this woman again. You got me?"

"Got it." The groom gave a succession of quick nods, apparently not intimidated at all. "Thanks for taking such good care of her, Kevin. Of us."

"My pleasure," was the gruff response.

As Kevin strode over to his reserved seat, Julie could've sworn his eyes held tears.

"Ready to do this?" Jack's low voice drew her back to his dark emerald orbs, and she struggled to think straight while his thumb, oh, so slowly caressed hers.

"Mm-hmm," she finally managed, her knees a little weak.

They took their places, and somehow, Julie got through the ceremony until she heard the pastor say, "I now pronounce you husband and wife. You may kiss the bride," then her eyes automatically slid shut. A second later, her husband's mouth found hers, and he tasted like manna from heaven. She couldn't help but kiss him back ardently, to the delighted cheers and clapping of the crowd.

When the kiss ended, she groaned.

Jack pulled her into a tight embrace and whispered in her ear, "I know. I missed you too."

***

Their photographs had been taken, speeches given, and the three-tiered wedding cake cut. Charlie had caught the bouquet, while David's son Brad had won the garter belt toss. They'd danced to their favorite songs and mingled among the guests in the enormous marquee for long enough.

Tucking his wife's hand safely in his, Jack tugged her closer. "I vote we find a quiet place where I can kiss you without my every move being watched," he said softly.

"I like that idea." Julie smiled seductively, then looked over his shoulder and sighed. "I'm afraid your brilliant suggestion will have to wait, though."

"What? Why?" He shifted to track her gaze.

Steven and Melanie were headed in their direction, with Zac and Alex right behind. Checking for an escape route and finding none, Jack sighed deeply.

Julie patted his arm. "Patience."

The couples, their expressions unreadable, calmly surrounded them. Melanie gave her brother, Zac, a subtle wave—to encourage him to speak on their behalf?

Jack's stomach clenched.

"So, Jack," Zac said, casually, "we figured it was about time you made an honest woman of Julie."

Right, so that's what this was about!

Jack exchanged a questioning look with his wife, who gave him an imperceptible nod. Cradling her in front of him, he addressed the group. "About that... Julie and I are celebrating today."

Everyone chuckled politely.

"We kind of guessed that since we're at your wedding," Steven smirked, but then Melanie's eyes lowered to Julie's midsection, and she gasped.

"Oh, you mean you're pregnant!"

"I most certainly hope not!" Julie sounded horrified.

Jack flinched. Should he be relieved or alarmed? A baby would undoubtedly throw a wrench in the works, but would it be *so* bad? Maybe now wasn't the time to worry about their decision to hold off on starting a family for a couple years.

"My wardrobe manager would so kill me," Julie continued, her tone ultra-serious. "She's had my outfit designer busy for weeks, sewing all my clothes for the next six months."

A measure of relief filled Jack. It wasn't that his wife didn't want children, but rather the various booked events and expectations of the label that concerned her. It was about not letting anyone down.

Grunts of understanding came from Steven and Zac, and Melanie said, "I suppose it's not the best time."

Realizing Alex had been too quiet, Jack glanced at her peaky-looking complexion. "You okay, Alex?"

"She will be." Zac pulled his wife of six months closer, pressing a kiss to her temple. "Won't you, sweetheart?"

"Hopefully, by the end of next week." Alex smiled weakly, her eyes skimming over the group before resting back on Jack. "We didn't want to steal your thunder, but Zac and I *are* expecting," she said happily, despite her obvious discomfort.

"Wow, that's fantastic news! Congratulations." Jack beamed at her, then Zac. "I know how much you guys wanted this."

The others echoed his sentiments.

Never one to let anything go, Zac gave Jack a pointed look. "So what are you two celebrating if not the fact that you're the last of us to get married?"

Leaning down, Jack's lips grazed Julie's ear. "This is going to make my day."

"Me too," she replied with a cute giggle.

Keeping his expression neutral, Jack met Zac's eye. "Unfortunately, Dr. Danvers, you've got your facts wrong."

"Julie," Zac implored. "Could you please set your new husband straight? Clearly, he's forgotten he attended *my* wedding six months ago."

Laughing prettily, she shook her head. "Sorry, Zac, but today's our anniversary."

"What?" Steven looked confused, as did Melanie and Alex.

Zac's puzzled look was rather comical. "You mean since you got back together again, right?"

"No." Jack was loving every second of this ridiculous competition. "We secretly tied the knot; a year ago, today."

Their friends' stunned faces were precisely what he and Julie had predicted.

***

"It's freezing!" Julie squealed as her toes hit the sapphire blue water, seconds before the wave receded. "How can it be so clear and look so pretty yet be so cold?"

Jack's low chuckle warmed her insides as he snatched her hand and pulled her to him. "I tried to warn you."

Wrapping her arms around his neck, she stared into his amused eyes. "Well, I should've listened to you, my darling husband."

"Mmm." He leaned his forehead on hers, his fingers stroking her bare arms. "I love hearing you call me that," he murmured.

She giggled. Thank goodness the year of keeping their marriage under wraps was over. Now she could boast about her husband all she wanted. Of course, the press would have a field day if they ever found out. Luckily, it was Kevin's job to ensure that never happened. Not that it would be the end of the world.

"So, have you patted yourself on the back yet for organizing this little escape from the party?" she asked Jack, combing her fingers through his silky hair.

"Yes." His hands dropped to her hips, his eyes to her mouth. "I've also given myself permission to kiss my wife senseless."

Before he could make good on his promise, she snuck in a peck, whispering against his lips, "Is that so?"

When she attempted to ease back, his arms swiftly circled her waist. Then, without warning, his lips descended onto hers with purpose. Strong, warm, and gentle.

Breathless afterward, Julie marveled at how she could still stand. Likely the only reason was her being enveloped in Jack's muscular arms. Not that she was complaining.

He flashed her a mischievous smile, suddenly lifting her and spinning her around.

"Jack!" She laughed, feeling slightly dizzy. "Put me down!"

"Okay, okay," he said, setting her feet on solid ground, well, sandy beach.

Looking deeply into his eyes, she tried to swallow the lump in her throat. All she could think was, she never wanted to be anywhere else but with this man.

"You know, I love you more every day," she said softly.

"Oh, honey." Jack's voice cracked a little on the endearment. He wove his fingers through loose tendrils of her hair at the nape of her neck, his eyes never leaving hers.

Then, when he nudged her closer, his lips touched hers again, moving slowly and deliberately. Delicious tingles rushed over her entire body, and as the kiss deepened, a contented moan escaped her lips.

She could happily stay like this in his arms for the rest of her life.

If only.

Eventually, Jack drew back, the love shining in his eyes hard to miss, the smile curved on his glorious lips impossible not to see.

"I love you so, so much." His voice was husky with desire. "You know this thing we've got going on between us is—"

Julie pressed a finger to his lips. "I know. It's only forever."

The New Haven Series

Acknowledgments

Thank you for taking the time to read Jack and Julie's story! I hope you enjoyed reading it as much as I did writing it. From the moment I created these two characters in *Bad Reputation* (New Haven Series: Book One), I knew they needed their own happily ever after.

The first draft of *Only Forever* was written years ago, and the revision and editing process involved several people. I couldn't have finished the book without their input.

So, first I'd like to say a huge thank you to my friend Eve. Her brilliant suggestions and encouraging feedback during my early drafts were invaluable.

Thank you, Mary, for spotting the errors I had obviously glossed over, especially after what seemed like the hundredth re-read!

To Wayne, thank you for all your help with the whole package—your input and advice mean a lot. I look forward to our next project together.

To my husband and daughters for entertaining yet another question about sentence structure or word choice—thank you for putting up with me—I love you.

Lastly, but never least, thank you to my heavenly Father. You have blessed me with every good gift in my life. I'm forever grateful.

About the author

SAMANTHA J. BALL never thought she'd be a writer. An accountant by qualification, she used story-telling to help her sleep. A dear friend heard one of the stories she'd composed in her head and insisted she write it down. She didn't. Years later, her husband, after hearing yet another 'make-believe' romance from his wife, encouraged her to put pen to paper. She did. Writing has since become her passion, with ideas and inspiration coming from movies, books, and real-life characters. She lives in London with her husband, two beautiful grown-up daughters, and a gorgeous Tibetan Terrier.

Printed in Great Britain
by Amazon

80500317R00147